MURDER IN THE CARDS

GINA CHEYNE

First Published in 2022 by Fly Fizzi Ltd,
Pyers Croft
Compton, Chichester,
West Sussex PO18 9EX
www.flyfizzi.co.uk

Cover design by Kari Brownlie

ISBN 978-1-915138-03-3 (eBook)
ISBN 978-1-915138-04-0 (Paperback)
ISBN 978-1-915138-05-7 (Hardback)
ISBN 978-1-915138-06-4 (Audiobook)

❀ Created with Vellum

To anyone who has ever felt like murdering their partner during a game of bridge

You have to know the past, to understand the present

— CARL SAGAN

CONTENTS

FOREWORD

Author's Note

Part of this book in set in the 1960s and uses terms which were current at the time to add authenticity to the voice including Polari.

Polari was the secret language of the gay community and was particularly prevalent before the 1967 law when homosexual acts in England and Wales were legalised, on the condition that they were consensual, in private and between two men who had attained the age of 21. There was never an explicit ban on homosexuality between women.

Most of the Polari usage should be understandable from the context but there is also a glossary at the back of the book which covers the terms used and some others cant (slang) of the time. It is important to note that Polari was a flexible language, could mean different things to different people and is not fixed to tenses or grammatical structure.

Some, although not all, of the chapters have Polari headings, these are explained in the glossary.

Bridge, the game, is a recurring theme in the book and a few bridge terms that I thought might lead to confusion have been added to the glossary. There is reference to a notorious murder during a 1920s bridge game: Mr Bennett's murder, which is explained in the glossary.

CHAPTER 1
JACK'S PLACE, LONDON 1963

Jack shrugged the rain off his leather jacket like a wet dog shaking its fur and headed for the bar. He skirted around a table where four people were engrossed in a game. One of the players was humming 'Surfin' USA', and the irony of the Beach Boys' light melodies wafting from the jukebox across the dark smoky air of the club was not lost on Jack.

'Bloody hell, Clinton,' he said as the tall thin barman turned towards him polishing a glass, the way he did when listening to customers' complaints, 'it's Armageddon. First, we freeze our balls off all winter and now we're like as anything to drown on Greek Street. Might as well be back in Ireland.'

Clinton silently pushed an open packet of fags across the bar and Jack lit one, inhaling deeply before looking around the club through the haze of smoke.

'What's doing tonight? I see Bev. She minding herself?'

Clinton nodded. 'Yes. She brought in a choice new girl. They've been playing all evening. Big stakes. Don't look like she'll be giving French lessons tonight.' He licked his lips,

but carefully; Jack required his staff to always show gentle-
manly behaviour.

Jack looked over at the card players. Both Bev and her
partner had piles of cash on the table. Their opponents
were drinking whisky and one had a cluster of paper
bunched around his glass. Some of the liquor had spilt and
wet the paper, giving off a sour smell that percolated
through the warm air of the club. Both men had the glassy
stare of the losing gambler.

'Not if they win, certainly. Who's the other bird?'

Clinton shrugged. 'Bev called her Fran, but you never
know with Bev's girls – change their names with their
dresses. Nice legs.'

Jack played his eyes across the girls. 'Aye, but legs is as
far as she goes. She'll get nowhere with that catch of jubes.'
He mimed what he considered a girl's best feature. 'Best
hope she wins at cards.'

He laughed and was about to walk away when Clinton
said quietly, 'Le Duce was done over today. The lily law
charpering the place. Words out there's a sharpy polone
planted in one of the clubs.'

Jack's mouth hardened. 'Is there, bejesus?'

A police informer. And a female one at that. Jack had
never heard of the lingo of Polari until he arrived in London,
but now he found it a useful asset; he could converse with
Clinton, and anyone else in the know, without snoopers.

He walked over to Bev's table. She had some new gold
bangles decorating her arms and rings on her fingers. Jack
shook his head mentally; OK, she was a thief, but it was
unusual for her to display her loot so openly.

Bev was concentrating on the cards, but she looked up
briefly. 'Jack.'

'Bev.'

The girl Fran was dummy, so she looked up at Jack and smiled shyly. 'Hello.' She blinked through long eyelashes. 'Thank you for letting us play in your club. It's fabulosa.'

Posh girl, thought Jack. Where did Bev snaffle this one, this innocent? The way she mouthed 'fabulosa'. She might catch on, despite the lack of willets. Nice eyes. Long arms. Looked young. He might fancy a sample himself.

He walked on through the haze of smoke to the next room, where they were setting up to play skiffle. As they began jamming, Jack watched them lazily, thinking about young Fran at the bridge table. Too much greasepaint flagged up every time. Thought it made them look sophisticated. Probably fourteen. Maybe younger. Where did they come from, these girls and boys? Young ones usually frequented 2is or Speakeasy, not grown-up clubs. It was a dangerous game having them here. The sudden arrival of unhappy parents accompanied by lily law could cause havoc in a decent club. But Bev knew that. She wasn't usually a fool.

He glanced at his Rolex. Still early. They hadn't got much of a crowd yet; that usually came after 11 p.m.

Almost through a dream, he heard the whistles. From the other room came the crashing noise of rozzers doing the work of perfidious magistrates. Le Duce last night. His tonight. Those dilly boy charpers were hotting up and it was making it hard to run a club. He was fed up with this. He paid his money. He should be protected.

Ha ha.

He crushed the remains of his cigarette into his hand. Whipped back into the gaming room to stop the charge, but he was too late – tables overturned, broken glasses, policemen holding clients up against the wall. He looked around furiously. Then he noticed something.

No sign of the card table. Bev and Fran had cut out with their money and their notes. Only the men were being hauled out of the club.

How the fuck?

He hoped Bev wasn't pulling a fast one here. She'd better not be the undercover sharpy polone. He'd have words with that zhooshy tart later. He looked around for the betty bracelet in charge.

CHAPTER 2
DOG AND BONE IN OWLY
VALE 2020

Miranda shifted her arms along the table, feeling the hard wood cutting into her chin. Was she drunk? No. Her mind was clear. She lifted her head and looked around to point this out to someone, but Phillip was asleep on the sofa, his gentle snores reminding her the hoover needed fixing.

Flipping COVID restrictions, she thought, picking up the bottle and draining the last dregs. It was Christmas Day, and they were in Tier 4 liberty. Or should have been. Except yesterday, Trap and Trace contacted Phillip. His quick coffee with some infected colleague meant his family had to go into isolation. Instead of turkey at her sister's and oodles of presents, they had tantrums (mostly hers, although the children were very supportive) and something from the deep freeze.

Finally, Felix and Peta, bribed by promises of spectacular future gifts when they were released, had agreed to go to bed, but Miranda felt irritable. She lifted the empty champagne bottle again and, disappointed, wondered whether to open a second.

The phone rang.

She stared at it. The landline face said 'No caller ID'

Not Cat or Steph, her colleagues in the SeeMs Dog Detective Agency. They used her mobile.

Not her mother or sisters. They'd had a FaceTime call a couple of hours ago. Her youngest sister was a full-blown policeperson now, but even she had been on the family call.

Unlikely it was one of Phillip's snooty work colleagues (*Oh, hello, Miranda, I didn't expect you to answer the phone*) on Christmas Day.

Probably a spam call.

The phone went to answer machine and ended. It rang again.

Grudgingly, she picked it up.

'Do you play bridge?' asked a raspy voice.

'What?' Did she hear that right?

'Do you?'

What kind of spam call was this? And on Christmas Day! 'Yes, why?'

'Then you can help me,' said the voice, now with a firmness that echoed the kids' most lethal teachers.

'Only,' said Miranda, her oomph now returning, 'if I know who you are.'

'First,' said the voice, 'tell me about your detective agency.'

'I might,' said Miranda, 'but not until I've opened another bottle. You sound like the sort of caller I'll need alcohol for.'

The caller laughed. 'OK, you can keep the phone on. I love the sound of opening bottles.'

Miranda got a bottle of champagne out of the fridge and opened it right next to the receiver, hoping to deafen him.

She went back to the sofa with a glass, picked up the phone, but didn't speak.

'I know you're back, Miranda,' said the voice. 'Don't try to be clever with me.'

'Bright boy,' said Miranda defiantly, even though her skin shivered at the use of her name.

She waited for the caller to make the next move. There had been a time when she wasn't so subtle, but now she had learnt to let the client, if that was what he was, make the moves first.

'You're a cool one,' he said. 'I like that in a detective.'

'Thank you.'

'So,' said the caller, 'to the crime.'

Miranda drank some champagne, toasting herself.

'It involves the game of bridge. That's why I need a player. I don't need an *Andrew Robson*, but someone who knows about invitational and forcing play.'

Miranda felt a smile forming itself on her face; this was fun. 'Are we talking low for like, high for hate? Signals.'

His laugh gave her the impression 'signals' meant something more to him, but his voice was neutral when he continued. 'Nice! I see you've got the gist.'

Miranda rolled her eyes; sadly, they were not on a video call.

He was silent for a few moments, then said, 'Do you use BBO or Trickster? I assume since you are a detective in Tier 4, you *are* abiding by the rules.'

'Oh, wow. An assumption indeed,' she said leaning back in her chair. 'Haven't you seen our website? An agency that smashes the assumption and goes beyond what SeeMs to be true.'

His laugh was so cold that she expected a lie to follow.

'You underestimate me, young woman. I researched well. I know that your main fare is finding stolen dogs, and that, thanks to recent success in a quadruple murder case, you're branching out. You'd do better to ask me why I chose you as a partner.'

'OK,' said Miranda, refusing to let him depress her and instead feeling that familiar surge of excitement; a case was starting. 'Why *did* you choose me?'

'Because, Miranda, although you sometimes ruin your play by spontaneous guessing instead of analytical thinking, you are clever. And I'm interested to see if this extends beyond the bridge table.'

Miranda rolled her eyes again. Hadn't he heard of instinctive play? Or, as Andrew Robson called it, educated guessing.

Then her brain clicked in. If he knew about her bridge playing, then everything he said before was calculated to give the wrong impression. Who was he? What did he want? Did she know him? She listened to the tones of his voice more carefully.

'So, BBO or Trickster? Which of those online bridge sites do you use?'

'Both.'

'Excellent. Then you will play bridge on Friday 8 January at 6.30 p.m., BBO. I will invite you and your partner will be Simian. Your login is MirandaZ, am I right?'

'I'm impressed.'

'Don't patronise me, Miranda. Many have made the mistake of underestimating me. All have regretted it. Be there.'

He rang off. Miranda took a gulp of champagne. Had she imagined the entire conversation? But the excited beating of her heart told her no, this was a new game, a new mystery to enjoy and hopefully the entry to a case with a big income. But what was the crime? Or was that still to come? And why fix a bridge game two weeks ahead? Why not tomorrow?

CHAPTER 3
THE BIG SMOKE 1963

After skipping out of Jack's, the girls went on to Muriel's. Fran squinted at the bright green environment laughing ecstatically. 'Is she trying to bring the sunshine inside?' she asked Bev, stroking her arm affectionately. 'Should've brought my ogle shades'.

She danced across the room, doing a couple of jumps around the tables to the surprise of the much older drinkers. 'Love the bamboo and plastic plants. Madam hoping they'll grow?'

As she sashayed away, Bev beamed. Fran was crazy, but at the same time she could be Bev's road out of hell. For too long, Bev and her children had been at the rough end of the male sex. Men and pimps came and went. The only stables in her life were Jack's and Muriel's, otherwise there was little care for a half-caste doxy either from state or individuals. And now crazy Fran was showing her an alternative life, how to cheat at cards, how to stay ahead of the pimps and lily law. It was worth the risk.

Muriel had seen them enter, and she watched the new girl drop down to the rug, stroking the leopard's head before rolling sensuously over its skin, her short skirt almost at her waist.

The girl waggled her shoulders across the fur laughing. 'Oh Jean Paul, you sexy devil, yes, yes. Take me to France on your flying carpet. I'm going to rule the world. Give me some plastic plants, show me your *quongs*.'

'Wash your mouth out, you little bitch,' said Muriel. 'This is a private club. Like it or get out. Who is this anyway?' she asked Bev, staring straight at Fran, who was still lying on the rug. 'Your latest cunty?'

Bev knelt down beside Fran, pulling her earlobe to quell her antics.

'Ow!' said Fran, her voice petulant.

'You behave or I'll tell your father where you are,' Bev said sharply. Fran looked up, startled, then laughed slightly nervously.

Bev's voice softened. 'OK. Now I'm going to introduce you to Muriel. She's the rudest woman in London, but she's my petrol.'

Fran sat up slowly. Rubbing her ear, she raised an eyebrow. 'BP? Best pal, with a spark?'

Bev laugh bubbled up like molten sugar. 'You crack me up, little girl.'

'Your magic won't work in here,' Muriel butted in. 'I like 'em tougher. My Marys are special.'

Before Muriel turned to Bev, cutting out the girl with her shoulder, Fran caught the amusement hidden behind the eyes. She and Bev exchanged glances. Before long Fran was going to be Muriel's petrol as surely as Bev.

'Charpers everywhere,' said Muriel. 'You'd better park your game for the night.'

'We're cool,' said Bev. 'Fran here has taught me a whole new lay. I may even give up the trade and move to bridge.'

Muriel stared. 'Bridge? Bridge! The card game?'

'Yup, bridge is the packet, with Polari signals, using that cant language in a way the inventors never considered. That's our new caper.'

Muriel's face wrinkled with laughter. 'Bev-er-ley! You were ever a mug for a pretty face.'

CHAPTER 4
ZOOMING THROUGH OWLY
VALE 2020

Zooming her colleagues Stevie and Cat the next day, Miranda discovered that they'd had the same caller. All three girls were booked to play bridge online on Friday 8 January at 6.30 p.m. with an unknown player called Simian. He knew all their login names.

Stevie went to the Internet and began looking up 'Simians'. 'There is a reason,' she said, 'for every one of our actions.'

'Speak for yourself,' said Miranda yawning.

'There will be a connection between his name and who he is,' continued Stevie with the doggedness she had needed to become an airline pilot. She wrinkled her nose as a new page filled the screen. 'Hey! There used to be a band called Simian.'

Miranda rubbed her temples. She had a headache and was wondering if it was COVID or a hangover. Could be a mixture of two. Better if it was a hangover, then she could drink it away later.

Cat, crossing one slim leg over the other in a manner

Miranda, glancing at her own pudgy legs, found annoying, asked, 'Anyone want a doughnut? Were they any good?'

'The doughnuts?' asked Miranda.

'Ha, ha.'

'So,' said Stevie away in her research, 'ah ha!'

'What?' asked Cat, while Miranda wondered where she'd put the paracetamol.

'*Planet of the Apes.*'

'What?'

'Know what caused the growth of apes and the descent of human beings?'

'No.'

'A pandemic. And what are we in? A pandemic. And what are we waiting for?'

'Spring,' said Miranda, throwing two paracetamol into her mouth and gulping water.

'The vaccination,' said Cat, getting a lipstick out of her voluminous bag.

'Precisely. And what happened with the injection ALZ-113 in *Planet of the Apes*?'

'Oh, yes,' said Cat, 'I remember the film. It made the apes more intelligent, while making humans appear to recover while actually infecting more and more people who then died.'

'Close enough. Still want a vaccine?'

'Yes. I'm an optimist.' She picked up a doughnut.

'Well,' said Miranda, 'who is Simian? Someone who works in the zoo? Or films.'

Cat put down the doughnut uneaten but scarred red from her lips. 'Certainly someone who knows you better than us. And yet knows we all play bridge, Stevie better than me, perhaps better than you.'

'I wish,' said Stevie. 'OK, right. I've made a "party list" of potential Simians. It should be in your inbox. Firstly, Miranda's weekly bridge four.'

'I think we can discount women,' said Cat, looking at her iPad. 'That was a man's voice.'

'Unless,' said Stevie, 'she was using a synthesizer to change her voice. Or was gender fluid. Don't forget the caller talked about Miranda's bridge style. He must have played bridge with her.'

'Pharr,' said Miranda sticking out her tongue at the screen, 'I think Cat and I have enough experience of men and women to tell which sex we're talking to, even with voice-over thingies.'

Stevie raised an eyebrow. 'OK, humour me then. You have three main female players in your group, right, all elderly or middle-aged women. And then one or two fill-ins when the others aren't available, right?'

'Right,' said Miranda. 'The extras usually come from the bridge club in Chichester. But all women. Can't be any of them.'

'OK,' said Cat, examining the list, 'ignore them for a while. That leaves the four locals with whom we've all played. First, Percy Bigby, we've all played with him, but in my case only once.'

Stevie nodded. 'He's a serious bridge player. I've played with him twice.'

'You mean Piggy Big Noise,' said Miranda, cheerful now her headache was receding. 'Did he scream at you, Cat?'

Cat pulled at her wavy red locks, grimacing slightly. 'Yes, for not knowing what a splinter bid was and going four hearts when he only had one and I had three. We lost that game big time.'

Miranda chuckled. 'Did he shout at you, Stevie?'

'The first time we played was fine. I had no cards at all,

didn't bid, so he assumed I was better than I am. Then the second time, I replied four spades when we had a slam. He went so red I thought he was going to have apoplexy at the table. He had to leave the room and come back in after a few moments.'

Miranda laughed happily. 'I've heard he goes and shouts at the cars in the car park. I'm so, so careful when I play with him. He will still play with me – if everyone else is busy.' She grinned.

'Then there's Terry Plump,' said Cat. 'I've played with him once or twice.'

Miranda chortled. 'I'll plump for a beer! Calls himself a bridge player, but he's a good time boy – two beers per hand.'

'Yes,' said Cat, 'an expensively educated illiterate. Have you played with him, Stevie?'

Miranda stopped laughing and bit her lip. People who wasted their education were her red flag; she and her sisters had had to fight for their education after her father died. Eventually, she dropped out of school to help her mother in the shop, so the others could learn. Then someone like that threw his parents' money away. It irked.

Stevie's voice forced her back to the present.

'No. But I have played with Paul Sweet. He's lovely, but he can't bear to win.'

Miranda's humour kicked back in. 'You are so right! Brilliant brain, but so kind he makes mistakes on purpose. He likes to tell you what you've just bid or played.' She put on a male voice. 'My partner has just played a spade, oh look, it's been trumped, what should I throw? Oh, dear me. What won't I need next?'

Cat laughed and Miranda added, 'I can't reconcile that

kindly nature with the man I talked to on the phone. Unless he's got a hidden side.'

'We all do,' said Cat.

'OK, Cat,' snapped Miranda, rubbing her temples, 'let's not have any psychobabble now.'

'So,' said Stevie gently, 'what about Brian Deliverer? He's a serious bridge player, he hates losing so much he shakes and his eyes go all starey in his head. He's a possible.'

Miranda nodded thoughtfully. 'The strong, silent type, no talking while playing. Loves bridge boxes. Seems rather different from our man on the phone.'

'Quite so,' said Cat tartly.

On the appointed Friday, all three girls signed in to BBO as agreed and soon were round the virtual bridge table with Miranda opposite Simian. Simian rang them on WhatsApp, but when he appeared on the screen it was as a monkey.

'You have a filter on,' said Stevie in a kind voice. 'Shall I explain how to take it off?'

'Thank you, but no. I am quite capable of doing that myself. I just thought you'd like to see me in my true colours.'

'Ha, ha,' said Miranda.

'Actually,' Simian said, 'we'll go back to speech only. My broadband is not good enough for video and speech. We don't want to be knocked out of the game.'

Miranda's instincts shouted *suspicious*. But she had to admit that their village broadband was very slow. *He must be in the village, and not near the BT box.*

The first hand was tricky. Neither Stevie nor Cat were good enough players to have left the tools of their school behind and, despite looking at crib sheets, they went four down doubled and the IMP scores against them shot up.

After a few more games, Simian won the last trick with a seven of diamonds. 'When the pub opens,' he said laughter in his voice, 'you'll both have to buy me a beer. Better watch my future seven of diamonds or I'll be legless.'

Miranda clocked that as a Junior Bridge competition convention, while knowing it would mystify Cat. Stevie might understand; she was curious about the history of everything and might have looked up the eccentricities of bridge.

Which one of their four possibles had played Junior Bridge? Could only be Piggy Big Noise or Brian Deliverer. But weren't they born too late? Could either of them have been under twenty-six in 1987 when Junior Bridge started? Unlikely. Brian Deliverer was seventy, if not older, and Piggy must be in his sixties. Perhaps they'd cut their 'suspicious' list too fine.

'But,' said Simian, 'you already know my drinking tastes, don't you, Miranda? I've bought you a white wine or two.'

'Have you?' asked Miranda. She had certainly drunk with Terry Plump and Paul Sweet, but had she had a drink with the other two? She couldn't imagine Brian Deliverer in the pub at all, and Percy would soon be yelling at the barman for pulling his pint too slowly, or perhaps too fast.

Perhaps she could trap him into revealing himself. 'OK. What kind of beer did I buy you?'

'Bitter, my sweet,' said Simian. 'We laughed over the name: Tea.'

The only person she remembered in that scenario was a limping elder, who had collapsed into a chair beside her. They talked about her children. But he was a stranger to the area. Wasn't he? Had any of the others drunk Tea?

The game was continuing, so she put her thoughts away and concentrated on the game. As Cat and Stevie kept bidding, trying to discover what was in their partner's hand, Simian hooted, 'Well, girls, I have a pretty good idea of what's in each of your hands. Must feel like being undressed in public.' Giggling, he added, 'And now we will watch the naked ones go down!'

Miranda laughed with him, but she felt uneasy, knowing that the others were not enjoying themselves. Too creepy. Why was he teasing them like this? Giving them clues? What did he want?

Miranda's next hand consisted of an ace, ten, six and three of spades, ten, eight and three of hearts, four of diamonds, ace, nine, eight, four, two of clubs. *Eight points,* she thought disappointedly.

Simian opened the bidding. 'One spade.'

Stevie, on Simian's left, made an overcall. 'Two diamonds.'

Miranda, looking at her four okay spades and single diamond, thought they might just do it. She went four spades.

Somewhat to her relief, Cat said, 'Five diamonds.'

'What?' Simian yelled into WhatsApp, his voice no longer light and flirtatious. 'You silly bitch! You can't make it.'

Cat gasped and Miranda imagined her hands flying into her bag to get her lipstick for support. It certainly sounded like Piggy Big Noise.

Hm, she spun her tablet around reflectively, if he really thinks his hand is *that* good, should I go up to five spades?

Then something flashed through her memory: she'd seen this hand before.

Of course! It was in Andrew Robson's Sunday podcast –

the podcasts she did daily in the vain hope of improving her play.

Mr Bennett's murder: a failed bridge game in the 1920s where a wife shot her husband after he played the hand badly. She used his own gun, and she was acquitted. Was this the hand they were asked to play for? Why? Was there some correlation between this game and the crime Simian was about to reveal?

Miranda was in the position of Mrs Bennett. Simian was Mr Bennett. The other two were Charles and Myrna Hoffman. Would either of the others recognise the game?

Miranda wished she could see Cat and Stevie so they could swap glances; BBO and WhatsApp were not so satisfying. Even in libertarian Sweden they would have been able to roll their eyes through the plexiglass screens.

They played the game and, as predicted, Stevie and Cat went one down.

'Ha,' said Simian. 'Now we will replay the game as it should be done.'

'All right,' said Cat, and Miranda visualised the lipstick being chucked back into the bag with resignation.

'How do you do that?' asked Stevie curiously. 'Replay a game on BBO?'

'Simple,' said Simian, his triumph resonating through their phones as he explained about pulling down the hamburger and resetting.

'Brilliant,' said Stevie.

Miranda frowned, musing about his clear comfort within the system. He would have been able to set up the game the way he wished without issue. But the question remained: why?

This time Cat let the four spades bid stand, and Simian began to play. His first two tricks replicated the Bennett versus Hoffman game, but then he branched out, trying to win the contract.

As Miranda was dummy, she had time to consider who their strange partner might be. Take it in steps, she thought. He is a very good bridge player and he knows his way around the bridge Internet. This game has some deep significance for him. He drank beer in the pub at least once. The two lesser bridge players, Paul and Terry, did that, but kindly Paul would not be here forcing an issue. Whatever Cat said about hidden personalities, it was not Paul.

And Terry 'plump for another, thank you, darling'. Could he really be this subtle? She couldn't see it. Besides, he didn't have this level of ability.

Which brought her back to the two better bridge players: Percy and Brian.

Did she share a drink with them? Bitter? Tea?

Simian's cry of delight as he won the game broke into her thoughts.

'Ha, did it! If you let West overtrump on the fifth trick, he – or she, in this case – loses her trump advantage. The secret lies in preventing East from getting the lead too early. If she cannot lead through my king of hearts to West's ace, then we play our clubs. We win and Mr Bennett doesn't get done in! Wait until I tell Francis!'

Miranda felt a shiver down her spine. Brian Deliverer had a son called Francis. Village gossip proclaimed they had fallen out and Francis moved to Australia. Perhaps this was an olive branch.

So, it had to be Brian Deliverer at the other end of the village. And yet her instinct shouted *no*.

She ignored it.

Pausing, she wondered whether to discuss the unveiling of the mysterious Simian with Cat and Stevie, but her ego got the better of her caution. She pulled up her contacts list. There was his landline number.

Listening through WhatsApp, she dialled the landline. She could hear Brian's phone ringing in the background.

'Well,' said Simian chuckling, 'I've shown that the hand can be won! You won't need to shoot me, Miranda.'

In the background, and on Miranda's phone, Brian's landline went to answer machine. She rang again.

'Are you ringing to congratulate me, Miranda?' asked Simian. 'Or to congratulate yourself?'

'What are you talking about?' asked Cat, her voice jumpy.

'I think,' said Stevie, 'Miranda has unveiled the statue.'

'Two clever little piggies,' said Simian unctuously, 'one stayed at home.'

He picked up the landline. 'Hello, Miranda.' His voice echoed through the Wi-Fi with feedback.

'Hello, Brian,' Miranda replied, 'you made it too easy for me. Gave me too many clues.'

'So, it would *Seem*, Miranda,' said Simian, and all his lines went dead.

'He's gone,' said Stevie unnecessarily.

'I wonder,' said Cat.

'What?' asked Miranda. 'Can't you believe I got there first?'

'Perhaps,' said Cat her voice staccato as she reapplied her make-up. 'To me, this seems odd. What is this crime? Don't tell me we've been asked to discover the truth behind Mr Bennett's murder?'

'Oh,' said Miranda, surprised. 'Did you know about that?'

'Of course! You're not the only one who reads about bridge.'

'OK,' said Stevie, 'so what is the crime behind this?'

'Given that it was clearly Brian Deliverer leading us on,' said Miranda, 'it must be something someone did to him, which he wants us to discover. Clever of me to identify him.'

'Hm,' said Cat, 'you think? It seems too easy. Perhaps he wanted you to win. Perhaps it is Paul Sweet after all.' She half laughed.

Miranda jeered. 'Pah! See you tomorrow. I'm off to celebrate.'

CHAPTER 5
A DEATH IN OWLY VALE 2020

T wo days later, Miranda, still feeling chuffed with success, sat the children down with their home-schooling screens and books. The children were quiet, so she got out her tablet to check the pod emails. Pods were the subgroups within the village that kept an eye on each other. The leaders of the pods communicated with each other under the interesting name 'jailers', so that all the villagers knew the same news. Mostly, there was nothing special in the emails. Sometimes there were appeals from the village shop not to forget they were there, or from the pub reminding people that they could buy vouchers for the future. Miranda had already bought so many pub vouchers she was expecting to treat the whole village to a night out when the lockdown was finally over.

Their pod was called 'Top of the Village', and was run by Professor Dee, who started every email 'Top of the Morning to You All!'

Miranda loved it. It still made her laugh, even though she'd had some fifty emails since lockdown began.

However, this one started differently.

'I'm sorry to say,' began Professor Dee, 'that down in the Lower Village Pod one of the residents has died. We don't have any details as yet, but the rumour mill tells me he was one of our older members and it may be a heart attack. I will be in contact again when I have more information.'

Miranda's nose twitched and she grabbed her phone and called Stevie on WhatsApp.

'Read your pod this morning?'

'Yes. Know who it is?'

'No,' said Miranda, 'do you?'

'Brian Deliverer.'

'No! *Wow*! They're saying a heart attack – is that right?'

'End of Village saw police and ambulance arrive, but the police always come in on a sudden death, so it's not necessarily suspicious. Mid Village rumour is daughter found the body when he didn't do their nightly Zoom on Wednesday. Perhaps our bridge game on Tuesday was his final hurrah?'

'Oh, that's awful! No wonder he was behaving so oddly. Poor Brian. Know him at all?'

'No, but his wife died a couple of years ago, and his daughter and grandchildren live in the village. You remember the rumour that he fell out with his son who moved to Australia. Presumably, he'll be back for the funeral.'

'Can he?' mused Miranda. 'I thought COVID funerals were restricted matters. More the point, can you travel freely from Australia?'

'Well, he'd need a negative COVID test. I don't think Australia is one of the red-list countries. I'll check the rest of the regulations. Any reason why you're so interested in Brian Deliverer's family? Something to do with our bridge game, or just compassion?'

'Not sure, Stevie, my detective nose is twitching. Something here is too neat.'

'Yes, no, maybe,' said Stevie, and Miranda could feel her amusement through the ether. 'I prefer to stick to facts and the Internet "near-facts". OK, back to lost and stolen dogs. Thefts are increasing daily under lockdown and we've had several new clients.'

A week later, the girls (thanks to a fluid interpretation of Stevie's demented mother's care bubble) were in the SeeMs office in Stevie's house when Cat's mobile rang.

'Is that the detectives?' screeched an anguished voice. 'The dog ones.'

'Yes,' said Cat, 'have you lost a dog?'

The owner of the voice burst into tears. 'No, a father.'

'Oh, dear,' said Cat, 'we would like to help. Can we start with your name?'

An hour later, all three detectives were on a Zoom call with Karen Middlebrow, nee Deliverer.

Although Cat didn't find Zoom a very satisfying way of interviewing – too few hidden clues, or rather over-hidden clues – it was the only way under lockdown. Neither of the other girls, perhaps because they were younger, had any problem with what Stevie called IAI (Internet Alternative to Interviewing).

'Every evening,' Karen said, her red jumper clashing strangely with the pink walls of her living room, 'my father read Orla, my daughter, a story via Zoom. She's seven, so she goes to bed at six o'clock and the stories helped to make her sleepy.' She wiped away a tear. 'He did it as usual on Friday night, but then when I sent the Zoom link on Saturday, he didn't sign in. I called him but got no reply. He had started forgetting things ... you know – keys, glasses, that sort of thing. And recently I'd seen him staring into space, talking to himself.

'I worried he was getting dementia. Thought he might have forgotten Orla's reading. So, I went round to his. Let myself in. I have a key. I insisted on having a key. I was always worried this type of thing might happen.' Tears started to drip down her face and she turned away from them, brutally muting her screen with an angry finger .

The detectives waited patiently while she composed herself and unmuted.

'I went in and found him. Dead on the sofa in the living room, sitting there with a glass of whisky like he was watching television. It was so loud. Cricket. He didn't even like cricket. It seemed so unfair.'

She burst into tears again and this time ran out of the room, leaving the detectives staring at the pink wall behind the sofa. Laughter from a children's TV programme filled the unmuted background.

After a while, Karen came back into the room and sat down. She looked for the mute button, realised she was already unmuted and nearly burst into tears again. 'Sorry. I called 999 and the ambulance came out. They jumped on his chest and ...' She stopped again, but this time stayed on the sofa breathing hard.

'It was awful,' she said eventually. 'I knew he was dead. I said I hadn't talked to him since yesterday, but they said they had to do it, so they attached all those pads to him and tried to jump-start him. I burst into tears. It was horrible. Just ... just bad.'

She swallowed and eventually continued. Miranda wished she was with her to put a sympathetic arm round her shoulders.

'Eventually, they said he was definitely dead. The police

arrived and a young constable stayed with the body until the undertaker arrived to take the body away. At first, they said that he'd had a heart attack. Later the policewoman rang me. She was very kind. She said she could come round, but I said I preferred doing it via the screen. I have a duty to my family. To keep safe. You don't know where those police people have been. In and out of germy houses.' Karen took a breath. 'She said that the post-mortem showed he had taken an overdose of amitriptyline.'

'Amitriptyline?' said Cat unconsciously searching for her lipstick. She knew that drug. It was used against depression. She had been given some after Charlie died. 'Why did he have any of that? It's a prescription drug.'

'Yes,' said Karen, 'my mother had terrible fibromyalgia. It came and went. So, she used to store large amounts for when she needed it. If she got a migraine, she would take a big dose and go to bed until it was over.'

'And lots left in the house after she died?' asked Miranda.

Karen's sigh held years of unexpressed family guilt. 'Yes. I knew it was there, but I never thought …' She compressed her lips. 'The policewoman said his stomach was full of whisky but given the state of his liver it was unlikely that would have any effect, except perhaps to make his death easier.'

'Was he a big drinker?' asked Miranda.

'Depends what you mean by big. He probably had half a bottle or so every evening. He told me whisky was the purest alcohol, much the safest to drink.'

Miranda could see Cat looking at her, no doubt wondering how pure her white wine consumption was.

Karen went on, 'The policewoman told me he probably died shortly after seven o'clock on Friday evening, right after we finished our story. No wonder he kept staring into the distance and talking to himself. Perhaps his body was already drifting on speed clouds. But why would he do that?'

Miranda broke in, seeing her own shocked face reflected in the screen. 'But that's impossible – he was playing bridge with us until ten o'clock, and we know it was definitely him because I rang him on the landline. He answered and we could hear it through the Internet via WhatsApp.'

Karen stared at her. 'Could the police be wrong?' she said eventually, and her voice held a surprising element of hope as though she was suggesting it was someone else who died, not her father. 'The police think it was suicide,' she added. 'They found a note. He left it in the bathroom, which is why I didn't find it first.'

'In the bathroom?' said Miranda. 'Why would you?'

'Maybe he was fetching the pills from the bathroom cabinet and put down the note and then forgot it was there,' said Cat.

'What? How can you forget a suicide note? It's not a shopping list.'

'Well,' said Cat, 'Karen, you did say he was starting to lose his memory.'

'Yes,' said Karen, but she sounded doubtful. 'He did keep losing his keys and glasses and things. But I can't imagine why would he take the suicide note into the bathroom. No pen was found in there. He wrote in pen,' she added, 'not pencil, not biro, pen.' She leant back and stared at the ceiling and for a moment no one spoke.

'So,' said Karen, 'shall I read you the note? It is addressed to me, but I think it might help you.'

'Yes, please,' said Cat.

'His writing is very bad,' said Karen, 'a scrawl. I was the only person who could read it, so I've transcribed it.'

'OK.'

She leant forward and opened her tablet, its floral cover seeming somehow appropriate for a death.

Dear Karen,

I am very sorry to leave you with this mess. I hope you will realise that my death in no way reflects on the love I have for you and the children.

'Here,' said Karen, 'his writing went really jagged. Perhaps he was already failing.' A tear slid down her face onto the screen, but she wiped it away and went on.

I have decided it will be best for everyone if I now pass over to the other side. You will remember from your Dante that suicides go to purgatory until they are cleansed, so don't fear for my soul.

Karen stopped again. 'I don't think he's right,' she said crossly. 'I think suicides stayed in purgatory for eternity.'

None of the girls spoke and Karen, after glancing at the screen, continued.

A long time ago, I did something terrible. Useless to explain – I did not intend it to end the way it did; the consequence was horrific. I have lived with this for 57 years. No one ever knew about it. Now your mother is dead, I have no reason to continue living with the pain. Forgive me.

Please tell the children I love them both very much and you too.

Your ever-loving father.

'He signed it,' Karen said, gasping. 'He signed it Brian

Deliverer. As though I might confuse him with someone else. Why didn't he sign it Dad?'

She hugged herself and the detectives wondered if she might mute them or leave the room, but she continued. 'The police think it's done. He killed himself because of the pain and that was that. Gone. They've taken a few things from the house, but now they've finished their work they said they could bring them back if I needed them. The detective who rang me said they won't be investigating any further unless something odd comes up.'

'But they haven't contacted us,' said Miranda crossly.

She felt cheated. Now she would never know the truth behind the mysterious bridge game. Why play bridge, win, and then kill yourself? And the relationship with Mr Bennett's murder? Was he suggesting that was somehow suicide? Was it that having won the game he now felt vindicated and could die? It didn't make sense.

Cat's voice talking to Karen brought her back to reality.

'And you don't believe them?' asked Cat. 'Or you want to find out why he killed himself?'

'Both,' said Karen. 'I certainly don't think he would kill himself. Anyone could have written that note, copied his handwriting. What father writing to his daughter signs himself with his surname? He'd sign Dad, wouldn't he? I don't believe it. He loved spending time with my daughter, even though, thanks to COVID, we've only been able to see him through Zoom, the window or going for walks. He loved all of that. He wouldn't leave her. She's really upset.'

'And your son?' asked Miranda.

'Ah,' said Karen, playing with the toys on the table in front of her, building a stack of pens, which immediately fell down. 'Yes, there was some friction there. I don't know why, but the last few years my father and Tom have been rubbing each other up the wrong way. I spoke to Tom about it, and he said Granddad didn't like him anymore. When I asked my father, he just clammed up and said I should mind my own business and look after my children like a good Christian mother.'

'Oh?' said Cat, her voice jumping. 'A good Christian mother? What did he mean by that?'

'He doesn't ... didn't think I ought to go out to work,' said Karen. 'He didn't understand the modern world. I'm a physiotherapist and my salary really helps our family. My husband's a brickie and he's really good, but tradesmen are not paid as they should be.'

'I quite agree,' said Miranda. 'There's a shocking imbalance in income and it's not getting better. Did your mother work?'

'No, she didn't have to. My father was an only child. My grandmother set up a trust for when my father got married so his wife would never have to work. In fact, she wasn't allowed to work. If she got a job ... no money.'

'Oh,' said Stevie, 'what an odd trust. I've never heard of anything like that before.'

Karen's shrug looked somehow exaggerated by the Zoom screen.

'I think there were some religious issues there. I didn't really know my grandmother. She was always sick.'

'We need to look at your father's house,' said Miranda, 'but we'll have to do it without you being there. The police may be allowed to act as though COVID isn't happening, but detectives are still hampered by the rules. Can we do it?'

Karen shrugged again. 'Of course. He's no longer there. The body went long ago. There might be some yucky stuff I didn't wipe anything, and I expect the police have taken all the computers and everything of note. They always make a mess. I remember my father complaining about it.'

All three detectives were silent. They looked at each other, then Cat said quietly, 'When did he complain about it, Karen? Had he been involved with the police before?'

Karen looked surprised. Miranda got the feeling hers was not a family where they questioned statements made by their father.

'I don't know. Francis, my brother, might have a better idea. He's older and he used to ask questions all the time. I never did.'

'Thanks,' said Stevie. 'Send over his details and I'll send him an email while the other two go and look at the house.'

CHAPTER 6
LOSING A FATHER AND
FINDING A LANGUAGE
OWLY VALE 2020

After the call, Cat turned to the others. 'We need to decide who will be lead detective on this one. Last time, being completely equal didn't work.'

Miranda saw Cat was directing a rather rude glance her way. Ever since the Black Widow case where Miranda had rather distinguished herself, even if she said so herself, Cat had been jealous of her interviewing skills. OK, Cat did speak four languages fluently, but could she talk to normal people like an equal? However, Miranda thought with a flash of understanding, really Cat's imperious behaviour came not from having a big house in a small village, but from her belief that she was the only adult here. That total lack of understanding caused her difficulties with her children as well as her friends.

'I'll be lead detective,' Miranda said in a rather gentler voice than she might have used. 'After all, Simian partnered me.'

'Fine by me,' said Stevie.

Stevie had only once been lead detective when it was an aviation-related case. Otherwise, she was perfectly happy just doing the Internet research or flying her Tiger Moth when the weather was good enough. Basically, she didn't do people; machines were her thing.

'Fine,' said Cat. 'But you will take the case seriously, won't you? No pissing off drunk halfway through.'

The other two girls gave theatrical gasps.

'Bit bitchy, Cat,' said Miranda.

'Girls,' said Stevie, 'remember we *are* all on the same side.'

Cat moued and reached into her handbag for her lipstick. 'Sorry. I just feel sorry for Karen. Terrible thing when your father commits suicide.'

Miranda gasped for real this time. 'You think I don't know that?'

Cat blushed and dropped her lipstick. 'Sorry, I wasn't thinking. Spoke ...' she stopped, her hand waving vaguely. Clearly there was nothing she could say, how could anyone, let alone a close friend, have forgotten that Miranda's father had killed himself. Cat put her hand tentatively on Miranda's arm.

Miranda hugged her. 'It's OK, Cat. We all speak before thinking sometimes. I still love you. Let's go and visit Brian Deliverer's house. After that I think we should interview the three other people on our list. I'll do Piggy Big Noise.'

'Right,' said Cat, glancing at Stevie. 'Do you want to do any interviews?'

'Rather not.'

'OK,' said Miranda; she was in charge here, not Cat. 'Cat, can you do Paul Sweet and I'll do Terry Plump?'

'Right,' said Cat.

. . .

Karen had left the keys to the back door on the stoop. There was an alarm, but it wasn't set; perhaps the last policeman in the house didn't know the code. There was tape and fingerprint dust everywhere.

'Good at searching,' said Cat, 'not so good at clearing up. Probably men!'

'Ha ha.'

They agreed to start in the bathroom, where the note had been found. Going upstairs, they saw the bannisters had been dusted for fingerprints. Both women were wearing protective surgical gloves, COVID's answer to fingerprints.

'Why would they even do that?' asked Miranda.

'What?'

'Finger-dust the bannisters.'

'Maybe checking there was no one else in the house,' said Cat. 'Presumably they didn't find anything suspicious, or they'd still be investigating. We could ask Karen later. I'm making a list of questions to ask her.'

'OK.' Miranda drew out the word. Did Cat remember that she, Miranda, was the lead detective?

Upstairs the house smelt of mould tinged with maleness.

'Smells like Phillip's parents' house,' said Miranda, 'that grandparent smell that hits you when you go into old people's houses.'

Cat twiddled her phone; she was herself a grandmother, several times over.

The bathroom was vast, with a fireplace on one side and an armchair next to it. The Georgian wallpaper had peeled in the moisture of the room, which had an atmosphere of neglect.

'Unusual,' said Miranda, 'I've never seen an armchair in a bathroom before. Must rot the fabric.'

Cat nodded, pouting thoughtfully. 'Hm. It was popular in the 1960s, but surprising here. This bathroom looks as though it was done up ... when do you think? 1990s?'

'Popular in the sixties? Why? Bathroom parties.'

'I suppose. I was born in 1961, so I didn't partake. But my parents had a sofa in their bathroom before they did it up.'

Miranda sniggered at the follies of past generations. Would she have married Phillip if she'd seen him in a bathroom party first? Was it like swinging? Did they all drop their keys in the bubbles and dive in searching for them?

'Nice bath,' said Cat, indicating the feet under the base. 'In keeping with the period, I suppose, but I've never liked taps in the middle.'

'Makes it easier to share with a friend,' said Miranda.

'Hm, do you think Brian shared a bath with anyone?'

Miranda laughed. 'He must have had a hidden side after all.'

They looked in the bathroom cabinet but there were only the usual assortment of out-of-date prescription drugs, plasters, half-used cough medicine bottles and a few bottles of aspirins, strips of Nurofen and paracetamol.

'This lot wouldn't do for you,' said Cat. 'Not nearly enough hangover relief.'

'Ha ha, Cat, very funny.'

They left the bathroom and walked through the rooms, noting the dust as they went. There were three spare rooms. Two had cobwebs and a fine layer of dust over everything, even though cleaners were still allowed to visit under lockdown. The third had recently been cleaned and the bed made up. A water jug, a glass, and some biscuits sat on a small bedside table.

'We'd better ask Karen if Brian was planning to have someone to stay,' said Cat.

'Even if he was,' said Miranda, 'he wouldn't have told her. Not allowed under lockdown, is it?'

'Ah. Give you that.'

One for me, thought Miranda, hiding a grin, pretending not to point score.

'The cleaner might know though,' said Cat. 'Do we know who Brian used?'

'Probably Dolly – everyone in the village uses her. I'll ask her when she comes tomorrow,' said Miranda.

Miranda peeked her nose into a shower room that smelt of green mould. 'I must admit, I still can't remember ever having had a drink with Brian in the pub, or that he was so good at bridge. Brian knew all the conventions, but he really wasn't spontaneous or imaginative. He was rather a dull player.'

Cat glanced up and her foot caught the step. She grabbed Miranda's shoulder to steady herself. 'Different from the man last week, you mean?'

'Yes, as far as his playing, and even his attitude is concerned. Brian was a really quiet man. Last week's man was full of bravado, flirting, annoying even ... but different.'

'Perhaps his last night was an act. A last hurrah before he killed himself.'

'Really. You think Brian was such a good actor? I think a more possible scenario is that someone else played bridge with us after killing Brian.'

Cat turned and looked at her shocked. 'Why do you say that? The police didn't think so. They seemed quite happy the note was genuine, and Brian was alone in the house.'

'Maybe, but then the police didn't even come and talk to us about the bridge game.'

'Oh, actually ... they did ring Stevie, after she sent them a message saying we were playing bridge, but only to tell her none of Brian's computers had ever been used for BBO or Trickster. Brian hadn't played bridge through the whole lockdown. However, he did have a login name.'

'Oh. Thanks for telling me.'

'Sorry.'

Miranda bit her lip. Again, Cat seemed to have forgotten she was lead detective.

'What was his login name? And when was it created?'

'Simian. You'll have to ask Stevie about when it was made.'

'Simian!" said Miranda. "So, it *was* him. And yet he never used it on his computers. That doesn't make sense. The phone rang in his house. If he wasn't playing, then the killer was playing in his place. Using Brian's login but his own computer.'

'The killer brought his own computer?' said Cat lifting an imaginary computer and banging it downwards. 'Does any take their own computer when they visit a friend? Anyway, would you murder someone with a computer?'

'Possibly,' said Miranda, ignoring the flippancy but surprised by Cat's comment. She always took her own computer with her to other people's houses. 'Anyway, all the computers here look way old. BBO was started in 2011.'

'Oh, OK.' Cat nodded. 'Perhaps he was playing on his phone.'

'He wasn't, was he? We had WhatsApp on the phone, you can't do both.' Another point to me, thought Miranda, pinching herself to stop herself smirking.

'Hang on,' said Cat, 'even if we follow your crazy theory, there are two different problems. Let's suppose from the made-up bed that Simian knew Brian, and Brian gave him the Internet code and the login. How would he force Brian to take an overdose?

'Alternatively, if we assume he was a stranger, after all, Brian might always leave a bed made up – I do – why would Brian give him the Internet code and the login? Neither theory makes sense. I think he played bridge and then killed himself, and perhaps the police got the time he died wrong.'

'Unlikely,' said Miranda. 'These things are pretty accurate these days. I reckon someone came in, perhaps with a gun, and forced Brian to kill himself. Then he played bridge and hopped it taking his computer with him.'

'Maybe,' said Cat. 'Let's think it through. How long does it take to die after taking an overdose? If he took the drugs around ... when, six thirty? Just before he read to his granddaughter? Given that he was still playing with us up to ten o'clock, could it take three and a half hours to kill him? I'd have thought it was possible.'

'So long,' said Miranda. 'What if he took the overdose at five, then read to his granddaughter and died. Then it must have been someone else. Why are you so keen to cling on to the suicide theory?'

Cat twisted her nose. 'OK, I'll ask Gloria about timing of drugs and how long death takes. I guess her work in psychiatry might well include drugs and suicide. I should have thought about that before.'

Miranda laughed gently. 'Any excuse to talk to your favourite daughter-in-law. Not that you have any choice.'

Cat said nothing, looking suddenly wistful. Miranda realised she didn't want to dwell on her children's strange family structure and the fact her daughter-in-law lived with both Cat's son and Cat's daughter. And then there were the children ... neither Cat nor Miranda knew if Cat's son was their physical father or only their biological one.

In Brian's bedroom, the bedclothes were thrown back as

though someone had just got up, although there was a film of dust over everything. Above the bed was a crucifix.

'Look at that,' said Miranda. 'I haven't seen one of those since our trip to Poland to discover our roots. Looks like a Polish design.' She reached up and brought it down, moving in gently in her hands. 'Pretty. Looks pre-war, I wonder where he got it from.'

Cat nodded. 'We know he must have been religious. He talked about purgatory in his note, and clearly thought he was going to a better place.'

'Yes,' said Miranda, 'although Karen disputed that, didn't she?'

Cat nodded. 'Would that alone invalidate the suicide note, when everything else, including his writing seems genuine?'

Miranda was silent; she wasn't going to point score anymore. Cat needed to come to the same conclusion at her own speed.

The cupboards were full of shirts – work shirts, dress shirts, one of silk, which looked bespoke. Most were in good condition.

'All the right way round,' said Miranda.

Cat glanced at Miranda raising her eyebrows.

Miranda grinned. 'I sometimes turn Phillip's shirts inside out to see if he notices. I like the idea of him arriving at work with his shirt askew.'

Cat shook her head. 'Does he?'

'I imagine so. He often leaves in the dark, before I wake up, but he's never said.'

Brian's shoes were lined up neatly like soldiers. Most were black. All were polished and shining.

In the drawers were a few jumpers, still in their packaging. Cat opened a second cupboard and sucked her breath in. 'He liked his dark suits,' she remarked. 'There must be ten or fifteen here, black coats and wow, how many gloves?'

Miranda joined her. 'Look at the ties – obviously preparing for a lot of funerals.'

Cat snorted. 'Hm. Clearly not an embarrassing kipper-tie man.'

'No. Don't you remember him? He was always impeccably dressed, coat buttoned to the top, gloves, sometimes a hat. I thought he had some skin problem exacerbated by the sun. Never saw him in anything other than business clothes, did you?'

'No.'

'More hang-ups than a wardrobe and looking at that he had plenty of those too,' said Miranda raising an eyebrow.

'No women's clothes either,' said Cat thoughtfully, ignoring Miranda's joke.

'Who? What? Brian? You think he was trans?'

'No! Idiot. His wife only died a couple of years ago. I kept Charlie's clothes for five or so years before I threw them out. Widows often do.'

Miranda twisted her lips. 'Yeah, but Brian was not like you. I imagine him getting someone else, probably Karen, to sort out the clothes, and then sending them all to the charity shop.'

They went downstairs and into the living room where local landscapes and sailing paintings, mostly from another era, covered the walls. An elegant yacht speeding over the water, its sails ballooning out triumphantly, sat on a bookcase.

Miranda looked at the books. 'Lots of books about sailing here, and accountancy. Nothing on bridge. And the pictures are so old, with such a masculine feel. Do you think Brian threw out all his wife's pictures and books when she died, or just she didn't have any? No novels. No chick lit. No books on gardening or cookery. Weird. You would think from this room that Brian was a bachelor. Everything is from another era, nothing modern. Did he inherit all his furniture and pictures? Bought nothing himself?'

Cat twisted her nose thoughtfully. 'So, just following your theory of someone else playing bridge. Let's imagine Simian was using his own laptop. It doesn't necessarily make him a killer. He could have been in another room. Doing his own thing, while Brian killed himself. Perhaps Brian didn't even know he was there.'

'Indeed,' said Miranda, although she thought that unlikely.

Cat nodded to herself, thinking out loud. 'OK. So, perhaps Simian didn't know Brian was killing himself next door. He did answer the phone the second time it rang, not the first.'

Miranda bit her upper lip, trying to remember if the voice she'd heard on the phone sounded like the Brian she had met. Trouble was, she hadn't known him very well. An older man, and there were a lot of them in the village, Brian was more notable for his absence than his presence.

'The phone,' she said.

'What?'

'Where's his phone? The one he did WhatsApp on.'

'Maybe the police took it.'

Miranda raised her eyebrows. 'Karen didn't mention it. All right, on the list for Karen, but if it's not there, that is very odd. There must have been someone else and he must have known Brian was dead.'

Cat moved to the table, squeezing past a Victorian mirror on animal feet. 'Odd place to have a mirror,' she muttered. And then stopped. 'Look over here, Miranda.'

Miranda walked over to where Cat was looking down on a small table.

'It's been set out for a bridge game,' Cat said.

Miranda stared at it, examining the game. 'Do you recognise it, Cat?'

Cat stared at it for a while. 'That does look like my last hand on BBO.'

'It is. Someone laid this game out for Mr Bennett's murder.'

They stared at each other.

'I'll take a photo,' said Miranda, 'one of the table, another of the whole room. This obviously means something but is it a clue from Brian about who killed him or a warning from the killer to Brian?'

Off the living room was a small snug. It had been turned into a study by Brian, and a large desk crowded the space. The desk was empty apart from an inkstand half full of black liquid and a penholder.

'I've never seen such a tidy desk,' said Miranda. 'You should see mine.'

'Character,' said Cat.

Miranda yawned.

'You may not like it, Miranda,' said Cat, 'but you only have to see your desk to see you have an untidy mind. Brian clearly had a well ordered, if rather too restrained mind.'

'Cheek,' said Miranda, swatting her friend. 'I know where everything is.'

Cat frowned and started going through the drawers. The contents were as tidy as the top. 'Look at this.'

Miranda left the window, where she was watching a pheasant strutting across the lawn. 'What?'

'A stack of pre-signed letters.'

Miranda stared at the pile of unused paper, each with an

engraved letterhead at the top and 'Brian Deliverer' signed at the bottom.

'Wow! Who does that? Who even writes letters nowadays?' said Miranda. 'And an engraved letterhead? It's like something out of the darkest past.'

'Well, it explains why his suicide note had his full signature on it. There's no other paper in the desk.'

'But how odd. What if he wanted to write a second sheet?'

'Probably,' said Cat, 'he'd learnt that no one reads the second sheet. If you can't get it on the first page, don't bother writing it.'

Miranda grimaced, thinking of her many four- or five-page sheets of scrawl to her mother, who didn't like the computer.

'I wonder if he pre-signed cheques too,' she said. 'I bet he still used a cheque book.'

'He certainly thought things out in advance,' said Cat. 'I wonder how long he had been preparing to kill himself.'

'*If* he did it,' said Miranda. 'But think, a killer could also take a sheet from here and copy his handwriting. I bet I could do it.'

She grabbed a sheet of paper and sat down at Brian's desk. She wrote a short note in Brian's handwriting.

Cat leant over her shoulder. 'How did you do that? Just from the signature?'

'Yes, I've always been good at forgery. I think it goes with remembering faces. I'm an OK artist too. Remember details. But to be honest I'm probably making lots of mistakes, but since you aren't trained you can't see them.'

Cat frowned, 'you think the police used trained handwriting experts? You are a dark horse. Lucky I send every-

6

thing by email these days. My kids would be amazed to get a letter from me, especially the sort of thing you'd write.'

'Ha, ha.'

They moved into the basement, entering by a door under the stairs. It was so dusty and the entrance had so many cobwebs it was clear the police hadn't bothered to look down there. Down some rickety wooden steps, they entered a small chamber. Beyond the room the basement stretched under the house, but the ceiling was only waist high. Red wine, elderly champagne and sailing gear filled the room. Everything was dusty and covered with cobwebs. There were more old computers, laptops and tablets all under thick layers of mould and dirt.

'Did anyone ever come down here?' said Cat.

Miranda picked up a blue cardboard book saturated in layers of dust. On the cover was a title written in childish script.

The War of the Houses

There was a child's drawing of two houses separated by a swamp. The writing inside said:

The village had two big houses.
One belonged to Prima Dona, Queen of Rubber Bridge.
The other belonged to Hetti Omi, Emperor of Chicago.
Between them lay the conduit of corybungus, quagmire of
quongs, and the mud of meshigener.

Miranda laughed. 'I wonder if Karen made this. It's certainly not Brian's illegible scribble. Looks like a secret language. It must relate to bridge playing, with the Queen of Rubber Bridge versus the Emperor of Chicago. Obviously children who played the game a lot. We did too as kids. I wonder what quongs are, or meshingener ... it might be wonderful onomatopoeia; if we knew what it meant!'

Cat, always fascinated by linguistics, hurried to her side saying. 'Oh, we'll have to ask Karen if she plays like her father—'

Her foot caught in an old lifejacket, and she sprawled onto the floor, grabbing a heap of boating equipment as she fell. 'Bugger! I think I've broken my arm.'

Miranda put down the book and had a look. 'Rubbish, you're fine. Cats have nine lives anyway.'

'Thanks.'

Miranda moved to give her a playful pinch and stopped. 'Look what you've unearthed.'

Cat turned and saw, tucked away under the low part of the cellar was a whole stack of old cine film rolls, the type that families used in the 1950s and 1960s.

'I wonder when these were last looked at,' murmured Cat, standing up and reaching under the low ceiling to pick up the closest reel. An avalanche of dust accompanied it as she pulled it from the pile.

Miranda coughed. 'Last century!' she said gasping cheerfully. 'Look, there's an old projector too.'

Cat pulled it slowly out, her sore arm forgotten. 'It's got a modern plug on,' she said. 'I'm sure plugs were different in the sixties.'

'Were they?'

'We'll have to ask Stevie to look it up, but I remember my parents using round plugs in the sixties and seventies.'

Miranda was fiddling with the projector. 'How do you work these things?'

Cat wrinkled her nose. 'There are some benefits of being older,' she said. 'I know exactly how it works. My step-brother loved films and we had hundreds of me running naked in the garden or him fishing or birdwatching.'

'Kinky!'

The reels were labelled 'Boat trip June 1957', 'July 1957', 'August 1957', 'June 1958', and all the summer months every year up to 1963.

Then there was a different coloured label: 'Climbing trip in Nepal 1957'.

'Is there a screen down here too?'

'Can't see one, but the walls are white upstairs, and we can take down a picture or two.'

'OK, let's take them all upstairs. If they were kept here hidden away, they must hold some clues.'

CHAPTER 7
INNOCENTS IN JACK'S CLUB, 1963

O ne diamond,' said Bev, winding her ring slightly.
'Pass,' said Mr Tank, on her left.
Jack, watching the game, could already imagine a leer forming on Tank's internal face. Of course, there would be nothing visible; Tank and his partner played poker in the club far more often than they played bridge. Tank had the king, queen, jack and two little diamonds. Although he only had a count of seven, his partner would certainly have something, and they would have enough to get the girls down. Tank loved playing with green molls, and anyone could see the girl Fran was an innocent for the plucking.

'Oh ... three clubs, I think,' said Fran, her eyes hardly flickering over the winding ring on her partner's finger.

'Pass,' said Mr Ruby.

Jack imagined Tank's annoyance. He was no doubt hoping to play with diamonds as trumps, given the hand he held. He wondered what tricks that clever little innocent was pulling tonight.

'Five diamonds,' said Bev.

'Double,' said Tank.

Tank obviously intended that call to be a lead-inducing signal. Whatever the girls played in, clubs or diamond, provided his partner led diamonds the boys would certainly knock them into cinders. This was a war Tank was ready to win. Although his face remained impassive, Tank was clearly cheering inside, ready to enjoy this game.

Fran spent a lot of time deliberating, almost speaking then holding back, thinking. Tank loved it. You could almost hear her little brain ticking over, he thought. She'd got herself in too deep for sure. He was going to put a big, big bet on this one. He might even get the girl, as well as the money, for the night.

'Seven no trumps,' said Fran.

Tank almost wet himself in delight. There was going to win big tonight. He pushed all his money into the centre.

'Double,' Ruby said.

'Redouble,' said Bev.

Jeeezzus! Did those bitches never learn?

Behind him and unseen by any of the players Jack made a signal for Clinton to send over the security, discreetly. Whatever the outcome of this game, the amount of money involved meant emotions were going to be charged.

Fran went no trumps, so Mr Ruby had the lead. He led a small diamond, as per Tank's signal. Even if they lost the first trick, he would win many others, and the girls would lose the game. With each point worth a penny and the redouble meaning that was multiplied by four hundred, he and his partner were going to win a lot of money. Tank knew he wasn't a genius at sums but that could be leading to a tidy pony or more.

Bev put down her hand. OK, thought Tank, so she had the ace, and she had six little babies, but did she really think that was enough to go five diamonds? What an idiot. If her partner was relying on her diamonds for the length she was going to be corked.

Mr Tank's legs did a jig under the table.

Fran said, 'Thank you, partner,' in what sounded like a strangled voice. She had spent a lot of time preparing her strategy, much that that would help her, silly greengage.

She took the first trick in dummy. Tank was surprised to see she had no diamonds; even less brainpower going no trumps with no diamonds at all. She'll get stuck in her hand, or I'm a donkey's aunt.

Fran then led a club from dummy back to her own hand. No surprise there. She took the next six tricks in clubs. However, Tank could see dummy held the ace of hearts, so she'd have to go back there eventually. He stored his diamonds in preparation; dummy was also keeping hers. Obviously, the dumb youngster thought she would squeeze them into throwing their high diamonds and she would win on length. What a plank!

Fran went over to the ace of hearts in dummy and led herself the last spade on the table. She then took the rest of the tricks because her hands held only spades.

'Seven no trumps, bid and made,' she said. 'Gosh! Wasn't I lucky?'

'Looks like you owe us a monkey,' said Bev blandly.

Tank was about to jump up in fury when he felt Jack's hand on his shoulder. 'Wasn't she lucky?' Jack said. 'Those diamonds would have been killers. How fortunate for her she couldn't get back to dummy earlier.'

Tank stared at his money on the table, which the girls were now scooping into a bag.

'Time to go,' said Bev. 'Thanks, guys.'

And they disappeared quicker than the fairy dust they must have spread in his eyes.

The girls were relaxing in the Culture Club when Jack came over.

'You a member, Miss Jack?' said Muriel snappily. 'I don't remember seeing your subscription. We've got a better class of people here. Didn't you see the sign? No dogs. No Irish.'

'Leave it out, Muriel,' said Bev stroking her hand lazily down Muriel's arm. 'He's my guest. Sometimes you need the muscle.'

Muriel shrugged her hand off and, turning away rudely, went to talk to some of the members.

'You're getting greedy, Bev,' said Jack hitting his fist against his palm to control his emotion. 'That was too transparent. Even a thicko like Phil Tank can see when he's being done over big time like that.'

Bev winced. 'It beats walking the streets.'

'For you, maybe – what about Fran?'

They both looked over at the girl, who was now playing bridge with a group of young women, all of whom were members of the club. Fran looked up and waved, blew Jack a kiss, but went straight back to the game.

'See. All she wants to do is play bridge,' he said. 'She's better than that. She's clever. She could play without cheating and still win.'

'Like you know? You getting soppy over her? Or what? She isn't for you, lover. Not your type.'

Jack growled. 'You know what my type is, do you?'

Bev looked him up and down as though ascertaining his worth as a client, but then said in an apparently loving voice, 'OK, OK, I'll send her down to visit her mother in

Chichester. But it can't be too long. You're not the only one who falls for her. She's dynamite, and not just in diamonds.'

As she turned away from the man, Bev grinned at her own deceit. Of course, there was no loving mother in Chichester to go home to, and to send her home to Daddy would mean death. Fran would merely hide in the open, but Jack, like any big muscular man, would not understand what that meant or even why it was necessary.

CHAPTER 8
CLASSIC FILM NIGHT IN OWLY VALE 2020

Miranda and Cat carried all the film spools and the projector upstairs and set it up in the living room, so it faced one of the white walls.

Miranda took down a couple of pictures of sailboats from the 1930s while Cat wound the spool around its head and started up the machine. The first few frames were a mixture of brown and white lights and shapes, with odd flashes, numbers and lines.

Then the first film started. The label was 'Boat Trip at Sundown 1952' and showed a man in a striped jacket with loose-fitting trousers, more reminiscent of a 1920s musical than the 1950s. He was carrying a small child, two or three years old, wearing a dark blue skirt, a red and white top, and a sailor hat, while a second child in blue shorts walked beside him. The man climbed onto the boat from the dock, put the girl down on one of the bench seats, helped the boy onto the deck, then disappeared below. The little girl was holding a toy boat. She pushed it and it fell off the edge of the seat; the boy reached for it, but she pushed him aside and fell off herself. Her face slowly welled up and the screen filled with crying child. The man rushed back on deck, examined her, gave a flamboyant shrug towards the camera and shook her.

Miranda laughed, but Cat stared at the flickering pictures, her lips pouting in disapproval. 'That shake looked a bit too rough,' she said.

'Hm,' said Miranda. 'Theatrical. Don't forget there is someone else there, probably the mother, filming. But then I can't imagine you disciplining your children at all. That's probably why they're so characterful.'

'Ha ha,' said Cat, but Miranda could see her opinion hadn't changed.

The next one was from 1953, with the same crew except the children were bigger. The girl was in a blue and white sailor suit and a white hat, while the boy's outfit looked almost Victorian. Several more reels of the boat followed from the years 1954, 1955, and 1956. Always the same boat, sometimes with just the man, sometimes the girl was carried by a woman in loose trousers and a dark blue top with an anchor on the shoulder, and sometimes it was just the boy. Other films without children were shown. Occasionally there were other people on the boat, some of those with children.

The same boat appeared in 1957, now looking very spruce as though it had just been painted. In this one, the boy was wearing a sailor suit but there was no sign of the girl; however, the way the camera moved around shakily made the detectives wonder if a second child was filming.

As they moved through the 1960 reel, Cat stopped. 'Look at the boy now – he looks about ten years old. Do you think that could be a young Brian Deliverer? The boy has that blondish red hair he kept until the end.'

Miranda nodded. 'Could be. I was told to look at the ears

and nose. Apparently, those are good indicators. Shall we call him Brian anyway, to distinguish him from the others?'

The potential Brian was wearing slacks and a striped jacket. His clothes made him look like a small replica of the older man.

By 1961, Brian's dress had remained the same but there were two other boys with him wearing shorts and T-shirts. Father was at the helm and clearly enjoying himself. The other boys seemed to be taking it in turns to do the filming because Brian appeared in most of the shots with one or other of the boys.

'Oh, blah,' said Miranda as they looked through Boat Trip 1961. 'This is so boring. Not even in colour and certainly no choreography. The old dad obviously liked himself and his boat. How many more?'

'Have a break,' said Cat, 'let's look at this one on Nepal in 1957 and then go back to the boat trips.'

'Ha, OK, might as well.'

The Nepal film showed pictures of Dad with several Sherpas and groups of young boys. Neither of the women knew anything about climbing, but even so they could see the equipment was archaic: no helmets, and the climbers wearing cotton shirts, woollen jerseys, floppy cotton trousers or voluminous breeches and anoraks. On their feet were boots or noticeably tattered gym pumps. There was no sign of the boy on the boat.

'Weird – Brian didn't go climbing then?'

'Too young,' said Cat. 'It says 1957 on the tin, when he was only seven.'

'But there are some other young boys with the father. Any idea what Brian's father was called?'

'We need to ask Karen.'

'OK.'

They watched two more boat trips from 1961, 1962, and the last one was 1963.

'Perhaps he sold the boat,' said Cat.

There were also some rolls where the labels had fallen off.

'Keep going,' said Cat. 'There's a reason Brian kept all the films but couldn't bear to watch them anymore. There has to be something here.'

'OK,' said Miranda, 'OK.'

Right at the bottom of the pile was another one without a label.

'OK,' said Miranda, 'looks like the last one. Thank Heavens. If I get one more look at that blooming boat, I'm going to be seasick.'

'Ha, ha. Very funny.'

This film started in the normal way, on the approach to the same boat, but then became much more theatrical. There were distant shots out to sea and then close-ups of each one of the actors. Whoever was now handling the camera had learnt much more of his or her craft and become more expert. Again, there was Brian, but this time the schoolfriends seemed to be much more in the picture, doing useful things like holding sheets and casting off. When all three boys were in the frame, the quality of the filming was lower. Seemed like Dad was not as artistic as the boys.

'They must be relations,' said Cat. 'They've been in most of the films, just more in prominence in this one.'

'Could be friends,' said Miranda, she sucked her lip thoughtfully. 'But ... hang on.'

Cat glanced at her. 'What?'

'Remember that film about climbing in Nepal. Those

two boys were there too,' she said pointing at the screen.
'They were younger ... what was the date on that one?'

Cat fished it out of the pile. '1957. But Brian wasn't in the
Nepal pictures. If you were going to take a relative, wouldn't
you take your son?'

'Perhaps they were older. Seven does seem a bit young.
Let's see that Nepal video again.'

Cat rewound it and put the spools up again. They slowly
watched the film unfold.

'There,' said Miranda, 'look at that one, the skinny boy.
Definitely not Brian.' She shook her head. 'That boy is
slightly built. Look at the way he walks – lithe, athletic.
Remember Brian on the boat in the early sixties. He was
diffident, uncertain. Also, he's a different build to this boy.
Bigger, lumpish. Now look at the third boy, with dark hair
all over his face. Look at his ears, how they stick out. Then
get up that 1961 film.'

Cat wound up the other reel, put it on to the projector,
and played the film.

'See,' said Miranda. 'A boy with sticky-out ears, and that
same slightly broad face. And the petite lithe one. It's the
same boys. I'm sure of it.'

Cat nodded.

Miranda studied all the people in the film, committing
their faces to memory. 'OK, back to Nepal.'

'Pity we don't have sound,' said Cat, putting up the Nepal
film again. 'Look at this bit where clearly the skinny boy is
doing something that's really making the old dad laugh.'

Miranda looked. All the Sherpas had gathered around
the boy, who was performing. They were relaxed and laughing. Happy faces filled the screen.

'He looks like he might be doing imitations. What do
you think?'

'Yes, or maybe that's another element to Brian. If he was doing imitations, he would look different,' said Cat. 'We could ask Karen if her father did imitations. Or if she had a cousin who did.'

Miranda shook her head. 'That is not Brian. Trust me. But he might be holding the camera. I wonder what happened to the girl. After the first few reels she disappeared.'

'Oh dear, we'd better ask Karen. She might have died,' said Cat. 'What was the mortality rate for children in the 1950s and sixties? I know it was very high before the war. My father was one of ten children born and only five survived to adulthood.'

The film came to an end. Cat packed up the home cinema and put the projector, the film of Nepal and the last film in her car.

'Why are you doing that?' asked Miranda. 'Nobody's going to come here. Karen has the only key, and it's not as though the police are interested.'

Cat looked at her. 'Evidence,' she said. 'Something doesn't feel right to me. I think we're better off taking anything we find suspicious home. Otherwise, it may not be here tomorrow.'

'Okey dokey,' said Miranda, 'but to me that feels like belt, braces and more braces.'

'Impossible for a detective to be too suspicious,' said Cat picking up her monster handbag full of reassuring lipsticks.

CHAPTER 9

YASHMACKS, PONTEFRACT
AND A LITTLE BIT OF FISH

When Cat and Miranda got back to the office, Stevie had news. 'Karen's brother Francis sent me an email,' she said. 'Interesting email address, he calls himself Frank@Anglinout.'

Miranda raised her eyebrows. 'Big fisherman?'

'No. It took me a while to find out what it meant, but I'm pretty sure it refers to the only successful escapees from Alcatraz. One of them was called Frank, which can be short for Francis, and the other two were brothers called Anglin.'

'What?' said Cat. 'Bit far-fetched, don't you think?' She got out her lipstick and redid her red lips, giving herself time to think.

'I think it's quite clever,' said Miranda. 'Maybe it refers to his escape from the UK.'

'I'm not sure I see the relevance,' said Cat. 'Is he suggesting he was in prison here?'

'I asked him in my second email, but all he replied was that he was too emotional about his father's death to talk to us now, but he would arrange a date in a week or so.'

'Poor thing,' said Miranda, hugging herself. 'It's even

worse when you've fallen out with the person who dies –
now he'll never be reconciled with his father. Awful.'

'A week or so,' said Cat pragmatically. 'Not very helpful.
What did his sister say to that?'

'She said she would try and get him to talk to us sooner
but he didn't seem to feel any urgency. He apparently said,
"Well Dad's already dead, so what difference will a few
weeks make?" She wasn't very impressed.'

'Hm, do you think her funds are running out?' asked
Cat, putting away her lipstick and checking her teeth in the
mirror.

'So, Stevie,' said Miranda, crossing her arms and
compressing her lips. 'What did the police say to you about
no computers in Brian's house with BBO or Trickster
installed, or even used?'

'Not that exactly. They're not magicians,' Stevie said with
the kindness she reserved for her Internetally-challenged
friends. 'What they said was that clearly none of Brian's
computers had been used for a while, and since Brian had
pretty much no security, anyone could use his internet. They
checked the router activity and there was some around that
time. BBO told me that the teacher who set up the Mr
Bennett game on the site used a VPN. Obviously, they
couldn't trace that.'

'Obviously,' said Miranda, cleaning her shoe on the back
of her trousers.

Cat, apparently less embarrassed about her lack of
computer knowledge, butted in. 'And all that means what,
exactly?'

'Someone was using Brian's Internet, when we played.
But for the set-up of special games he or she used a VPN –
an untraceable network.'

'Makes sense,' said Cat. 'Brian's house is on the edge of

the village. Someone could just have walked into the garden and used a computer there ...'

'It was raining that evening,' said Miranda. 'I remember because I had to run out with the dog before bridge and we both got soaked.'

'Ah, how about a shed in the garden?'

'There is one,' said Stevie, looking on Google Maps, 'but it looks too far away to get the Internet, unless he's run a cable there. We could check.'

'OK.'

'By the way,' said Stevie. 'Did you find any old computers hanging around?'

'Yes, the cellar was full of them. Why?'

'Your sister got info from Apple – I didn't ask how – apparently Brian had about forty computers registered in his name at some time or other. Usually, he only kept them a couple of days before they were reregistered.'

'Why on earth would anyone do that?'

'Was he a schoolteacher? Perhaps schoolteachers register computers under their own names, instead of the school.'

'Doubt it,' said Cat. 'That would allow kids to access all the adults-only bits. Anyway, he was an accountant.'

Stevie looked amazed. 'What? I didn't think you knew anything about computers.'

'No, but I have Netflix on TV and it has a separate area for kids and adults. I assume computers are the same.'

'Cool. How many did you find in the cellar?'

'There must have been four or five or so there, but certainly not forty. Most of them looked like old Apple Macs. Perhaps he was hoping to sell them.'

'Maybe. Obviously, the police didn't think them relevant because they left them there.'

'Maybe,' echoed Cat, 'but I don't think the police went into the cellar. There was a pretty significant level of dust everywhere.'

CHAPTER 10
ROUND AND ROUND THE HORNE

Miranda called Percy Bigby on his landline, hoping she would remember not to call him Piggy Big Noise.

His wife answered the phone. 'Oh, hello, Miranda. Yes, he's here, can you hear that noise?'

For a moment Miranda was flummoxed. His wife knew then, did she, what they called him? Did she agree? Think it funny?

'It's the chainsaw, terrible noise. He's out in the garden, but as soon as it rains I'll ask him to call you. What shall I tell him it's about?'

Thank heavens for nosy wives, thought Miranda. 'Bridge. You don't happen to know if he was playing bridge on 8 January, do you? Only we have a missing prize winner and I wondered if it was him.'

'Nope,' said his wife, 'as it happens, I know exactly what he was doing on 8 January, but you won't tell anyone. will you?'

'Scout's honour.'

She laughed cheerfully. 'Shouldn't that be girl guide's,

Miranda? The eighth is my daughter's birthday and even though technically we shouldn't, we popped over to her house and met up for a celebration ... outside, of course!'

'Thanks,' said Miranda, 'well that answers that. No need for him to call me back then.'

She was quite sure it had been raining on 8 January, but never mind. She had her answer.

She was about to call Terry Plump when she got a text from Cat.

'Paul Sweet, our other bridge player, had COVID in January. He was in hospital in Chichester. He's OK, back home now but still gets very tired. Xx Cat'

Only Cat, thought Miranda, would use correct punctuation in a text.

So that knocked two Simian suspects off the list. Now for Terry Plump.

No one answered Terry's phone and Miranda tried and failed to remember if he was married or not. In fact, he was one of those people she had had a drink or two with but knew absolutely nothing about. Wasn't that odd? She was usually so good at finding out things about people, and yet she knew nothing about Terry. Rather unwillingly she typed his name into Google. She usually preferred to let Stevie play Internet games, but needs must.

Apparently, Terry Plump was a range of make-up, particularly good for 'plumping up your lips'.

Miranda closed the machine and decided to wait until Terry deigned to answer the telephone.

CHAPTER 11
SIMIAN'S SHEESH GRAVE

The next day, Stevie got a message from Frank@Anglinout.com – a short email headed 'St Ruperts's Monastery Cemetery'. It said 'Have a look for a grave just outside the cemetery walls.'

'Bit cryptic,' said Miranda. 'Couldn't he have given some more details? A name, for example. Who do you think we're looking for?'

Cat nodded. 'Yes, is he teasing us? Like Simian. He could be Simian?'

Miranda looked at her, narrowing her eyes. 'He says he's in Australia, but he might have come over here before lockdown. Does he have a family or anything over there?'

'We should ask Karen. Let's add that to the list,' said Cat. 'OK, now can we all go in the same car? We're not the same family, so is that OK?'

'Of course we can,' said Miranda. 'We're in the same bubble. But anyway, it would be ridiculously unenvironmental to take three cars to the cemetery and back. Wear a mask if you're worried, Cat.'

As Cat pulled her mask out of her handbag, Miranda raised her eyebrows. 'Ah, the recyclable surgical mask.'

'Ha, ha,' said Cat. 'Just because you think of masks as a fashion item. What are we wearing today? The skeleton? The flying birds? The laughing mouth?'

Miranda swiped her. 'At least mine are hygienic. Yours must be covered in lipstick.'

The cemetery was set back from the monastery and only connected by an isthmus of land, most of which was paved, but some graves lined the path. A quick glance at the tombstones showed the graves along the isthmus were mostly inhabited by the friars who had once lived in the monastery, their names and dates inscribed on the tombstones. The graveyard was deserted, apart from an old man cleaning the stones.

'Only ten monks and friars live here now,' said Stevie. 'It's a dying profession.'

'Vocation,' snapped Cat, 'it's a vocation, not a profession. You can't decide to be a monk or friar, you're called.'

'OK, sorry,' said Stevie looking at her in concern. 'I only meant the number living here is dwindling.'

Cat put her hand on her friend's arm, forgetting that was forbidden under COVID. She shook her head slightly. Religion did this to her, wound up her normally calm persona, but how could she shout at Stevie? Miranda, yes, anyone could get annoyed with her, but Stevie, no; she was gentle and abstract, obsessed by flying and computers possibly a source of exasperation, but not a target for anger.

After the isthmus there was a low wall enclosing the rest of the burial ground. The women climbed over it and walked around the outside, clambering through overgrown clematis, jasmine and thorn bushes, some of which probably had a heady scent in the spring, but which now just scratched their legs. There were no graves there.

'Nothing,' said Cat as they got back to the isthmus, 'not a grave in sight. Waste of time.'

'Maybe,' said Stevie getting out her phone. 'I have an idea.'

She fiddled with her phone and then said: 'Yup, the boundary wall was extended outwards in 1970.'

'Why?' asked Cat.

'More stiffs than expected,' said Miranda doing a little jig. 'Perhaps the monks were incredibly good at converting sinners just before they died.'

Stevie laughed but Cat frowned. 'Now for the graves just inside the walls.'

'OK,' said Miranda, 'here we go again – round and round went the grave hunters in search of ... of what? Not Paradise, presumably.'

Cat turned her back on her. 'How much did the wall move by, Stevie?'

'Ten feet all round.'

'Wicked,' said Miranda. 'Probably only a hundred or so graves – piece of cake. OK, let's go from different directions this time.' Miranda took the left-hand circle and examined each grave as she went.

John Thomes, 1916 – 1970. May his soul rest in peace.
Margery Pumpkin 1899 – 1970. Joining Herbert Pumpkin in
peaceful rest.

And on and on and on. She yawned. Couldn't they have something more interesting like 'Just missed damnation, lucky bugger!' Or 'Bet he needs a whisky in hell'? At least that would make you laugh.

However, just as she was about to reconnect with Cat and Stevie, and at the furthest point from the monastery, she came across a grave with an elaborate marble headstone.

An old man with a bucket of water was cleaning it, easing over the letters gently with his sponge. 'Good morning, ma'am,' he said.

'Hello,' said Miranda, amazed to be called *ma'am*. 'Lovely day. You're doing a super job.'

'Thank you, ma'am,' he said. He got up slowly and, lifting his bucket, walked away.

On the marble headstone the words 'Frances Deliverer 1949 to 1963. By their fruits ye shall know them' were engraved.

'This must be it,' said Cat coming up beside her. 'At last.'

'But he's still alive,' said Miranda, 'and sending us messages from Oz.'

'Look at the date,' said Cat. 'Born in 1949, buried in 1963. Oh! And the sex. This says Frances Deliverer. Perhaps this is the little girl in the first cine reel we saw.'

'Oh yes. I'd forgotten about her. Except – hang on. What happened to her between 1953 and 1963?' said Miranda.

'Ten years,' said Stevie, 'perhaps she didn't like sailing. Refused to go on the boat.'

'But she can't be Brian's sister, or Karen would have mentioned her,' said Cat.

'A cousin then,' said Miranda. 'Another unaccounted-for Deliverer.'

'Perhaps it wasn't worth mentioning an aunt who died before Karen was born,' said Stevie, getting out her phone again. 'Why would she even remember her? Let alone talk about her. Unless there was some scandal connected with her.'

'Actually,' said Cat, 'in those days, even more of a reason to pretend she hadn't been born. But we still have the original question to answer: why was she buried outside the church boundary? Do you two know what it means to be buried outside the cemetery walls?'

'Not enough space inside?' asked Miranda, raising her eyebrows and rolling her eyes.

'Ha, ha, I'm serious.'

'OK, OK! Go on.'

'It means she did not get forgiveness. Because of something she did, she could not be buried in the cemetery but only outside.'

'What sort of thing?' asked Miranda, narrowing her eyes.

'I don't really know,' said Cat, 'but I remember being taught that if you commit blasphemy against the Holy Spirit, you cannot be buried in holy ground. Remember my religion lapsed long ago, around her age in fact.'

'She was thirteen or fourteen! What could such a child do that would constitute blasphemy against the Holy Spirit?'

'I'm not sure. Life was both stricter and easier then,' said Cat unhelpfully.

'But,' said Stevie thoughtfully, 'couple of points: one, she still has a tombstone. Surely, if she were to be one of the unremembered dead, they would not give her a tombstone. And two, Francis Deliverer, the brother of Karen, was born in what, 1980 or so? How would he know a grave had gone inside the walls in 1970? He wouldn't have seen it until it had been inside the walls for years. That means both that someone told him and he wanted us to know the walls had moved. Why?'

'Good point. I wonder when the gravestone was put

there,' said Cat. 'It could have been later on. It might have even been put there by Brian.'

'One thing's for sure,' said Miranda, blowing out her cheeks. 'Karen has not been telling us everything.'

On the way back, Miranda sent Karen a text. 'Got a couple of questions. Can we have a Zoom this afternoon?'

'Yes, 3 p.m. suits me.'

'Perfect.'

At 3 p.m., Stevie sent Karen a link and there she was on her floral sofa with the pink walls behind, but this time wearing blue. Perhaps she'd seen the previous clash of colours reflected in the screen.

'We've just been to the cemetery at the monastery,' said Miranda, 'on your brother's suggestion. We found a grave for a Frances Deliverer buried in 1963, with a date of birth of 1949. Do you know anything about this girl? Could she be a cousin or something? Or even Brian's sister who died?'

'Dad was an only child,' she said. 'And I never heard that Grandpa had any brothers or sisters. We certainly never met any cousins on that side. On my mother's side it was different. She had loads and loads of brothers and sisters and they all had about four children. Francis and I were overrun with Smasher cousins, but I never met any Deliverers.'

'Well, if this was a cousin, she'd have been dead before you were born anyway,' Stevie pointed out. 'She died in 1963. When were you born?'

'1982.'

'Did your father ever talk about a cousin? Or an aunt?' asked Cat.

'No, nothing,' said Karen. 'I'm afraid you'll have to ask Francis. If it was his idea, it means something to him.'

'Also,' said Miranda, 'and this may seem a strange question. Do you play bridge?'

'No.'

'Does Francis?'

'Yes. He did all the Andrew Robson courses, went up to London for them. I think he has a group in Oz. Dad was against it, which probably made Francis keener.'

Miranda frowned. 'Why was your father against it? He played himself.'

'Yes, but Dad used to say it was like a shotgun – fine if you knew what you were doing, but dangerous in the wrong hands.'

Like Mrs Bennett, thought Miranda, wondering if Brian Deliverer kept a gun.

'Hm. Where does your brother live in Oz?'

'In the Blue Mountains. His wife has a property or some woodland or something there. I know they've narrowly missed being burnt on a couple of occasions. His children are about the same age as mine, but they've only ever met on Zoom. We'd love to go over there and see them all, but you know how expensive it is for a family to travel out there.' She fidgeted in her chair. 'Well, we'll see what we get for Dad's house. I keep optimistic that we might finally be able to meet.'

'That would be fabulous,' said Miranda enthusiastically, 'how lovely. I love meeting new relations. People who share so many of your genes and yet are strangers. I find it so exhilarating.'

Karen laughed, and Miranda realised that was the first time they heard her do so. 'Thank you. Yes, I really hope it happens.'

'Did your father have a phone?' asked Miranda. 'Did the police take it?'

'Oh, yes,' said Karen, 'I meant to say. They found a Nokia, one of those old things that people used to have yonks ago. But they said it didn't look as though he'd used it for a while. The battery wasn't even charged, and they couldn't find a cable. I'm not sure if he still had it or it was lost. I know he was thinking of getting an iPhone, but whether he actually did, I'm not sure.'

'OK,' said Miranda. An elderly Nokia wouldn't work with WhatsApp, but perhaps that phone belonged to the other Simian. She was quite certain now that there had been someone else playing bridge with them from Brian's house, but who? The only person left on their 'possibles' list was the elusive Terry Plump. Perhaps they needed an 'also ran' list.

'Incidentally, what happened to your mother's things after she died? There didn't seem to be anything of hers in the house.'

'No,' said Karen sucking her upper lip. 'Dad didn't want anything in the house that reminded him of her. He asked me to take everything I wanted, send stuff to Frankie, and the rest to the charity shop.'

'OK, thanks.'

'One other thing,' said Cat. 'I wanted to ask about your grandmother and grandfather. What were they like? What were their names?'

'Karl and Hannah,' said Karen. 'We knew our grandfather. He was a frighteningly strict man. I seldom saw him smile. Our grandmother was always ill. She occasionally came to see us, pushed in a wheelchair, but mostly she stayed at home, in bed. I can only just remember her. She died when I was eight and Francis was eleven. My mother said she never got over her son's death ...'

She stopped, staring up at the ceiling as though hoping to find something there.

'What?' said Miranda. 'What son? Did she have a son by a previous marriage?'

Karen brought her gaze back to the screen. She fiddled with something on her lap. 'OK,' she said after a few moments' pause. 'Maybe. Look, I'm not sure. It was just something my mother said, and then ... well ... Look, I don't know what sort of family you're from,' said Karen, now pulling her earlobes one after the other as though removing earrings, 'but we weren't encouraged to ask questions. My parents said "Children are to be seen and not heard". It's not like that now. I encourage my children to ask questions.'

'Well done,' said Cat. 'I always did too.'

Miranda rolled her eyes. Cat's children were the most critical family she'd ever met. The only good one was the daughter-in-law, and she was a huge complication of religious angst.

'Francis is older than me by three years,' said Karen. 'So he went to local parties long before I did. One Christmas, he was at a party in East Harting. He was probably about fifteen or sixteen. But you know what those parties were like – eight to eighties we called them – everyone came. Anyway, he could see this old girl over the other side of the room asking someone about him. The way you can always tell someone is talking about you. Some sixth sense.'

Miranda nodded.

'So,' Karen went on, 'she toddled over to see him. "Hello," she said, "I'm Maria Hearthop. You must be Francis Deliverer. You have such a family look." Francis was amazed. He looks nothing at all like my father, who is, sorry, was, a big, rugged man, like his own father. Francis is quite tall but small boned. I'm the strapping great big one like Dad. Lucky me, eh! Not. If anything, he looked like Mum, but she was quite well built too, even if not as much as Dad.

'So, he says, "That's nice to hear. I thought I was adopted, so little family resemblance." And he said it with a little laugh, not wanting to sound rude to an older woman.

'"Nah," she says. He said you could see she was that sort of woman, say what she thinks, no holds barred type, if you know what I mean. "Not Deli Deliverer – you look like your uncle. The first Francis."

'Well, Francis was stunned. He didn't say a word. His mind was reeling. No one had ever mentioned his father had a brother. There were no photos in the house. No occasional references to a dead uncle. Neither parent nor my grandparents had ever referred to another child in the family, let alone another boy. So, when he got home, he came into my room. I wasn't asleep. I didn't sleep well as a kid, always thinking about things. He wanted me to ask Dad about it. I was always Dad's favourite and, well, to be honest, Dad and Francis never got on well. Francis didn't dare ask Dad, or not then at any rate.

'Next morning, I tried to bring up the subject at breakfast. I was having my muesli – Mum liked us to eat muesli, she thought it was good for us. Francis always refused. Even as a baby he threw it on the floor. I asked how the party went last night.

'Mum said it was fun, lots of locals there, and she started to list who was there. She was lovely, my mum, a real people's person. I missed her so much when she died ...'

Karen stopped, blushed, obviously realising she had gone off the point. 'Dad didn't say anything. He was reading the paper. He always read the paper at breakfast. So, I said, partly to Mum, because I thought she was the only adult listening, that Francis had met Mrs Hearthop yesterday.

'Before I got any further, Dad jumped up. He threw down the paper as if it had bitten him. He towered over me looking in a funny way. I can see his eyes still ... they narrowed, and his mouth drew in like he was trying to eat it. His voice, when he finally spoke, was no more than a whisper. "Mrs Hearthop," he said, "is a witch. Never mention her name in this house again." He walked out of the room, even though he'd only just started his breakfast. I thought his eggs would get cold.'

She pouted like that unhappy child. 'I felt sick. I'd only ever seen Dad quiet or gentle. Never that odd, angry tension. I was so scared. But my mother was there too, and she saw how upset I was. She got up and put her arms around me. I burst into tears. I kept sobbing, saying that I didn't know, I didn't mean to upset Daddy. I didn't understand. And who was Mrs Hearthop anyway?

'Then she told me it wasn't my fault. It was just that Dad had seen Mrs Hearthop last night at the party. She had walked up to Dad, and said, "Eh, Brian. Looks like Francis came back from the dead, don't it?" Dad apparently turned round and walked away. He grabbed mother's shoulder. Swung her round and told her to get her coat. Said they were leaving. She didn't even have time to say goodbye to the hostess. They just got in the car and Dad drove so fast that Mum was scared. She said she'd never seen him drive like that.

'Then Mum said that years ago she'd heard a rumour about a brother or sister who disappeared. She didn't know the family at that time ... anyway, she was much younger than Dad. Once, she said, she tried to ask Dad about it, and he went completely white and came at her like a madman. He said she was never to mention it again, or he would kill her, and he was not a violent man – rather the opposite, rather closed and taciturn. So she told me to forget it, and pretend I had never heard the rumour, and I did.'

'But,' murmured Miranda, too quietly for the Zoom receiver to pick up, 'Francis was not so biddable. He presumably either approached his father on the subject or went back and found Mrs Hearthop, and now he knows a lot more than his sister and isn't telling – or may tell in a week or so ...'

Cat and Stevie, still looking at Karen on the sofa, nodded.

Why a week or so? Miranda wondered.

'Is Mrs Hearthop still alive?' asked Miranda loudly enough for Zoom. Then, thinking about Stevie's mother. 'Still lucid?'

'I doubt it,' said Karen. 'I was about ten then, so it would be about 1992. If she was seventy-ish then ...'

'Hm,' said Stevie. 'She'd be pushing a hundred, pretty unlikely to be still alive, and even if she was ...'

She thought about her mother, Blinkey, and her crazy stories, her occasional belief that her daughter was her sister, and her refusal to let anyone in the house unless they knew the 'password'. Dementia can have sane moments, but they'd be lucky to find a hundred-year-old with a complete set of memories.

'Look, girls,' said Stevie when the call was finished. 'There must be someone else who knew the Deliverer family. An older person in the village. Someone nosy, who knew at least a few of the family secrets. Could be my mother knows, but her dementia isn't letting her tell us anything. Who else was living round here before 1963?'

'None of my family,' said Cat. 'I was born then, just, but we lived in Oxfordshire.'

'My father would have known,' said Miranda sadly. 'As a local builder he knew all the secrets, but too late.' She shrugged. 'But hey! What about Pete Drayton again? Chief village gossip. He was so great in that Black Widow case. Bet he knows a thing or two.'

CHAPTER 12
SMOKE SIGNALS FROM UP THE HILL

Miranda rang Pete to arrange a meeting, wishing they could meet in the pub as they had in the previous cases, but under lockdown, pubs were closed, and outside your immediate bubble, you were only allowed to meet on walks.

'Walk then,' said Pete on the phone, 'and come up Signals Hill. We're working on the place, and we can walk more from there, if you want to, and have a chat.'

As she climbed up the hill, her wellingtons slipping and sliding in the January mud, Miranda wondered why she put walking on her CV as a hobby. Should have said 'walking in the dry', but then people would imagine she wanted to walk in the desert.

Phillip, who joined her walking the dog at weekends, said he loved the mud.

'Reminds me of the Somme,' he said, although the closest he got to the Somme was watching *War Horse*, and even then, he fell asleep in the cinema. Miranda felt a sudden bubble of laughter. Phillip could be very tiresome, but he was kind and he worked hard and, even though he did fall asleep when she was talking to him, he was fun to be with. Besides, she thought, tightening her grip on the lead, he had given her this dog, who was now dragging her up the muddy slopes.

When she finally reached Signals House, Pete was in the drive hauling a wooden bench out of the utility room. 'We can sit here until it snows,' he said cheerfully, pulling a beer out of the cold sack at his knees and handing her a thermos of coffee. 'Well, Miranda, I think I'd better join your agency. I seem to be the source of information in all cases.'

Miranda winked at him, feeling a rush of fellowship. 'It's because you were so brilliant in the Black Widow case that we know you're an oracle.'

He swigged his beer and grinned in delight. 'Gossip fountain, you mean. OK, lovely, what did you want to know?'

'I wanted to know about Brian Deliverer's family.'

'Funny coincidence then. This was where Karl Deliverer's family lived. They was a posh family, kept to themselves.'

Miranda looked at the house in surprise. 'It looks pretty modern. When was it built?'

'It is – old one burnt down in 2000 and took Karl with it. The old girl was dead by then. We built the new house with the insurance money. Brian sold it.'

'No kidding. What happened, what caused the fire?'

Pete laughed. 'Want the pub theories? I can tell you my mate Jeff, what drinks in the Foxy Den with me, he said there were two sources of fire. You'd better ask him for more details.'

'Odd, certainly,' said Miranda. 'Two fires starting at the same time. Did the police think it was arson?'

'Not the police. The fire brigade. They did the investigation, found the two sites. Pub had all sorts of theories.' He winked at her. 'You'd best ask Jeff.'

'Who's Jeff?'

'Don't you know him? Drives a beaten-up old Land Rover, got a couple of manky spaniels what he says are "fire dogs".' Pete laughed. 'Anyway, he was the fire investigator at the time. The police came over, too, because of the dead body. Jeff said the post-mortem showed smoke inhalation, so Karl could've been asleep when the accident happened, but he wasn't dead. What you'd expect.'

'Karl was born in 1916,' said Miranda, 'so he was quite old, probably did like a sleep in the afternoon – was it afternoon?'

'It was. Jeff said there wasn't much of the body left, but they're good at doing reconstructions. Seems he'd run into a mirror.'

'Weird. So what was verdict, the outcome?'

'Death by misadventure. What we reckoned in the pub was that the old boy got drunk. Hardly came out of his house after his wife died. Saw himself in the mirror and drunkenly thought it was a burglar, ran at it and knocked himself out. Then, of course, his cigar started the fire and it was bye-bye time.'

'Wow.' Miranda massaged her chin. 'What a way to go.'

'Hm. Probably too pissed to feel anything.'

'I wonder,' said Miranda, thinking about Brian's confession that he had done something awful. 'Did anyone think Brian might have been responsible for his father's fire?'

Pete waggled his head. 'Pub talk? Yes, well of course we discussed it. But he had a good alibi.'

'What?'

Pete laughed. 'He'd gone shopping with his wife and

daughter. The girl, Karen, was eighteen and they wanted to buy her something special.'

Miranda nodded.

'There was one thing Jeff, the fire investigator, mentioned ...'

'Go on.'

'Well, they got the impression that Karl wasn't alone when he died.'

'How did they know?'

'I can't recall, perhaps it was just because the firemen were called so quick, but if you like I'll give you Jeff's number. You can ring him.'

'Thanks, that would be good. What else do you know about Karl Deliverer?'

'Karl Deliverer,' said Pete, and the way he smiled made Miranda smile too. Looked like quite a lot of information was coming her way.

'Karl Deliverer was at school with my dad,' Pete said grinning. 'He was a cocky fellow, full of himself, thought he was God's gift, that's what my dad said.' He took a glug from his can. 'My dad wasn't the only one to think so. One night a group of boys got together and held him down and ... OK if I tell you this, love? It's a bit smutty.'

Miranda nodded, her eyes flaring open; what could be coming? 'Fire away.' She stuck her lip out, realising it was an inappropriate phrase.

'Well, five of them held him down while another one wanked him off.'

'What? You're not serious. That's weird. Why?'

He looked at her impishly. 'We wasn't so prim in those days as you lot are now. They was fed up with him, but really it was a bit of harmless fun. But he got to thinking they was all queer – sorry, love, that's what they called it then – and after that he was hungry to hunt down queers and get them arrested. He became a school maniac. My father said he was a nightmare from then on. Of course, none of the boys was queer at all, it was just a game.'

Miranda drank her coffee wishing it was wine. She wasn't even sure if she was shocked, just totally amazed; did boys really do things like that to each other? Now, as well as then? What would Cat and Stevie say? She almost wanted to run down the hill and ask them. 'When was that? Pre-war?'

'Yes,' said Pete. 'Funny you should mention the war. My dad said it changed a lot of people, but Karl changed completely. At school, well apart from the queer incident, he was more or less normal. An affable enough boy. Cocky, yes, but OK. Sporty. Fun. But when my dad met him again here, in the forties, he'd become a right little Hitler. Snobby. Didn't recognise me dad at first. Only when me dad said, "Hey, Karl, forgotten me, have you? Schooldays too long ago," did he acknowledge him. Odd how the war changed people.'

Miranda nodded. 'I'm not surprised. I expect there were a lot of unrecognised mental-health issues. Nobody understood them then, did they?'

'Guess not,' said Pete, taking another beer. 'Those were the days, 'eh. What else did you want to know about Krazy Karl?'

'Krazy Karl? Is that how he was known?'

'Yup. He was so extreme. We did a job up here when I was still in my teens. We liked to horse about, you know how kids are.' He winked at her. 'Well, beforehand, Dad warned me: careful when Krazy Karl's around cos it doesn't take a lighted match to blow his fuse. Of course, my brothers and I took no notice. Anyway, there was a big loft in the old place then and one of my brothers, it was probably Ralph, I think

Tom had already left to be a diver by then, and I climbed up the ladder and found an absolute treasure trove up there. There was old clothes from before the war, wartime uniforms, those old tin hats that wardens used to wear, and gas masks ... loads of brilliant stuff. So Ralph and I, we have the tin hats on and the gas masks and we're jumping about fooling around. Well, you know what it is when you can't see. Well, I tripped, flew across the loft and into the back part. Well, blimey! If we'd thought the other part was full of treasure, this was the golden chest. There were whole rolls of cine tape, an old projector, but what really got us was the guns. Twenty or thirty of those flintlocks. You know what I mean, love, the ones with the long barrel and a bit on top. You see them in movies, they blow on them to cool 'em.'

He picked up a piece of wood from the drive and blew on the end, half closing his eyes like an Owly Vale version of Errol Flynn. 'So, dressed in our warden's gear we had a duel, we were back-to-back and just doing our paces across the loft: one, two, three ... when "Stop right there!" It was Krazy Karl, and he was ballistic. Ralph was closest and Karl punched him, knocked him right over, there and then, and Ralph was no baby kitten – he was six foot four or more and built like a brick shit house, sorry love, but he went over like a skittle.

'Then Krazy Karl came for me. Well, I'm not as big as Ralph but lighter on my feet, so I dodged him, got him with my shoulder and he went over. I dropped the pistol and jumped through the hole in the loft, down those stairs, and I was out of there before you could say burnt sausage. I was still wearing the helmet and gas mask. Ralph was right out behind me and before long out came Krazy Man, but now he was waving a knife ...' He took a gulp of beer.

'A knife,' Miranda reiterated, feeling herself shaking. 'What happened?'

'My dad. He was bigger than Ralph and calm. He saw Krazy Karl running at us, and he picked up a log of wood and whammed it into Krazy's midriff. Karl went down and lay still. The knife flew off somewhere. For a moment, I thought Dad had killed him, but my dad put his foot on Karl's chest. "You stay down, sir," he said. His voice was so powerful like a king. "Take a deep breath and count to ten, sir. You need to stop before you kill someone." I've never seen my dad like it. His face was white, like a ghost, while Karl was sort of purple.'

'Did that work?'

'Yes, Karl calmed down. I thought we'd lose the job, but actually he just said if we ever went into the loft again, he'd take the job away. We never did.'

'Wow.'

'Yes, it taught me something. My dad was brilliant with clients, even the mad ones. I'll never be half what he was.' He opened another can.

'So there was no comeback?'

'Only that Krazy Karl removed his porn.' Pete's face cracked up.

'His porn?' said Miranda. 'You didn't tell me about that.'

'Yup, next day Brian came up and removed reels and reels of cine film and a projector. Took it down to his own house. Made us laugh in the pub. Can't say I'd want to watch porn with my dad, but,' he shrugged, 'it takes all sorts.'

'Are you sure it was porn?'

'Well, I didn't see it, but what else could it be?'

Miranda shrugged. Her mind wouldn't immediately jump to porn, but clearly Pete's did; men were definitely different. She moved on. 'What about Hannah, Karl's wife, was she ever there?'

'Nope. I don't know where she was when we was building. But you never saw the old girl, anyway, after the two children disappeared ... Pub talk said she took to her bed and never got up.'

'Two children?' asked Miranda. 'Whose? Hers? Karen said something about a son, and there's a film including a little girl we saw in Brian's house. Were those her children by an earlier marriage?'

'Maybe. We didn't socialise. But pub talk was there was a girl – don't know what happened to her.'

'So, he did have a daughter?'

'You heard that too?' said Pete, clearly glad to have the rumour confirmed.

'Well, there's a gravestone in the Catholic churchyard with Frances on it. But then Karen said something about the mother being distraught at the death of her son. Well!' She pouted. 'Brian's only just died.'

Peter nodded, rubbing his chin. 'I have to say, I was never very sure. I remember the mother ... as you said she was Hannah or Henrietta, or something posh. Sometimes we saw her shopping in Petersfield. My mother liked us boys to carry the shopping. My dad didn't come shopping, although sometimes he drove my ma into Petersfield and sat in the car with a newspaper.'

Miranda laughed. She'd seen old boys, sitting in the car, waiting for their wives in the supermarket car park.

'There weren't all those Tescos and the like in the fifties,' said Pete, as though reading her mind. 'We'd go first to the butcher, who was also the fishmonger on the other side of the shop, and then fetch the bread from the bakery, then on to the tool shop. Best shop in Petersfield, that one.

Gone now, of course, like all the good ones. Anyway, Hannah'd be there with two little kids running beside her, one in a tutu, the other in those funny shorts kids wore post-war.'

Miranda poured some more coffee from the thermos and wished even more that he'd thought to bring her some wine. 'I wonder what happened to the daughter. Sounds like she died early.'

Pete shook his head and shrugged simultaneously. 'They was a funny family. Pub talk said that Karl wouldn't let any of his kids go to boarding school after his experience.' He grinned. 'Mind you,' he said, 'I seem to remember some tale about an adopted child too, son of a hippy in India or some far place.'

India, thought Miranda. No one had mentioned India before; could this be a confusion with Nepal? Some connection with the reels in Brian's house? 'Who? What? Hang on – a boy with big ears and a wide face?'

'Now you've got me, love. Boys don't really look at other boys, well, unless they're that way inclined.' He flexed his wrist.

'Wow,' said Miranda, 'this has certainly given me a lot to think about. Did they go about with the kids, socially, I mean?'

'Not with us. Not our class, love.' He laughed and pulled the pin on another beer, chucking it away as though it was a hand grenade. 'Sixties! They wasn't like now! The village had stratas.' He lengthened the word for emphasis and put a finger under his nose. 'Definitely them and us! It's much fairer now.'

'Is it?' asked Miranda, thinking of the many local big houses owned by Russians and hedge-fund managers. 'Is it fairer, or just different?'

Pete shrugged. 'As long as they need building work, I like 'em. Did I give you enough information, love?'

'I'm not sure,' said Miranda truthfully. 'I don't suppose you know anything about Karl playing bridge, or his son?'

'Nah. I did play whist with my nan when I was a nipper. I was pretty good, but life's too busy now.'

Miranda nodded. She got up and stretched herself, wondering if all this walking was making her lose weight. Unlikely, alas.

'There's an old girl in Petersfield who might know about the bridge,' said Pete. 'Old as Methuselah, but she still organises the local bridge tournament every year.'

'Who's that?'

'Name of Mrs Hearthop. She's about a hundred, lives with a carer in her old house near the lake in Petersfield. Used to sit on its own, but the town grew round it. When she goes, that land will be worth a bob or two. Pity! It's a smashing house, but whoever gets the contract will pull it down and built loads of affordables in the space. Won't be Draytons. We've lost our oomph after that bitch of Tom's stole all our money.'

Miranda made a sympathetic face. Pete had helped her in the case of the Black Widow, but he never forgave Anastasia for taking half his family firm.

She brought her mind back to Mrs Hearthop. 'About a hundred? Will she remember anything?'

'They say her mind's a sharp as a bell, just her body is feeble.'

'Thanks, I'll try her,' said Miranda, her mind now distracted by the slippery walk down the hill she was about to embark on. Perhaps if she kept the dog close, he would make a soft cushion for landing.

As she was about to leave, Pete said, 'Oh, love, I've just thought of something else.'

Miranda turned back, raising her eyebrows. 'When we were mucking around, before we found the duelling pistols, we found a whole stash of Pervitin.'

'Pervitin?'

'Yep, course, you youngsters would never have heard of it, but us wartime blokes, we knew about drugs. It's methamphetamine, used to be known as the pilot's chocolate.'

'Really? Karl had a stash of crystal meth in his house. Was he a druggie?'

'Doubt it. This was old stuff. The Nazis gave it to their soldiers and their pilots to keep them awake on a charge. It's normal. Our lot used Benzedrine. Wartime leads to some odd habits.' He laughed. 'Literally.'

Wow, thought Miranda, as she and the dog meandered down the muddy hill. Why would a British soldier have a stash of crystal meth used by the other side?

CHAPTER 13
DRESSING-UP IN JACK'S CLUB 1966

Bev had a new companion in the club.

Clinton made a face when Jack walked in. 'Bloody hell, boss, couldn't you have left it alone? Bev's new bridgy is no looker at all. You seen her? Right meese!'

Jack took a fag from the open pack and swung over to the table to inspect the new girl. Older than Fran, she was still a youngster, but while he might have complained about Fran's lack of jubes, this girl had the sort of willets that could knock you off the table. Legs like trees in trousers and black-rimmed ogle fakes that magnified her eyes so you felt you were looking into the soul of a cow.

'Hi,' she said, seeing him inspecting her and taking off her glasses. 'I'm Carile. Jack, are you?'

He nodded.

She put her glasses back on and went back to the game.

'New omees,' he mouthed at Bev tilting his head at the players.

She waved her hand like a duchess at a soiree. 'Guys, meet Jack, he's your host for tonight. Butch here's a dona.'

Butch took Jack's hand and squeezed it hard. 'Good to meet you, Jock. We're looking forward to the game. Carile here tells me she's just learning, so we're sure to be kind to her. We will, won't we, Pete?'

Her partner inclined his head, smiling. 'Sure will. I always love a little learner. Don't you, Butch?'

Jack watched Carile play. Different from Fran, she made small mistakes, frowning when she did so, but finding other ways of winning the game. Occasionally, usually in the early games, she lost, going down, but never when vulnerable and never badly. The opposition inevitably increased their stakes, and she won the next few games, always when the opponents were vulnerable.

Jack frowned. He gave Carile a long look. There was a pattern in this play, and he doubted he was the only one seeing it. One day Bev would come unstuck. He just hoped her girls managed to escape. Especially Fran. Fran. He liked to think of her as the girl who played with fire. Perhaps one day he could persuade her to play with his fire. He wondered where she was. Oddly he felt her presence, as though she was actually here and laughing at him.

Three weeks later, Carile had gone, to be replaced by Enid.

Enid favoured stiletto heels and gloriously long red ringlets, which jiggled as she emphasised her speech. 'Darling Jack,' she oozed at him. 'I am Scarlet Enid von Herse. You can call me Scarlet, as long as you call me often.' She lifted her fan, brought it demurely down in front of her face, then swung it in a wide arc provocatively demonstrating her large bosom, which was enclosed in silky material high in the neck but slit all the way up her thighs. 'I love muscular Irish, don't you, boys?'

The men she was playing with said nothing, concentrating on their cards, possibly dazed by her endless speech.

She tapped Jack gently on the shoulder. 'Love a man with a packet. Speaking of which, come on, boys – money on the table, no half-crowns. Here we like men with full measures in their hearts. Vada the cards and digest them well. Think like a trendsetter ...'

'Six hearts,' said Bev.

Jack, already aware from Scarlet's Polari speech that she had the ace and seven small hearts, glanced at Bev's cards. The woman had a couple of aces and some small cards. He sucked his cheeks thoughtfully. Was Scarlett a good enough player to make the contract? He was intrigued and waited to find out.

'Darling, darling boys,' Scarlet said in the middle of the game, which should have required her concentration as well as that of the defenders. 'Bridge, like life, is not about who wins it but who loses it. Take you heroes born without a packet but earning their own way with extra strong ogle fakers, then suddenly you get in the eye of Jennifer justice and down you go, without even a cottage to call your own. Looks like you're one down here too. Darling Jack, could we cash up or will you be cleaning the kitchen?'

When Scarlet left, Bev was joined by Ranelf, a lively Italian who played with jerky movements that distracted the opposition almost as much as the fast staccato Polari he talked.

Ranelf was replaced by Vince. There were many more, their only apparent connection their ability to play bridge and speak Polari.

Where did Bev find all these bridge-playing girls and boys, Jack wondered. Was she creating them in some home factory?

CHAPTER 14
PLAYING THE GAME 2020

When Miranda rang the number of the bridge circle, the secretary gave her a telephone number for Mrs Hearthop.

'Is she OK?' asked Miranda. 'Compos, that is.'

The woman's laugh bordered on hysterical. 'She's probably sharper than you or I. Me, I hope I'm like that when I'm eighty, let alone when I reach her age.'

Miranda rang the number and a young-sounding woman with a New Zealand accent answered the phone. 'Hearthop House, right,' she said, making Miranda giggle.

'Good morning,' said Miranda politely, 'I'm a detective making an inquiry into the unfortunate suicide of Brian Deliverer. I gather Mrs Hearthop played bridge with him and I wondered if she would mind me asking a few questions.'

'Hang on, chook,' said the New Zealand voice. 'I'll find out.'

Mrs Hearthop herself came onto the phone. 'Who is it wants to visit?' she asked, her voice astonishingly strident for someone nearly a hundred years old.

'Hello,' said Miranda. 'I'm from the SeeMs Detective Agency. I wanted to ask you a few questions about the Deliverer family.'

'Oh, it's you ... the dog detective. Which one are you? The chatty one, who goes to the pub? The young one, who flies airliners? Or the pussy Cat?'

Miranda choked. Cat would not enjoy being described as a pussy. 'I suppose,' she said, not feeling very chatty, 'I'm the chatty one.' She remembered they were COVID bound. 'I wonder, should I just ask my questions now on the phone? I mean, you don't do Zoom, do you?' Perhaps she was being rude, assuming just because someone was old, she couldn't use the Internet.

'And what,' asked Mrs Hearthop, 'is a Zoom? It sounds like something children do with their arms out.'

'Sorry, it's a way of communicating via the Internet. I suppose then, er, given COVID rules, we'd better meet outside and go for a walk. Would that suit you?'

'Damn me, *no*,' said Mrs Hearthop. 'You come here like a civilised person. I've had a jab. I'm healthy as a fish, and if you turn up in a mask I'll tell the girl to deny you entry. I'm not sitting with someone with a mask on their face. Makes me feel like I'm being robbed.'

'Oh, OK, thank you.'

'Yes, and come now. At my age every day may be your last. How long will it take you to get here?'

Miranda said probably twenty minutes.

'Good, and you'll stay to lunch.'

She had put the phone down before Miranda could bleat that that wasn't allowed under COVID rules.

As she drove over to Petersfield, Miranda felt guilty. Even with Pete she had thought they were brushing the line of legality; now she was definitely breaking it. To ease her conscience, she wore her mask in the car, and kept it on for the walk across the yard to the door.

A large black woman opened the door. They greeted by touching elbows but seeing Miranda's mask the woman laughed. 'You'd better take that off, chook,' she said.

Miranda felt the unexpected shock of touching a wire fence. She remembered the accent on the phone had been New Zealand, but she hadn't equated this woman with the accent. Did that count as unconscious bias? Was she showing some racist tendency by thinking a black woman must be African?

The New Zealander was still talking. 'She'll be asking me to throw you out if I let you in wearing a thing like that. Hurts my back chucking out *manaakitanga*.'

Miranda pulled off the mask and slipped it into her pocket. '*Manaakitanga*?'

'Guests, eh.'

The woman laughed and Miranda echoed her. Had she seen she was nervous? Was she trying to reassure her?

'What is Mrs Hearthop like?' asked Miranda. 'She seems not to care about the COVID rules.'

'She's OK,' said the woman. 'She appears rude, but it's just her manner. Brittle. She's generous. She can be kind. Ignore her attitude and you'll be fine.'

'Thanks,' said Miranda, but she felt her legs shaking as though she'd run here.

'I'm Jean,' the woman said. 'It's not my real name, but she couldn't manage that, so we opted for Jean.'

Miranda raised a lip. What name would Mrs Hearthop give her?

Jean led her through the hall, opened a wide wooden door on the right side and showed Miranda in. Miranda's first impression was of a very small woman in a very large room. Both looked dusty and grey.

'Miranda Zielinski, Mrs Hearthop,' said Jean as she showed Miranda into the room and across to her chair.

The old woman stared at her without moving. 'That your name or your husband's?'

'Mine,' said Miranda. 'I kept my father's name when I married.'

'Hm, I remember him. Builder, wasn't he, started gambling and threw himself under a train.'

Miranda gasped. Jean had warned her, but she hadn't thought it would start like this. She was tempted to leave, but instead hovered uncertainly.

'Oh, do sit down,' snapped Mrs Hearthop. 'You're making me dizzy.'

Miranda automatically turned towards the door but before she could move Jean reappeared with a tray and winked reassuringly at her. She tilted her head at an armchair close to Mrs Hearthop's chair. 'I put the chair there. She's a bit deaf, eh,' she whispered.

'You like wine,' said Mrs Hearthop in a loud voice. 'I prefer sherry.'

Miranda took a glass. 'Thanks, Jean.'

'No worries.'

Miranda took a gulp. Either the normality or the sugar calmed her, and she walked over to the seat and sat down.

'Don't you want to know,' said Mrs Hearthop, 'how I knew you liked wine?'

It hadn't occurred to Miranda. She assumed everyone knew. 'You're not the only detective here. I rang the pub to find out.' Mrs Hearthop laughed.

Breathe, Miranda thought, and start again. 'Thank you for seeing me,' she said, raising her glass to the old woman.

Mrs Hearthop smiled, and her face gentled. 'I was glad to see you,' she said. 'I don't have many visitors at any time, and today only Jean and the district nurse. It's not an exciting life being old. Gets worse after seventy. Jean is expecting you for lunch.'

Miranda was about to refuse but stopped. The old woman was probably telling the truth; each day was filled with nothing of interest. Given her age and abrasive character she was unlikely to have many friends. Miranda felt bile in her mouth; her friends were her lifeblood. Even her tiresome husband and children and her crazy detective company were much better than being alone. 'Thank you, that would be lovely.'

'Excellent. You said you wanted to know about the Deliverer family.'

'Yes.'

Mrs Hearthop took off her spectacles and picked up a polishing cloth, wiped them and returned them to her nose. 'Karl and Hannah Deliverer moved here after the war. People were moving about then in a way they never had. They bought the place up on Signals Hill, above the village of Owly Vale. It had been taken over by the army in the war, and an airstrip was laid down in the field. When the army left, the whole place was in a terrible state. They would have had compensation, but it was never enough. Holes in the walls, rubbish everywhere, written ribaldry and worse.

'The Delivers got it for a song, but at least they employed local people to do it up, which spoke in their favour. Jobs were sparse after the war and men needed employment.' She took a sip of her drink. 'Karl lacked charm, but he wasn't stupid. He was the type of man who would remember a childhood insult but not notice the beautiful flowers in his garden. Do you understand me?' She stopped and looked at Miranda.

'I guess.'

Mrs Hearthop frowned and paused for a moment. Her eyes drifted across the room and Miranda wondered if she'd forgotten what she was talking about. However, when she continued it was back on the subject. 'Hannah was warmer, but she was weak. Limp handshake. Feeble smile. Never said boo to a goose, just smiled and nodded. Know the type?'

Miranda smiled and nodded.

'The money was hers, of course. You can always tell. He was forever talking about grand relations, who were no doubt poor as church mice. I think he once showed me a family tree. Sure sign of nouveau riches.'

She took another sip of her sherry. 'Then, after the house was finished, Hannah had twins, born at home. It was normal back then, with a midwife. The birth was fine. Two healthy little boys.'

'Boys? Someone said ...'

Mrs Hearthop looked at her sharply. 'Yes? Someone told you a girl and a boy?'

'Yes.

'She dressed them as girls. Post-war, people did odd things. Perhaps she thought they'd be safer if something happened and we returned to fighting. But they were boys. The midwife was the mother of my maid.'

'Perhaps she wanted a daughter,' said Miranda. She spoke automatically but her brain was humming. So, was the girl in the films a boy? Really? Or was there another unaccounted-for family member?

Mrs Hearthop was continuing. 'Hm, anything was possible with a woman like that.'

Miranda gasped but changed the subject. 'Did you fight in the war?'

'No, born in 1925. I'm only ninety-six.'

Mrs Hearthop's face lit up as she spoke, and Miranda wondered why. Was she remembering a happy part of her youth, or was she being funny? Or did ninety-six seem young when everyone thought you were a hundred? What would it be like, being a hundred and having seen so much?

'How did you meet the Deliverers?'

'We met at parties, and we often played bridge together. I ran the bridge club. Ran it for forty years. Stopped when I was ninety. I started forgetting conventions. Games are so complicated nowadays. In my day, we played proper bridge.'

Proper? Odd, that juxtaposition of words. Miranda taught her children proper behaviour, proper manners, but was there a proper bridge? Would it be played while drinking sherry?

'Not your modern versions,' Mrs Hearthop was saying. 'We played contract bridge, mostly rubber bridge. How can you have a game named after a town? Chicago bridge? And worse. Under Al Capone bridge the scoring is so dodgy you can win and still lose. Honestly.'

She made a sound that might have been a laugh but sounded more like an *eek* to Miranda. Mrs Hearthop drank her sherry and signalled to be topped up. Jean had left the room, so Miranda jumped up and got the decanter from the tray. She filled her hostess's glass.

'Dear one,' Mrs Hearthop said in thanks, but her face did not soften, and Miranda was shaken by the contrast between the words and the expression.

'Karl played a steady game,' said Mrs Hearthop. 'Not as good as he thought he was. My husband enjoyed playing with him, but you didn't want to play against him and Hannah.'

'Devilish team?' asked Miranda, raising her eyebrows.

Mrs Hearthop sneered, her glasses rising on her nose. 'Only in the abuse. She invariably played the wrong card, and he invariably shouted at her. It was embarrassing. Nobody wanted to play with her. They knew they would lose before they started the game. She was the only person I knew to call "no bid" with twenty-three points.'

Miranda laughed. 'What happened to the second son?'

'Francis?' Mrs Hearthop said, and for a moment her face showed the softness it lacked when speaking kind words. 'He was a lovely boy and only thirteen or fourteen when he drowned.'

'Drowned?'

'At the time they said he fell off his father's boat and drowned. I'm told the boom hit him and broke his neck, and by the time they turned the boat and got back to him he was dead.'

'Killed by the boat itself?'

'Yes. I heard the rumours from my girls.'

'Your daughters?'

'My maids – we still had a full staff then. All gone. Just me and Jean now.' She sighed. 'I do have a daughter, but she wouldn't tell me anything. Besides, she was only fifteen when Francis died.'

'What did Karl say about it? I mean, did you continue playing bridge?'

'No. Karl never spoke of it, and you couldn't even mention Francis's name in his presence. I tried once and he turned and left the house. He was a very rude man. I never liked him. And after that he stopped playing bridge with us. We only met him at cocktail parties or local funerals.'

'What about Hannah? I was told she was very upset.'

'I never saw her again. She took to her bed and apparently only got up to visit his grave.'

'So, no more bridge?' said Miranda thoughtfully.

Mrs Hearthop looked at her curiously, echoing, 'No, no more bridge.'

Lunch was clearly an important meal for Mrs Hearthop, although she ate very little. They sat in the dining room, next to each other so Mrs Hearthop could hear what Miranda said. However, they were buried in an elaborately decorated table with silver candelabra, condiments in silver jackets and three or four lines of cutlery. Course after course appeared, but until the crème brûlée was put in front of her, Mrs Hearthop only played with her food.

'You can't let standards slip,' she said. 'Once you do it's the end. The day I eat sitting in front of the *television* is the day I die.'

Miranda said nothing. The way she and Phillip ate there would be no standards to slip. They were better when the children were around, but when it was just the two of them, they usually ordered a takeaway. At least the tin container had a silver sheen, she thought smiling inwardly.

'I like my puddings,' Mrs Hearthop was saying. 'Sometimes I have two or three, but Jean doesn't really approve. She thinks I'll get diabetes. Die young!' Mrs Hearthop started laughing and finished up coughing.

While she recovered, Miranda, having tucked in hungrily, mused on the pros and cons of taking another walk; while it would reduce her waistline it would also distract her from thinking about the case. Could she think and walk at the same time?

Mrs Hearthop's renewed coughing brought her back to the dining room.

'Did you spend any time with Brian Deliverer and his wife?'

'We knew them, of course, but we didn't see much of Brian, or any of the family after Francis died. Weren't invited to Brian and Emma's wedding. Saw them at drinks parties, local weddings, funerals and hunt balls. Different generation. After Karl died in 2000, we started meeting Brian and Emma again. She was lovely. Whatever made her hook up with that slowcoach I will never know. Mind you, she wasn't from the first water, and whatever you feel about the Deliverers, their background was impeccable. I'm told they were descended from one of Charles II's mistresses, but then who isn't really?'

'Oh,' said Miranda, her eyes shooting open. 'Why? Are you?'

'No, certainly not,' Mrs Hearthop snapped. 'We didn't do bastardy in my family.'

'Oh, right. So Emma Deliverer was pretty?'

'Yes, and friendly, not like her standoffish husband. You young people would say she was a normal person, whereas Brian always looked as though he came from another planet. He hardly spoke at all. He drank a lot, but we all drank a lot in those days. It's only now everyone has become so namby-pamby that they don't drink and only eat certain foods. They should have tried living through the war with that attitude.'

Miranda said nothing. How would Mrs Hearthop have managed being the mother of five-year-old Peta, who right now would only eat spinach, but last week would not eat spinach, even when disguised with cheese?

· · ·

As Miranda was leaving, Jean stopped her. 'I heard you talking about the Deliverers, right?' she said, looking a bit cautious.

'Yes, did you know Francis?'

Miranda couldn't believe it. Jean looked about fifty, tops, and Francis Deliverer would have been seventy-one or seventy-two if he was still alive.

'No, but you could ask Charlotte, eh.'

'Charlotte?'

'Mrs Hearthop's daughter, right. She talks to me when she visits.'

Jean paused and ushered Miranda outside. 'Look, Charlotte doesn't get on well with her mum, right – personal reasons. Neither of them talk about it, eh. But she likes to come and pass the time of day with me in the kitchen.' Jean sighed. 'She cares for her mum, right. But the old lady is difficult, especially with her daughter. Wished for a son, right. Never forgave the girl.'

'Oh,' said Miranda, tears spontaneously jumping to her eyes. She was one of three girls, but her parents never gave any indication they would rather have had a boy.

'When Brian carked it,' said Jean, 'Charlotte told me none of the Deliverer family had ever been the same since Francis died. Francis was the best brother – kindest, most fun. He used to do imitations. Apparently he did wonderful ones of her mum and his dad.' She laughed. 'You should ask her about it. Apparently, her mum and father Deliverer fell out over how the game of bridge should be properly played. Bridge, 'eh? You Brits crack me up.'

'Really?' said Miranda; this was really useful. 'Thank you, Jean. Where does she live?'

Jean nodded. 'She lives in London, but because of

COVID she came down here ... said it was to be near her mum, eh. Hired a cottage in Owly Vale. You know it?'

Miranda laughed. 'I live there.'

Jean shook her head. 'Some things,' she said, 'are meant to be, eh.'

CHAPTER 15
A COTTAGE IN OWLY VALE 2020

Charlotte Hearthop was a tall, straight-backed woman in her mid-seventies with purple hair. Miranda imagined her returning home with it many years ago in an act of rebellion. A rebellion that never stopped.

Unlike her mother, Charlotte did want to obey COVID rules, so Miranda and the dog met Charlotte at the well in the centre of the square and their walk took them up the hill towards the windmill.

'Have you always lived here?' asked Charlotte, taking off her mask for the walk and waving it like a flag.

'No, we moved here a few years ago. We got married and left London. Rather traditional, I suppose.'

Charlotte laughed gently. 'I suppose. Frankly, all the traditions I grew up with have gone out the window. Even more so for my mother.'

'Yes.'

The path narrowed and they walked in single file. Miranda tried to hide her puffing. It was annoying that this woman, more than thirty years older than her, was clearly much fitter and raced ahead up the hill.

At last, the path widened, and they could walk side by side. Charlotte turned to her. 'They didn't do pony club.'

'Excuse me?'

'The Deliverer boys. They didn't ride. That was how you usually met boys. At pony club. I didn't like it. After the first set of pony club dances, I refused to go. All the boys wanted to do was touch you up. I hated it. My parents were furious.'

Miranda nodded. They seemed to be travelling up a dead end, and not just up the hill. 'How did you meet them then?'

'Sailing.'

'Oh?'

'Yes, if you live by the sea, you sail. My mother wasn't interested in sailing, she rode, but my father loved it and since I was an only child, he took me. We joined Bosham sailing club. They'd recently bought an MGB to make a clubhouse.' She stopped to let Miranda catch up again. 'Do you know what an MGB is?'

Miranda bent over, puffing and holding her sides. 'No, what?' She gasped for breath.

Charlotte laughed delightedly. 'Sorry, was I going too fast for you? An MGB was a motorised gunboat. They were used in the war and afterwards were going cheap, all left over and no homes. Bosham bought one and used it as a clubhouse. I seem to remember there were bunks and things too, but I never slept there. They sold it when I was about ten and got a proper clubhouse, but I always preferred the boat.'

'So, you sailed with Karl Deliverer and the boys.'

'Definitely not. My father said Karl was a menace on the water. He used to joke Karl's Swan was the only boat that sailed like a Duck. He refused to let me go sailing with them, although Francis did ask if I could. Sometimes he and I would sneak off in a dinghy, have a laugh. He was a lovely sailor. He was younger than me, but he was really nice, and I didn't have many friends.'

'Why not?' Miranda had asked the question automatically before realising it might be a bit personal.

Charlotte looked away. 'I don't know. Only child perhaps. No brothers. No sisters. You get used to your own company.'

Miranda nodded. 'Yes, I know. Stevie, one of my colleagues, is an only child and you can tell. She's very self-sufficient, never asks us to do anything for her.'

'Yes, I was like that too.'

They skirted round a tree that had fallen across the path going in single file, the dog leaping ahead.

Once side by side again, Miranda asked, 'What did you think about Brian?'

Charlotte tilted her head. 'I didn't like him, he was too ... it's a bit bad to talk about the dead, but then you are a detective, so I suppose it's OK.'

Miranda nodded encouragingly.

'Well, he was rather a mean man, closed up. He was even like that as a child. I knew him all my life and yet I never heard him laugh for joy or give anyone a pat on the back and say a spontaneous "well done" or anything. I always pitied his wife. He looked at you as though you hadn't lived up to his expectations. What that must be like to be married to ...'

Miranda moued sympathetically. 'What happened to Francis? Any idea?'

'They say he got hit by the boom, fell off the boat and drowned, but I never believed it, not even when I was fifteen. Francis was so light on his feet. He was a brilliant sailor. Not like Brian, who was behind on every turn. If you'd told me Brian had fallen off the boat, then I'd have believed it, no problem. But not Francis.'

She looked at Miranda and pouted.

'It seems funny to be talking about an old death, when everyone around us is dying daily of COVID. The cottage had its boiler serviced this morning and five of the boiler man's friends have died and his boss was seriously ill. But we British, we plough on, thinking of the past.' She laughed. 'Sorry, old age catching up with me. So where were we?'

'Do you remember the actual occasion? Of Francis's death?'

'No. I doubt anyone would. At least, not the details. The story was that they went out late on a Friday night in July. The harbour master said they drove right up to the quay, got the dinghy out and piled it high, then Silas drove the dinghy over with Francis ...'

'Silas?'

'Oh, sorry, yes, that was the boy they had.'

'The boy?'

Charlotte turned and looked towards Miranda, but she wasn't seeing her. Charlotte was looking away into the past. Where was she? With two boys on a dinghy? Two boys about to make their last ever sail. Miranda felt a wave of sympathy; it was hard to forget the dead people you have loved.

Charlotte shook herself and went on. 'It was a bit of a scandal at the time. Karl and Francis went to Nepal, climbing. Brian didn't go. I don't know why. But when they came back, Karl brought Silas back on his passport.' She stopped. 'You're too young to remember, but in those days children under sixteen could travel on the passports of any family member, no pictures. It changed in October 1998. Before then, Karl could easily bring in another child as his own. And he did. People said he was Karl's son from some indiscretion in the war. I'm told it happened all the time. He ran away after Francis died. Some people said he went back to Nepal.'

Miranda thought about that. Karl was not coming out in a very good light. 'So, how did you hear about Francis's death?'

Charlotte gave a half laugh. 'We almost didn't. Two weeks after it happened, I saw Brian. I never knew what to say to him, he was so ... so closed, so I said, "Hello, I haven't seen Francis recently. What's he doing?" He went as white as a sheet, turned, and walked away from me. After that he avoided me whenever he saw me coming. It was frightening. Anyway, I asked my father about it. He was the one that told me Silas was probably Karl's by-blow – that's what they called it then – what would we say now? Illegitimate offspring?'

'Maybe be non-marital child? Or illegitimate is fine, just not his bastard,' said Miranda. 'What did your father say about Francis's death?'

'He said he'd been in the churchyard – we're left-footers as they used to call us.' She stopped and looked at Miranda.

'Catholic?'

'Yes, the Deliverers were too. Anyway, my father was visiting Friar Jacques, the resident at the monastery, and Jacques showed him the grave outside the cemetery wall. No tombstone. Obviously, my father asked why it was outside the wall. Francis was only thirteen – what could he have done to blaspheme against the Holy Spirit? And Friar Jacques said that was on Karl's instruction. He was not to be blessed, but he could be buried.'

Miranda shook her head. 'I don't understand. Surely it's either in or out.'

Charlotte sighed. 'We're talking of a different era. I accepted it at the time, but now I wonder if something worse happened on the boat. Perhaps Francis didn't fall off. Suicide would be a reason to prevent him being blessed, but I find it impossible to believe Francis would commit suicide. He loved life.'

'Suicide? How awful.'

'Yes. Neither thing is easy to believe. On the one hand, I can*not* believe Francis, who was such an expert sailor, could have been knocked off by the boom. On the other, why would he kill himself? As for drowning – he could swim, for Christ's sake, we all could.'

CHAPTER 16

VADA BONA BEAUTIFUL BOSHAM

They finished their walk and Charlotte returned to her cottage, telling Miranda to contact her if she thought of anything else.

Although it had started to snow, Miranda got in the car and drove down to Bosham. Phillip was working from home and was *probably* glad of an excuse to look after the children; anyway, he just smiled, blew her a kiss and said, 'Fine.'

Miranda thought she would pop into the Southbourne farm shop on the way home, just to confirm her trip was legal.

She parked her car outside the Blue Anchor. A handwritten sign with a short menu offered takeaway or local delivery. Further down was a notice reminding car owners not to leave their cars here on an upcoming tide; she looked out at the sea, but it was miles away. She'd be fine.

The clubhouse at Bosham was closed, giving it the sad look of a beach hut in the winter. Walking through the yard, she glanced at the empty windows. Was there someone inside peeking through the blinds, watching her? Natural suspicion. Once a detective, always a detective.

As she walked down the quay to the slip, a few flurries of snow landed on the dinghies, shaken off the wires by the singing wind. She imagined Silas passing these same dinghies, taking everything out to the boat, the boys laughing together, splashing each other with water. Happy in the way only young things can be, little knowing that this would be Francis's last sail.

'Pretty, isn't it, in the snow?'

Miranda jumped about twenty feet and her stomach jumped higher.

'Whoa! I didn't hear you.'

'No. I've always been light on my feet. I didn't mean to scare you.'

The tall thin man behind her was probably smiling, but Miranda couldn't tell because his mask went over his nose, under his chin, and a hood covered his head. She understood why Mrs Hearthop thought it looked as though they had become a nation of muggers. Unlike Miranda, whose mask had been decorated by her children, the stranger wore a surgical mask giving nothing away.

'I used to sail here,' he said, 'many years ago.'

'Did you?' asked Miranda. Not surprising of course – this was a sailing area. Presumably almost everyone here sailed. 'I wonder, were you here in the sixties?' She faltered slightly. She couldn't see, under all those clothes, what age he might be. She hoped she hadn't been rude.

His eyes, enlarged by glasses, smiled at her, as though he realised her embarrassment. 'Yes, but I was young, even at the end of the sixties.'

'Oh.' Miranda couldn't keep the disappointment out of her voice. 'Pity, I wanted to ask something about 1963.'

He inclined his head. 'Try me.'

'Did you know a family called Deliverer?'

'I did,' he said immediately. 'And even if I didn't, I think the scandal around that name would mean anyone would remember the boy's disappearance.'

Miranda laughed. 'You'd think. But everybody seems to know the name and no one the actual story.'

'Really? What have you heard so far?'

'Some say Karl and Hannah had a boy and a girl, some say two boys who she dressed in girls' clothes, others say there was an adopted boy, possibly an illegitimate son of Karl. Some say Francis fell off the boat, others say he was too good a sailor to fall. I hear one thing, later I hear the opposite.'

He nodded and there was something in his eyes that made Miranda wonder if his mouth was cynically twisted. Masks were so annoying!

'I certainly knew Brian and Francis. They went to school with me.'

'Oh?' Here was a real chance at last. 'So, do you know what happened to Francis?'

He looked out to sea and back at her. 'Why do you want to know?'

'Oh, sorry, I should have said. I get carried away sometimes. I'm a detective with the SeeMs Agency. Brian Deliverer died a month or so ago. The police say suicide, and his daughter wants to find out why. She employed me.'

He nodded. 'Interesting profession, being a private detective. I would like it for myself. I'm naturally nosy. I expect you are too.' Again, his eyes smiled at her. 'So, what would you like me to tell you about the family?'

Miranda looked around her. 'Do you think we could legally sit on that bench? I'm so tired of walking up hills when I interview.'

The masked man laughed. 'Of course,' he said, 'let's do that. Isn't a detective a keyworker?'

'Sort of, but I'm not a police officer. Private investigators can do surveillance but if I sit on a bench and ask you questions, we're pushing the limits a bit. Still, it's better than falling over.'

They walked to a bench dedicated to someone who died in 1986. Would she have known Francis Deliverer? Miranda wondered. The stranger walked beside her with a lithe gait. Did one's walk change with age, or remain forever one's own? If the thin man was at school in 1963 then he was pushing seventy at the youngest.

They sat down.

'What were the Deliverer boys like at school?'

'Different,' he said, 'from each other, that is. Considering they were twins. You might expect them to be similar.'

'Twins? But Francis was born in 1949 and Brian in 1950?'

His eyes creased up and she imagined he was laughing silently under that surgical mask. 'Any idea of the day?'

'What? The day? What day?'

And then Miranda got it. 'Wow! You mean Francis was born on 31 December 1949 and Brian was born on 1 January 1950? Double wow. I never even thought of something like that.'

'Exactly. Rather like a Gilbert and Sullivan opera, isn't it?

'Is it?' asked Miranda. She had heard of Gilbert and Sullivan, but that was it. However, her new friend was happy to fill in the blanks.

'Yes, in *The Pirates of Penzance*. Frederick is enslaved to the pirates until his twenty-first birthday, but the problem was he was born on 29 February, so he only gets a birthday every four years. Hence he will be enslaved to them until he is eighty-four years old.'

'Oh, triple wow! Got it. Did you do Gilbert and Sullivan operas at school then?'

Her new friend's eyes lit up. 'We did indeed. Francis was always the lead because he was so talented. His voice was amazing, even after it broke. His acting was ...' he shrugged, 'well, I think if he'd lived ... Well, you'd have heard his name alongside that of Olivier and Gielgud.'

'Oh,' said Miranda, 'I'm sorry. Sounds like you really admired him.'

'I did. I always thought it was a shame the best brother died.'

Miranda made a face. There was something embarrassing about this kind of revelation from an older person, even though she was now realising older people enjoyed emptying their souls like this. 'Did Brian act too?'

'No. I expect he would have found it embarrassing. Kinder people would say Brian was shy, but the truth was he was a plodder. He worked hard but he didn't do well. He wasn't much liked, but he did have his group of friends. He wasn't one of those unfortunate boys who never fit.'

Miranda nodded to show she was following. Not that he needed any encouragement.

'When I think back on it, most likely the drama master started the operas for Francis. He was naughty. Before he took up acting, he would skip off school and go into Petersfield, hang around with groups of street kids. Always in trouble, but after the acting he stopped all that and started learning. Then we found out how clever he was.'

'Were you ... sorry, I didn't ask your name ...'

'John, John Marche. Spelt the French way but pronounced Marsh here. In fact, I'm thinking of changing it to Marsh to make it easier for everyone.'

'Thanks, John. I was going to ask if you were in the same

class, and what the boys made of it when Francis didn't return to school after he was killed.'

'Yes, to the first one. As for the second, Brian didn't come to school the first day of the Autumn Term, and we were all lined up, the whole school, and told, for those of us who didn't already know, that Francis had been killed sailing, that Brian was extremely unhappy about it and that we should not mention it to him.'

'And did you?'

'What do you think? We were young boys. Some of them probably stayed shtum, but most people couldn't wait to ask Brian what happened. Everybody was curious.'

'So, what happened?'

'Well, the first time someone asked him Brian punched them. They punched him back. Brian wasn't a good fighter, but he was big. There was a huge fight, and Karl took Brian away from school and sent him somewhere else. And that was that.'

'What an anticlimax.'

John laughed. 'You could say that.' He looked at his watch and got up. 'Look, sorry, I've got to go, but here's my phone number.' He gave her a card. 'Call me if you want any other information.'

Miranda got up too. 'OK, just one thing.'

'Yes?'

'Was there another boy who came to school with Brian and Francis, maybe a bit older or around the same age? Someone said he was called Silas.'

John looked as though he was twisting his mouth and there was a small ripple in the mask. 'No, I don't think so. I'll have a look in my school lists – sad boy that I am, I keep them – and let you know. Do you have a card?'

Miranda gave him one. 'Thanks, John.'

'Bye, Miranda.'

He walked away and Miranda sank down on the eighties-dedicated bench in shock. How did he know her name was Miranda? She hadn't said. She ran over their whole conversation but did not remember saying her name.

When, eventually, Miranda walked back to her car, the tidal water was splashing around her feet. Under her windscreen wiper a handwritten note politely pointed out that if she left her car here at high tide it would be damaged.

CHAPTER 17

THE VALUE OF SCHOOL

How did he know my name?' she asked Stevie and Cat on a Zoom call.

'Were you wearing that jacket with Miranda written on it?' Stevie asked.

'No!'

'I think it's pretty odd he was there at all,' said Cat. 'Isn't it a bit of a coincidence? You go down to the quay and suddenly an old boy turns up who knows the family and can give you information. You sure it was not the same voice as Simian, Miranda.'

Miranda sneered. 'Of course I'm sure. I'm not an idiot. You're not the only detective. But hang on...'

'Um?' said Cat.

'So, asking about Simian 'eh? So, you've accepted that Brian and Simian are not the same person and Simian aka the murderer is still alive?'

'Hm,' Cat muttered, 'just keeping every avenue open.'

Miranda was delighted but decided to be kind and went on with her story. 'OK. The voice was completely different.

That's a small area without many schools – I bet everyone knew everyone else back in the day.'

Cat was not so easily thwarted. 'Are you sure he said *Miranda* then? Not *my dear girl*, which from behind a mask might sound like Miranda.'

'Only,' said Miranda, delighted to have caught the Cat 'if you're getting a little deaf. Please remember I'm only just forty.'

Cat winced. They all remembered Miranda's Zoom fortieth birthday party and how disappointed she was not to be able to meet friends. How drunk she got. How cross Phillip was.

'I don't suppose you gave him a card, did you?'

'Yes. But if you're going to say it has my name on it, it also has yours and Stevie's, so same question: how did he know it was me?'

'Girls,' said Stevie, 'stop it! We're trying to solve a puzzle, not start a war.'

'You said he said something about school lists,' said Cat. 'Can we get those on the Internet, Stevie?'

'Should be able to.'

An hour later, Stevie had found not only a school list from 1963, but had found the name John Marche, and even an address where the family lived at the time. 'There's a phone number,' she said. 'You could try it – sometimes people take over the phone number when they buy a property. Not always, I agree, but sometimes.'

'Except,' said Cat, 'phone numbers were different in the sixties – shorter, fewer numbers.'

'Good point. OK, I'll see if there's a conversion. I remember my mother saying she kept the same last three digits but got extra numerals in front.'

'Right. Well, worth trying just in case.'

Miranda rang the number Stevie had found on the
Internet. A girl who, judging by her voice, would not have
been alive in 1963 answered the phone.

'Hello,' said Miranda, 'I'm sorry to bother you, but I'm
trying to trace a family who lived in your house in the
sixties.'

The silence emphasised the girl's amazement. Miranda
felt sure she knew what the next words would be.

'Hang on,' said the girl. 'I'll get my grandmother.'

The grandmother, when she came to the phone, had a
healthy-sounding voice that could have been any age.

'You are asking about a family who lived here in the
1960s?' she asked.

'Yes.'

'We lived here in the 1960s. I was a child then, but my
family has never moved. However, can I ask you, what
address are you looking for?'

Miranda pulled up the address and gave the address in
Bosham.

The woman laughed. 'Yes, I thought there might be a
mistake. We only recently got this phone number. Our
address is in Chichester, not Bosham. Phone exchange is the
same, place is different.'

Miranda thanked her and hung up. A dead end.

'Don't despair,' said Stevie when Miranda told her. 'At
least we know he did exist and did go to school with the
Deliverer twins. What was the number he gave you?'

'A mobile.'

'No address on the card?'

'No, just his name and mobile number. Not even a business address.'

'Well, never mind,' said Stevie. 'Think up a list of questions and give him a call. Then you can slip in questions about where he lives and so forth.'

Miranda spent all afternoon drawing up a list of questions, so it was getting dark and snowing hard when she finally made the call to John Marche.

The phone was answered by a Welsh voice.

'Hello,' said Miranda, 'is that John's phone, John Marche?'

'Yes, it is, and he's here, see, but he's just finishing the washing up,' the voice sang out. 'I'll give him to you in a minute, lovey. Let me just tell him, what's the name, lovey?'

Miranda could hear the Welshman telling someone in the background that a Miranda was on the phone, and then John's voice explaining he had met her down in Bosham that afternoon.

There was a bit of a scuffling noise, like someone moving things, and then the Welsh voice returned. 'Sorry about that, love, he'll be with you in a moment, see, he's just drying his hands.'

'Crazy accent,' said Miranda, 'do you sing as well?'

He chuckled. 'Oh, I love you! You hear a Welsh voice, and you think Eisteddfod. I'm as flat as a pancake in the sun, lovey. John's the singer, and he's not even a Welshman, and I'll tell you what, precious, I'm no good at rugby, either. I'm an embarrassment to the Welsh nation.'

Miranda laughed politely. 'Are you in Wales now?'

'No,' he said, 'in London. You *can* take the boyo out of Wales, whatever they say.'

John came on the phone. 'Miranda, thanks for calling. Now, I looked on my school list and there's not a single Silas there, let alone a Silas Deliverer. It *was* another Deliverer you wanted, wasn't it?'

Miranda, of course, knew that already, since she and Stevie had scoured the school sheets for any Silas between 1957 and 1964, just in case. There were none.

'Well, thank you for looking anyway,' she said. 'I wondered if you'd mind if I asked a couple of other questions.'

'Of course not, fire away.'

'Well, I wondered if the school had a bridge club, and, if so, if Francis and Brian played there.'

John was silent for a moment. Finally, he said, 'I'm not sure. We did have various clubs. I was a member of the COR, so I got to sit in aeroplanes and endure loops and so forth, while the real RAF members enjoyed themselves at our expense. But was there a bridge club? I'd have to look back in my old schoolbooks and let you know.'

'So, you didn't play bridge?'

''Fraid not. Although I can play whist, and still do occasionally, but I could never get to grips with that auction bit.'

Miranda laughed politely.

'Rhys did, though, if you wanted to ask a bridge question. But he wasn't at school with the boys. Shall I fetch him?'

'No, no,' said Miranda, 'that's fine. But, another thing, where did Brian go to school, after he left yours?'

'They sent him to Ampleforth. Know it? Catholic boarding school in Yorkshire.'

'Oh, thank you.'

She rang off and sat staring at the phone.

'Why would you send an upset child so far away? Didn't Pete say something about Karl swearing never to send a child of his to boarding school? What a time to change his mind, when his son was vulnerable after the death of his brother. And where did Silas go to school? Or did Karl keep him home like a slave?' Miranda really did not like Karl by now.

'What's up?' said Phillip, coming into the kitchen after putting the children to bed. 'You look worried.'

She sucked her upper lip thoughtfully. 'Honestly, Phil, I feel like I'm being played with.'

Phillip raised an eyebrow. 'How so? Cat being bitchy?'

Miranda shook her head. That was one of Phillip's favourite jokes, along with 'has Stevie gone loopy?' and 'Cat got your tongue.'

'No. I met a man at Bosham who knew all about the Deliverers. Cat says it's too much of a coincidence, and now I find he lives in London. Why would he be down in Bosham if he lives in London? It isn't legal under lockdown rules to travel around, we all know that.'

'Unless he was working,' said Phillip. 'Did you ask his profession?'

'No,' said Miranda, wishing she had.

Phillip smiled at her. 'Keep going,' he said. 'I would say bath the children and that will make you feel better, but Peta's asleep and Felix is reading in bed. They might be rather surprised if you wanted to get them up for a midnight swim.'

'Especially in winter! Why would you take your children sailing at dusk on a Friday night?'

Phillip raised his eyebrows at this change of subject, but after many years of marriage he was used to Miranda's elastic train of thought and he followed her deviation. 'Presumably because you wanted to spend the weekend sailing, and wanted to get an early start.'

'Hm, and how do you trace a man whose name you're

not sure of, and the only sight you've ever seen of him is of a couple of cine films when he was around seven to fifteen years old?'

At that moment Felix's face crept around the door. 'Mum! Peta's crying and she's keeping me awake.'

Miranda got up and went to be mother; at least it would take her mind off Simian and Silas. Were they the same person? Who were they?

CHAPTER 18
RIAH SHUSHER

H ello, love,' said the fire investigator's wife, Sheila, when Miranda phoned his mobile. 'Pete said you'd be ringing but, as I told him, Jeff's got COVID. He's here, not in hospital, but I don't want him fussed. Sorry, love. Don't get me wrong, but I can't bear to lose him. We've been together since school, couldn't live without him.'

'Oh, I'm so sorry,' said Miranda. 'Poor you. It is really difficult being the one that's OK, looking after the sick person. They, of course, feel terrible, but I know how it is – you live every moment with them. You feel their pain like yours. You poor, poor thing. Must be awful.'

'Thank you, love, you're so right, and no one under-stands. They all feel so sorry for him, and they get cross with me for protecting him. Don't get me wrong, but it's not my fault he isn't well.'

Miranda heard her moving the phone from one ear to the other; was it getting hot? Were her ears different shapes? One fitted a mobile better than the other?

Miranda forced her mind back to the issue. 'No, of

course it isn't. Is there anything I can do for you? Shopping or something? I know how difficult it is to get out these days.'

'Thank you, that is kind. Actually, what I would really like is a haircut. Don't get me wrong, but I don't suppose you can cut hair?'

Miranda suppressed a giggle. 'Yes, of course I can if you'd like me to. I cut the children's hair, but how should we do it safely? Would it be OK to sit in the garden and cut your hair?'

'Oh,' said Sheila, her voice suddenly lifting an octave in her excitement, 'would you mind? That would be so wonderful.'

Twenty minutes later, Miranda, wearing a welder's mask that she had borrowed from Pete, with a surgical mask underneath and a blacksmith's apron over her body, rang the doorbell at Sheila's house.

Sheila started, then recognised her. 'Oh, it's you,' she said, coming out and closing the door behind her protectively. 'I put a bench outside.'

Her hand flattened as she waved at a wooden kitchen bench on a patio surrounded by snowdrops.

Miranda's stared at the substantial bench. Sheila must be a lot more muscular than she looked. 'Good idea,' she said. 'Lovely flowers. Makes you feel spring is coming.'

Sheila sat down on the bench with a sigh. 'Wish it was – I'm that exhausted.' She puffed. 'Up and down, up and down – don't get me wrong but it's hard looking after an invalid. Very demanding.'

Miranda nodded. She moved behind Sheila and combed her hair. What a detective did to get information.

'How is he? I didn't want to disturb you, I just wondered if he remembered the fire up at Signals Hill twenty years ago.' She moved the scissors deftly around Sheila's ears.

'Yes, of course. I remember that OK,' said Sheila, 'that angry man up at Signals. Don't get me wrong, he wasn't much liked, but no one likes to hear of a house and owner being burnt. I felt sorry for his son. I mean ... they had so much tragedy in that family, it was awful.'

'Um,' Miranda agreed, measuring the two sides of the hair. Was one of her shoulders higher than the other or was it an illusion? Would they look equal to Sheila?

'Jeff doesn't really discuss his work with me,' said Sheila, apparently oblivious to Miranda's dilemma, 'but you know how it is, you pick things up.'

Sheila paused and Miranda wondered why. Perhaps the woman thought she might disapprove. She made encouraging noises, 'mm, yes, yes,' and went on cutting.

'Jeff said there were things funny about that case, funny *odd*, that is, not *ha ha*, if you know what I mean. We used to say that in the past but you young things with your language now ... I don't understand the first thing my grandchildren say.'

'Umm,' said Miranda.

'Well, you know they thought that someone else had been in the house at the time. Creepy that, isn't it? Watching him, probably. Jeff said it was hard to put his finger on it, but they felt it. I know Jeff thought it was odd. But they couldn't prove anything, and there wasn't anyone who would have benefitted by doing him in. So, the police let it go. However, one thing I do know is there was something not quite right about that family.'

'What's that?' asked Miranda, wondering if she dared put in layers; it would be a bit ambitious, but Sheila's looks would improve a lot. Risky.

'I used to do for him. Mr Deliverer.'

'Do for him?'

'I used to clean, up at Signals, when the old girl was still alive. After she died, he booted me out, said he didn't need a cleaner. Well, that's a laugh – if ever men needed cleaning more it was when their ladies died. It was the same for Dolly. The day Mrs Deliverer died that Brian was on that phone ...' She lowered her voice. '"No thank you ... don't need you anymore." No bonus either. Mean family they were, not that I want to speak ill of the dead. But, well, you know. They had money, and kept it.'

Miranda stood back for a moment surveying her handi-work. Amazingly the layers had worked, and Sheila's hair was much improved.

'The last day I worked for him, he was on his own in the living room. He called it the drawing room, but that was a laugh – now Hannah was dead no one drew anymore. No one did anything anymore. He had that old projector out and he was watching the reels. I sneaked in to have a look. Don't get me wrong, I'm not nosy, but I would have made a good detective, given what I've seen.'

'What was he doing?'

'Watching old movies of the little girl.'

'The little girl?'

'Yes, they had a little girl when I first cleaned there, always running around, she was, only about two or three, lovely girl.'

'What happened to her?'

Sheila laughed in an odd way. 'She became a boy.'

Miranda frowned. 'What do you mean?'

'Always was a boy, but her ma was odd. Definitely not quite right somewhere, but after the war they came back bonkers. She dressed him as a girl, then one day, blimey, she was a boy again. Reckon he refused to wear the dresses. Poor mite. As I say, there was the old boy staring at the child running around on the boat.'

Miranda pulled up a mirror, holding it behind Sheila's head like a genuine hairdresser. 'Did he catch you, watching him watching her? Is that why you got the sack?'

'Nah. He just didn't like people. Don't get me wrong, I know it's OK to like being alone, but I don't think he even liked his son and grandchildren.'

Miranda moued. She moved the mirror back and forth. 'How does that look, Sheila? What d'you think?'

'Oh, love, that's dandy. I was so fed up with my hair, it can't be worse. It looks lovely, thank you. I would give you a cup of tea, but of course I can't. But it was really nice of you.'

'No problem,' said Miranda. 'Say *get well soon* to Jeff.'

She frowned as she walked round the corner to her house. Pete had said the reels of film were removed, and yet here was Karl Deliverer watching the young girl in one after they should all have been in Brian's house. How did that happen?

CHAPTER 19
ORDERLY DAUGHTERS IN JACK'S CLUB 1973

When Jack entered the club, the rozzers were already in. Two policemen were sitting at the bar drinking coca cola.

'Jeezus!' he muttered to Clinton. 'It's been legal these six years, and still those orderly daughters find any reason to do us over. What the flatties doing here?'

Clinton shrugged. 'The big one there says they're just after having a drink and we're not to see them as betty bracelets, but as a couple of friends sitting at the bar enjoying the music.'

'To be sure! We all drag up the uniform when sipping with friends. Corrupt bastards. Lucky we're not black as well as queer or they'd be fitting us up big time. They hopin' for an auntie for themselves?'

Last year, Fran had made him take part in the first Gay Pride march, and the police behaviour had intensified Jack's lily-love. Now, seeing them sitting in his bar as bold as Jesus was enough to frizz up the hackles along his neck.

Fran herself had disappeared shortly after the march. Bev'd had to make do with Carile and Scarlet or any other willing aspra. He hadn't seen the silly bint since; she'd vapourised like a will-o'-the-wisp, but she'd be back. She always was.

He spun a mat along the bar. It knocked into the nearest policeman's glass and spilt some of the beer. 'I wouldn't trust a lily further than I could spit,' he said to Clinton loudly enough for the policemen to hear.

The policeman signalled to Clinton. 'Clean glass, mate,' he said smiling loftily.

The barman took over the new glass and the man poured most of the contents of his old glass into the new one, leaving a small amount in the old glass. He pushed it over to Clinton.

'Here's a tip for your boss,' said the policeman, and his smile would have made a mongoose scuttle away. 'You can tell him I saw him and his pretty girlfriend at the parade. Nice couple they made, didn't they, Jimmy? I was quite jealous.'

He leered at Clinton, never looking at Jack.

Jack forced himself to turn his back and walked away, but the policeman's action had hardened a thought that had been long growing in his mind.

Over the other side of the room, Bev's gold rings reflected the light. Jack watched the golden gleam, concentrating his mind. The club was raking in the dosh, and their name was good – outside lily pad, that was, but even those *nadas* in the *vada* only dared tread so far.

Two new omnis were playing bridge at Bev's table and tonight her partner was again Fran. Jack's already thumping heart leapt in a different direction. Not that he cared. God knows he wasn't one to go soppy over a doxie, any more than he'd lose his cool over a couple of bent rozzers.

He sauntered over. She looked up and their eyes met.

She lowered hers immediately, but she didn't fool him. He saw the light dancing in those green eyes. Little tart was glad to see him too. For one moment he imagined stripping off all her clothes, there and then, and bending her over the card table.

He laughed, and both omnis looked up curiously. Neither girl's concentration left the cards.

'Came back, did you?'

Fran smiled down at her cards. 'Feels like I never left.'

Jack sucked his breath through his teeth. Something registered in his mind; not sure, but he knew that little girl now. If she said 'Feels like I never left' then she hadn't. Could she really be that good an actress?

'Does it, bejesus?'

'You come in for the kill?' asked Fran softly, keeping her eyes on the cards.

He looked down at her cards. Fran was Mr Bennett of the infamous bridge game. This wasn't the first time she and Bev had tricked their omnis with that little match. Fran licked her lips.

Jack stared at the cards in her hands. He physically felt her longing. 'You pushing me, little girl?'

He felt Bev's hard stare from over the other side of the table.

'Want to play, tonight? At Muriel's?' Fran asked, too quietly for anyone but him to hear.

'I'll get my gun,' he said, and she nearly fell off her stool holding in her laughter.

CHAPTER 20
BONE CHASES DOG IN 2020

Miranda and Cat, and various dogs, went for a walk to discuss the case and to help Miranda clear her head.

The dog rescue part of the detection business had continued as usual, and Cat was now looking for a lost or stolen Water Spaniel.

'Dog thefts are getting worse,' said Cat. 'You can now get £3,000 for a puppy – ridiculous when you think how hard it used to be to get six hundred. It's all because of lockdown and people wanting a dog to walk.'

'Or puppy farms,' Miranda pointed out grumpily. Did Cat think she didn't know all this already?

'Yes, OK, puppy farms, but if the clients weren't buying then the puppy farms would not spring up. I heard that gangs are leaving drug smuggling and moving over to dog breeding. It's an easier option and the fines are minimal.'

'Ridiculous,' said Miranda. 'I hate to think how many dumped dogs there will be when lockdown ends.'

'I've been contacted by a couple called Brown – George and Sally. Do you know them?'

Miranda shook her head, although she was surprised; she knew most people locally. Perhaps these ones didn't frequent the pub; must be dull.

'They've lost a dog called Tea Leaf,' said Cat. 'Ironic name for a stolen dog.'

'Why?'

'Ur, ur! What's the matter, my friend, too much Aristotle? Bit of a Ben Dover! Forgotten your cockney rhyming slang?'

Miranda pretended to laugh. Sometimes Cat could be so annoying with her linguistic games. She remembered when the bullies would yell 'roly-poly' across the schoolyard, always catching that moment when she had just had a row at home or was feeling particularly low. This case was getting to her. If Simian was leading her to find something, then why weren't there more clues? She didn't want to fuck this one up – her first time as lead detective. Cat would never forget it if she made a mistake; she could hear it now, years into the future, Cat saying 'Can we trust Miranda with this one?'

'Humans are more complicated than dogs,' Cat was saying irritatingly, like the bullies reading her mind. 'You mustn't expect to be able to solve a problem immediately.'

'Thanks, Nanny,' said Miranda rolling her eyes.

Cat looked sideways at her and said slowly, 'Sorry, was I treating you the way my kids treat me? Must be catching.'

The tension fell away and they both laughed. 'You were. Need some more marital advice?' asked Miranda. 'I could tell you one of Phillip's jokes.'

Cat laughed. 'When I was married to Charlie, maybe, but Frank can out-joke me anytime.' Her face broke into a grin every time she thought of her crazy Liverpudlian boyfriend with his happy-go-lucky attitude to life, so completely different to her lovely but formal late husband.

As they walked up the hill Miranda was relieved to see Cat was as slow as she was on the mud-sliding slope.

'How did Karl Deliverer die?' Cat asked. 'Old age?'

'No, he was killed in a house fire in 2000.'

'So, no clues there? Odd, isn't it, that all those old cine tapes were in Brian's house, not Karl's? You would have thought that they might also have gone up in flames.'

'No,' said Miranda, 'remember Pete said some tapes were moved by Brian after Pete and his brother were found mucking around in the loft. But why do you think that was? There wasn't anything incriminating in them.'

'Perhaps there was – we just missed it. Should we look through them again?'

Miranda groaned. 'Oh, no! Of course,' she added, 'since Jeff's wife mentioned Karl had been watching the one with the little girl not long before he died, that does mean there were other tapes too. Ones Karl kept in his house.'

'What did Pete say about the tapes?'

'Well, "pub talk", as he says, was that they were porn, but we've seen them and we know they weren't.'

'Unless there were other reels that Brian got rid of. Perhaps Karl bought Silas from Nepal as a model. Dressed him as a girl ...'

'Oh, ugh. I hadn't thought of that, and we can hardly ask Karen if her dad watched porn.'

'Hm,' said Cat, looking at her watch. 'Well, keep asking around. I'd better go. I'm Zooming in half an hour with the distraught owners of the stolen Water Spaniel. Let me know if you find anything else.'

Cat turned and took her two dogs back down the hill,

while Miranda struggled on in the mud that covered all the paths.

CHAPTER 21
CHEAPJACK AT MURIEL'S
1973

Fran was already at the club by the time Jack arrived. She was playing 'Gypsys, Tramps and Thieves' on the piano. She saw him watching her as he walked towards her and she turned her head towards him, still playing.

'Muriel taught me. She thinks I shouldn't play bridge at such a high level of finance. Risking my neck in the stock market with the big girls, she says.' Fran laughed. Jack didn't.

'I like to think of you in Ireland,' said the girl, turning on her seat and leaving the keys. 'Shirt off, muscles bulging, sweat dripping down your back as you lift huge bales onto the truck.'

Jack gave a shout of laughter. 'What the hell they'd make of you in Killarney,' he said exaggerating his accent, which had now rounded down to English vowels. 'Where are you from, anyway? Sure as sure, it's not the bogs.'

'I'm from everywhere and nowhere,' said the girl grinning. 'My father would say Hell, my mother would say Heaven. Take your pick.'

She was laughing, but there was a sadness in her eyes that made Jack feel strangely protective. 'Why d'ya run away from home? What happened?'

The girl looked down at her long fingers now resting on her knees. She was silent for a while, then she said, 'My father tried to kill me.'

Jack had spent a lifetime judging whether people were lying. This well-refined ability had kept him alive to the age of forty. She was telling the truth; where he came from a small insult could lead to death. Fran, with her provocative manners and unusual predilections, would be a risk candidate wherever she lived. For a short moment, he wondered if and how her father discovered what she was and that was why. 'You beat him in one bridge game too many?' he asked, his eyes smiling at her.

She looked up at him. 'You're a clever man, Jack Club, not just the scrumptious muscle I took you for.'

'And?'

She slipped off the stool, took his wrist and led him to the sofa. 'It is a long tale, and it starts with the bridge game that you and I know as Mr Bennett's murder ...'

Jack called over the waitress and ordered two beers. He'd already judged it was time to sell the club and move on. Years of building it up made his club a good sales proposition. He wanted a new challenge and a life with Fran would be nothing if not a new challenge.

Tomorrow he was interviewing a new fella for the bar. Clinton Steman was leaving after all these years. Moving to a bridge club, of all things – said he had the chance of a windfall. *These young guys, eh!*

CHAPTER 22

TEA LEAVES LOSE A PACKET
AND FIND A BITCH

C at sent a Zoom invitation to Tea Leaf's owners, and they were soon sitting opposite her on their stripy blue and white sofa.

'Hello, dear,' said Mr Brown, 'are you there? Can you hear me?'

Cat said she could, impressed that this couple in their seventies didn't struggle to unmute the screen or find themselves upside down. The reason was soon forthcoming.

'We Zoom every evening with our grandkids,' said Mr Brown. 'Oh, and call me George, dear, no need for formality on Zoom. And she's Sally.' He waved in his wife's direction.

'Hi, George and Sally. Shall we get started? Tell me a bit about Tea Leaf.'

'Hi, Cat,' said Sally.

'Now, Cat,' said George, 'seems funny talking to a Cat about a dog, but I'm sure he wouldn't mind.'

Sally laughed encouragingly.

'Well,' said George, 'we've had Water Spaniels for the last fifty-seven years. Probably longer than you've been alive, love.'

Even though he stopped, Cat didn't say anything, hoping he would get to the point.

'All our spaniels have been called Tea Leaf. Ask me why, will you?'

'Why?' asked Cat politely.

'Well, there's quite a story ...' Cat's heart sank. 'But it's worth it, isn't it, love?'

'Yes, it is indeed,' said Sally, getting her few words in.

'Well, I'll start with the bit my wife doesn't like.'

'Honestly, George,' said Sally, 'do you have to?'

'Oh, darling, it may have been fifty-seven years ago, but I'd do it again like a shot. You were irresistible then and still are.'

Even on Zoom, Cat could see Sally's eyes lit up with delight. 'All right, go on then.' She giggled.

He winked at her. 'Well, Cat, my love,' he said, 'Sally and I both lived with our parents fifty-seven years ago. We were both seventeen and deeply in love.'

'Nice,' murmured Cat, making a few notes on her iPad while he told the story.

'But, of course in those days even holding hands was infra dig. Even smiling at each other could get my mother going on about PDAs, – Public Displays of Affection.

So, of course, we had nowhere to go necking – as we called it then. But my father had a boat, and I knew an island about three quarters of an hour from Bosham where we could be completely alone.'

'Lovely,' said Cat politely. She liked to let people talk, it was often interesting what things they let slip, which might then lead to finding the dog, but she wondered how long George would spend creating the picture. Perhaps the dog had gone back to the island; they liked to swim, those Water Spaniels – obviously.

'So, we took the boat,' he continued, 'and went over to the island. We were so much in love I could hardly contain myself and I was dropping clothes off long before we got there: jacket, tie, shoes, all gone. Afterwards I found my trousers and shirt in the grass all stripped before ...'

His wife coughed meaningfully, and he stopped.

'Sorry, love, one gets a bit carried away telling stories.'

'You do,' said his wife, but not unkindly. 'Tell Cat the important bit.'

'Oh, yes, sorry.' He grinned. 'Well, afterwards, and it was quite a bit later ... you see, we went out there on a Friday evening in July. It was really warm, not that we'd have noticed the cold. But anyway, as I say, it was morning before we were ready to leave. We got dressed, at least she did. I had to hunt for my clothes.'

He winked at his wife again. 'We went back to the boat. Funny how as you get old you mind about time, but when you're younger time slips by and you don't even notice it – well, as long as you're having fun, I mean ...'

'George!' said Sally.

He covered his face with his hands. 'Oh, sorry, dear. Anyway, the point is, when we got back to the boat it wasn't there. The boat had gone.'

Cat's mind had drifted off, but when she heard the word *gone* she focused again. 'Gone? Where? Had it floated away on the tide?'

'Good point, but no. Even though I wanted to get on to the island super quick and was stripping off, I still remembered to tie up OK, otherwise Father would have killed me. Nope, this had been untied and motored away. And we hadn't heard a thing.'

'Tricky,' said Cat. Finally she understood where the dog's name had originated. 'Your boat was stolen.'

'Yup. Some tea leaf ...' He shook himself like the dog after a swim. 'So,' he said, 'after that we got a dog to protect the boat, so no one could steal it again. Hence Tea Leaf, which is cockney rhyming slang for thief.'

Cat sighed inwardly.

'And every dog since has been called Tea Leaf,' he said in the happy voice of one making a huge revelation.

'How did you get back,' asked Cat, 'swim?'

'No, it was far too far.'

'So, how did you get off the island?'

'My father found his boat had gone, and he guessed what I'd done. He'd met Sally several times and ... well, he'd lived through the war. He was a man of the world, if you know what I mean.'

'George!' said his wife.

'Sorry. Anyway, he started looking for his boat and asking around. He didn't bother the police, they were pretty busy in those days anyway, but he asked in the sailing community, and someone had seen his boat pulled up on the sand at North Shore. When he got there, he found my tie in the bottom of the boat. Not my jacket or shoes, though. The tea leaf had taken both of those and my wallet, dirty bastard.'

'George!'

'Sorry, love. Well, Father guessed I was on the island and, although he said he was tempted to leave me there, he heard there was a storm coming in, so he came over in the boat and fetched us back.'

'I was that embarrassed,' said Sally, 'I thought I would die.'

'But it was OK,' said George, 'because I told him we were engaged, and although he said we'd have to wait until we left school to get married, he was pleased. He liked Sally and he liked her folks. And it's been a great marriage, hasn't it, love?'

'Yes,' said Sally, smiling at him, 'but I was that red in the face, and my parents were furious. I was gated for a month. They were really worried.'

'Did you ever get the jacket and shoes back?' Cat asked.

'Not the shoes, but the police found the jacket in a bin. No wallet, of course, and I'd taken out money from the bank that morning to treat my girl, but they sent the jacket back because the tailor's name was inside the jacket with mine below. Do you remember? They used to do that then.'

Cat nodded. 'Where did they find the jacket? The police.'

'Oh, yes, I'm thinking it was in London, wasn't it, dear?'

'Yes, darling. You remember it was the Camden police because we laughed about how the jacket had gone camping.'

Sally blushed her whole face flaring red. 'I mean you could say that, then. It just meant, well, you know, camping.'

George waved her aside.

'Right,' said Cat, 'we do seem to be getting a bit away from the theft. So when did you last see Tea Leaf?'

'He was in the garden,' said Sally. 'I was in the kitchen doing the washing up, I saw a van draw up outside the gate, and Tea Leaf ran over barking as usual. A boy wearing a parka with the hood up got out and opened the gate. I thought it was a delivery, so I got a towel and started drying my hands. I walked to the front door and opened it, just in time to see the van driving off. I didn't know what had happened. There didn't seem to be any parcel waiting, even nowadays when they leave the parcel and then stand back and yell your name. I called the dog, but he was gone.'

'Did you see any registration number?' asked Cat.

'No,' said Sally, 'by the time I realised what had happened the van had gone, and the dog with him.'

'Probably false plates anyway,' said Cat. 'We've had several incidents where the owners did see the registration, but it wasn't genuine. Could you describe the boy at all?'

'No,' said Sally sadly, 'I just saw him out of the window. All I could say was he was white – I am allowed to say that nowadays, aren't I? But he had a mask and hood, so I couldn't really see anything.'

CHAPTER 23

MUDDING THE WINTER WATERS

Every time Miranda put a foot forward it was dragged halfway back by the mud.

This is hell, she thought, but at least it can't get much worse. Woosh! Three bicyclists rode past at top speed (or top speed for three inches of mud) splashing her coat and decorating her face.

'You shits!' she yelled, and got three cheery waves.

That was enough. She was going to walk in the wood, even though last time the farmer had caught her and gave her an earful. On balance, his anger was better than any more boot-fulls of muddy endurance. Of course, it probably hadn't helped that when he yelled, 'I told you to keep your dog on a lead!' she gave him a Nazi salute and yelled back: '*Sieg heil mein führer*'.

This time she'd be more tactful; she'd just tell him his father belonged to the bachelor's club – one more of Phillip's favourite jokes. She laughed to herself, wishing there was someone there to share her joke.

Her dog skipped happily on; why did no one ever try and take him? It wasn't that she didn't like dogs, but this one seemed to have no potential for anything, except annoying his owners.

They went deeper into the wood and Miranda pulled out her walking app. She loved this app; no matter where she was, the app knew it too. Cat hated it, calling it the useless tracking app, but Miranda had replied wittily, 'Well, at least they'll be able to find my dead body.'

The wood was thickening and becoming almost as annoying as the mud when Miranda spotted a tall figure ahead with a hood over his head. *Oh no!* Not the farmer again, and, of course, her trying dog was rushing over towards him, full of joyous greetings.

She dragged out her whistle and tooted furiously. At least the farmer would think she was trying to control her animal. However, after a quick look back at her, the 'farmer' legged it. In a distant clearing, Miranda could see him grabbing a bike and then pedalling away at top speed. 'What the ...?'

She whistled and whistled but the dog refused to come back; in fact it had now buried its head in a clump of bushes and, with a furiously wagging tail, was sniffing away at something in the middle.

'Sodding dog!' she yelled at him.

As she got closer, she saw what was intriguing her dog: another dog tied to a tree.

'Fuck!' she yelled at the long-gone boy. 'Come and take your dog, you scoundrel.'

So, dumping had started already. Why couldn't the boy take it to the shelter, rather than leaving it out here to die?

'Little shit!' she yelled.

What sort of dog travelled on a bike, she wondered idly, turning her attention to the tied-up dog. The dog itself quickly produced an explanation: a neutered male. And it appeared to be tied by its legs to the tree. Clearly the 'farmer' was neither a dog lover nor an expert.

'I bet,' she told her dog loudly, 'that boy stole the dog, thinking he could sell it to some criminal puppy-farm breeder, and the breeder took one look and gave the boy a flea in his ear. I can imagine him saying, "And wot I'm supposed to do with that, no sperm, no womb, bloody useless. Now go and get me a young bitch, and look before you grab. Idiot!"'

Miranda chuckled. It was lovely when thieves were hoist on their own petard.

Her dog was now licking the tied dog's nose, in between jumping around him like a lunatic, while the large brown prisoner sat quietly waiting for her to release him.

She bent down and, releasing the dog, noticed someone had carved a heart with 'FD/SL' on the tree. Children! She stroked the bark. 'Sorry,' she said, 'I hope it didn't hurt you.' A tree tattoo. Yet another joke no one was here to share.

She took the dog's rope, smiling wryly, realising she now had two annoying neutered male dogs, and she much preferred cats. The dog was wearing a collar. What sort of idiot dumps a dog wearing a collar? The tag read 'Tea Leaf', with a landline number below. The number was in the village. Where had she heard that name before?

She looked at her phone, but there was no signal here in the wood.

She called her dog and headed back out of the wood and onto the mud, holding the brown dog on her dog's lead. Walking downhill must have stimulated the little grey cells because Miranda realised where she'd heard the dog's name before. 'Tea Leaf! Of course.'

She was about to solve at least a part of Cat's mystery.

Back in a transmission area, Miranda called Cat, who was still on a Zoom call with the Browns.

'Cat,' she said, 'keep talking to the Browns. I've found a dog that might be theirs.'

'Brilliant,' said Cat. 'Come round. Door's open. I won't say anything in case it's the wrong dog.'

Miranda ran all the way to Cat's house, the dogs bobbing along behind her like children's toys in the bath. She shoved open the door into Cat's kitchen and galloped over to where Cat was talking to the screen. Without even removing her coat, she lugged the dog into the viewfinder.

As they appeared on the screen, she heard Sally cry out, 'What? Oh! That's Tea Leaf! You've found him!' She burst into tears. 'Oh, my goodness. You are the best detectives in the world. Can I come round now?'

The dog, hearing his mistress's voice, wagged his tail hopefully, looking around as though wondering where the sound came from.

'Yes,' said Cat. 'Miranda will meet you at the door and tell you where she found him.'

Sally had already left her house and was running through the village. Miranda could hear her yelling, 'They found Tea Leaf,' to anyone listening. 'They found him. My baby!'

She ran through the still open door to Cat's kitchen and fell on the dog. 'Oh, my darling, darling Tea Leaf. Thank you, thank you, Miranda. You are the best. Thank you so much. I can never repay you. Tea Leaf is part of the family. We'd be lost without him. Darling, darling Tea Leaf.'

She kissed him happily, laughing and wiping tears from her eyes.

While Sally was away, George told Cat the story of how he had met Sally. Cat was still listening to him when

Sally and Tea Leaf appeared on the other side of the Zoom. Tea Leaf greeted his master effusively, happily licking his face.

George was delighted. 'I must tell you, you heroine, Miranda, the story of his name.'

'Lovely,' said Miranda, wishing she was there in person and he was handing her a celebratory glass of champagne.

'Would you like a coffee?' asked Cat, rising quickly to get one.

As George told the story, Miranda quickly became immersed in his words and its diversions, laughing happily at each aside, all of which embarrassed Sally as much as the first time. This time, however, she was able to bury her face in Tea Leaf's fur and clearly didn't care about anything except the dog.

As George paused for breath at the end of the story, Miranda asked, 'Couldn't you contact anyone to get you back from the island?'

George laughed. 'How? Semaphore perhaps. No one much went to that island, and of course it was long before mobile phones. But there was one funny thing. We went round the island. I knew sometimes people moored up in the bay on the other side and I hoped there might be a boat there. And I was right. There was a forty-foot Swan in the bay. They were just starting up and moving. I was so relieved. I waved and waved. There was a boy on there. He looked at me, and then he went out of sight. I saw a man at the helm and waved at him like crazy, but he just ignored me and motored out of the bay. I was so shocked. "What happened to the rules of the sea?" I thought. You're supposed to help other mariners in trouble.'

'Perhaps he didn't realise you were a sailor,' said Miranda.

'Maybe, but I was a human being stuck on an island. Anyone who sailed there would know that.'

Miranda nodded.

'Still,' said George, 'he got his comeuppance. The boat was scuttled the following year, so serve the dirty old bastard right.'

'You knew who it was?' asked Miranda.

'Not then, but later I saw the Swan moored in the channel. I asked about it. I was going to face up to him about leaving me on the island with my girl, but then his boat got stolen and scuttled and I didn't bother.'

Miranda smiled sympathetically, thinking she would have done the same. Then it struck her that Charlotte had said Karl and his sons sailed a Swan too. Perhaps it was the boat of the time, but considering they had also gone out on an evening in July, it could possibly be the same boat. 'Can you remember the date your jacket and boat were stolen?'

George grinned. 'I keep forgetting, but she can – she calls it our anniversary. When was it, Sally love?'

'Twenty-sixth of July 1963,' said Sally. 'It was a Friday evening.'

Miranda's heart leapt. 'And you said you faced up to the man who left you there. Can you remember his name?'

'Can I? It was only the most notorious family in the place – that Karl Deliverer, whose son fell into the Solent and drowned.'

'Where did they find your boat?' asked Miranda.

George swelled with delight. He had told this story so often and this was the first time anyone had listened for long enough to ask questions. He had always known that the girl Miranda was more intelligent than most.

'Funny you should ask that, love,' he said. 'The boat was dumped on the sands at North Shore, but there's nothing much around there now and there was even less then – no houses and only that funny old railway station that was closed the year before. The only way to get from there without walking for several hours was from the brick works. My dad used to joke it was stolen by a brick worker late for work.'

He roared with laughter and Miranda joined in.

'Really?' Miranda leant forward, her nose sniffing the screen in excitement. 'Did the line from the brick works go anywhere?'

'Well, they did send supplies up to Midhurst, so I suppose it might ...'

'Of course, he might have hitchhiked,' Sally broke in.

George frowned at the interruption. 'Oh, Heavens, honey, you've forgotten, there weren't really roads like today, it was mostly old tracks then. And anyway, people didn't have cars in the early sixties. You had to be really posh to have a car then, not like now when every man and his dog has one. Unless of course there's a tea leaf about.'

He roared with laughter again and turned back to Miranda, who was laughing too. 'Bit of an amateur historian, me. It really was not until after Beeching that the roads started getting developed and people bought cars.'

'More's the pity,' said Sally, 'and now the environment is suffering.'

'OK, OK,' said George. 'Sorry, girls, Sally can bore for England on that climate change thingie.'

Miranda smiled supportively at Sally.

'Google it,' hissed Cat.

But George was back to his history. 'Midhurst had a station until 1964. Although it's true it was only used for freight for the last ten years.'

'But if your "bricky" thief could get to Midhurst, he

could go on to anywhere? I assume trains were still quite good then,' said Miranda.

George nodded. 'You're right, love. Sally and I sometimes got a lift on the freight trains, didn't we, honey? Train drivers weren't so restricted then, and the stokers were lovely. Most of them had been in the navy and then got demobbed onto the trains. They had great stories. I loved to listen to their tales about the islands they visited where the people were cannibals and still lived in the trees. And the animals, you wouldn't believe the animals they saw. There was a frog, see, lived up a tree ...' He chuckled.

Miranda turned off the computer and went back to where Cat was making coffee in the kitchen, singing. Now, at last, they were getting somewhere.

'There has got to be a connection,' she said. 'Karl's Swan was out in the bay. The Swan helmsman ignored the stranded couple. And, on the same trip, on the same date, Francis died and Silas disappeared. Tell me there's no connection. I don't believe it.'

Cat nodded. 'Good catch. You were obviously listening to George better than me. But you're right. It's also quite possible that the boy on the boat who ignored George was Brian, and this relates to the bad thing he's been living with for years.'

Miranda nodded. 'All we need to do now is find out what happened on that boat forty years ago.'

Cat raised her eyebrows. 'Um, easy peasy!'

CHAPTER 24

THE PRICE OF THE MASK

Felix had not been concentrating at home, so he'd been allowed to join the children of key workers at his school. Miranda drove him to school at 8 a.m. and, wearing her skeleton teeth mask, accompanied him into the reception. The class teacher, Mrs Pogle, was waiting for him, sporting a more demure pure blue mask.

'We have a group of vulnerable children,' she said, her eyes narrowing like a crocodile above the mask. 'Felix can join them. Poor thing, I expect he's been terribly under-stimulated at home. You can come and pick him up at three o'clock.'

Miranda longed to say she was too busy on her PhD in astrophysics to help her son, but, as she was mostly self-taught, she just gave what she hoped were wolfish eyes over her skeleton mask and said, 'He may be distracted by the excitement of being at home, but you are *so* right – he needs to learn how to be bored.'

Turning, she stormed down the path, her mind imagining all sorts of tortures for Mrs Pogle.

She was still angry when she got home, so instead of

going to the office she whistled for her dog. As she grabbed his lead her mobile went off.

'Hi, Miranda, it's Karen.'

'Hi.'

'Look, I'm sorry, but I got a call from a weird man who wanted to sell me information about my grandfather. I'm afraid I told him you were working for me, and he could deal with you. I hope that's OK.'

'Yes, fine,' said Miranda, 'what does he want?'

'Money, I reckon,' said Karen. 'He said he was a detective, but I doubt it. He said he worked for my granddad, but I'm not even sure that was true. His voice sounded – I know this may sound odd but it's the term that came into my mind as he talked to me – putrid.'

'Thanks, Karen, I'll deal with him. Did you give him my number?'

'I did, but also he knows we all live in Owly Vale, so, well, you know. Take care.'

'Thanks.'

Miranda closed the phone and went into Phillip's home office, but he'd gone out, taking Peta with him. She hooked up the dog, who yelped with delight, and they set off across the square. As she passed the pub a tall, thin man blocked her way. He was wearing a black mask and a fedora hat as well as a long raincoat. He only needed to pull up his collar and she'd be calling him Raymond Chandler.

God, these masks are annoying for a detective, she thought. I have the information of the eyes but not its contrast with the mouth. What would it be like being a detective in a land where they wore burkas?

'Excuse me,' the man said. 'I'm looking for a Miranda Zeblonkski.'

She considered telling him she'd never heard such a name but softened. He might genuinely have information.

'I'm Miranda Zielinski.'

'Oh, thank you,' he said, his voice full of relief but his eyes holding some slyer message. 'Karen Middlebrow said I would find you in the village. I've been looking for you. May I walk with you a while?'

She smiled behind her mask. It sounded like an old-fashioned courtship. She looked at his leather shoes. *Bet they have leather soles too.*

'Oh course, but I need to walk my dog. Let's go up the hill. How can I help you?' She grinned happily, thinking of his smart shoes on the sucking mud.

'Well,' he began as they left the village and stepped onto the steep muddy paths through the wood. 'It is a delicate matter.'

My God, thought Miranda, listening to the serpentine timbre of his voice, could he be going to blackmail me? Tell me that Phillip has been chasing girls? Unlikely, especially now he's working from home.

The path narrowed and as the man in the leather shoes started slipping backwards in the mud, Miranda felt a silent giggle forming. Must have been the first time she'd ever outpaced anyone on a walk.

Behind her she heard him mutter, 'Nice piece of arse for a fat Russian.'

For a moment she couldn't believe what she'd heard. Russian? Russian! Rude comments about her arse were bad enough, but suggesting she was Russian. Cheek! Even now she could hear her father's ghost speeding back from Heaven to complain. Karen's 'putrid' was spot on.

When they arrived at the top, his trouser legs covered in muddy streaks and his shoes double in size, the Putrid

Detective continued doggedly. 'I understand you are a detective.' He attempted to increase his speed to catch up with her, but now the mud had changed to flint and chalk and his feet slipped from under him. His flailing arms looked as though he might slip back down the hill, then, at the last minute, he saved himself by grabbing the branch of a tree. The dog stopped and looked back suspiciously, raising a hairy lip.

'Yes,' said Miranda, unable to quell her growing smile.

'I am too.'

Miranda waited for more. If he thought his words would elicit compassion for a shared profession he could think again.

'I was employed many years ago by a Karl Deliverer, and I am quite certain I have some information that will be of use to you,' he said, his gasp for breath sounding like a snake ready to strike.

'Really,' she said politely. 'How kind of you.'

'As you know,' continued her new friend, his eyes filling with tears, 'times are hard for a detective under COVID. Our work has mostly dried up. One still has to live and costs have increased. There was no furlough pay for detective agencies, nor were they considered essential workers.'

Miranda felt a flash of boredom. He was an irritating man and she wanted to be rid of him. 'What is it you want?'

'I have some information about the Deliverer family which I am willing to sell you.'

'As one professional to another?' she asked, raising her eyebrows.

'It is of a delicate nature,' said the sleuth, misconstruing her response. 'But I'm quite sure his daughter will be glad to know it's no longer in the public area.'

Miranda was sure his smile was vile. Damn those masks

– his eyes seem to be leering. 'How do I know your information will be of use to me?'

'It contains pictures of a graphic nature,' he said, and his body appeared to wriggle in pleasure.

Miranda wondered if he had considered his audience. She, a young mother, was hardly likely to be impressed by graphic sexual images, was she? Or was he trying to sell her pictures of nubile young men, which he thought might be her bag? Or suggesting that she see the porn Pete thought Karl Deliverer had enjoyed. Her emotions swayed between fury and a desire to laugh. 'What sort of things?'

He stopped slightly ahead of her and, turning again, blocked her path. 'You will not be disappointed,' he said, reaching to put his hand on her arm.

Before Miranda could remonstrate the dog, already suspicious, clocked the man's sudden movement as highly aggressive. He jumped up and snapped at the man's exposed wrist.

'Oooh, the little shit!'

The detective dropped Miranda's arm and aimed a furious swing at the dog. It went wide and the dog circled delightedly and ran off into the field. Turning, it barked and circled again. The detective stopped, his arms waving.

'Your dog needs training,' he said angrily. 'They should be kept on leads, dogs.' He rubbed his wrist. 'He's broken the skin. I could sue you.'

'Go ahead,' said Miranda drily.

'Look, £1,000 and I drop the case, plus you can have everything I discovered about the Deliverer family. Karen Deliverer will not want it out in the open.'

She was sure she heard the man licking his lips under the mask.

Miranda's brain slowly processed the steps the detective

would have taken. It wasn't brain surgery to guess this man liked blackmailing vulnerable people. She turned and looked directly at him; inevitably eye to eye, but his were bloodshot above the mask. Was that years of dissipation? She shivered. Would her eyes one day look the same. She grabbed her mind and forced it to concentrate.

'You tried to sell this to Brian Deliverer, didn't you?' she said, speaking quietly so he had to lean forward to hear her. 'And he refused to buy it? So, you thought his daughter might be more willing. Particularly now she is sad and vulnerable after her father's death.'

His eyes looked scornful. 'Stupid fool. If he was going to kill himself, he should have made sure he got all the information first, shouldn't he?'

Miranda gasped, the implication of what he was saying filling her mind. She realised they had walked a long way from the village, and she was alone with an angry and possibly unstable man who wanted money.

'Let's walk on,' she said. 'We'll take the shortcut. I may be interested. Tell me more about it as we go down the hill.'

She whistled the dog. He came at once, baring his teeth with a low growl as he passed the man.

As they went down the steep hill to the village, Miranda could hear the detective slipping and sliding behind her. A man who thought leather soles were suitable for walking in muddy countryside would presumably believe he could sell strange pornographic images to anyone. Perhaps he didn't realise it was possible to buy wellington boots.

Once back in the village square, Miranda asked him, 'When did you try and sell your information to Brian Deliverer? How long ago?'

A spasm zipped through the man's eyes. 'You can't blame

his death on me,' he said. I wasn't there that day. I have witnesses to say I was in London.'

'Thank you,' said Miranda. 'I don't think I'm interested in your information, Mr ... what did you say your name was?'

His eyes sneered. 'You think you're clever, Mrs Zeblonkskie, don't you? Well, you'll regret this, I can tell you, and so will your employer, that Karen Middlebrow. You'll be sorry.'

And he turned and went into the village shop. Miranda watched him in amazement. Did he not realise that, under current COVID rules, the shop was not handling cash? That he could only pay there by credit card, and if he bought anything she would be able to get his name?

She took the dog home. She'd be back shortly for that information, which was possibly no more useful than the stuff he was trying to sell her, but it was worth trying anyway.

Half an hour later, having visited the shop, Miranda was on the phone to her detective sister, and they were having a very elucidative phone call.

CHAPTER 25

THE PASSWORD AND THE DOUCHEBAG

An hour later, when Miranda arrived at the office, Stevie's mother jumped out of the shadows. 'Password?'

Miranda jumped. 'Honestly, Blinkey, don't do that, you nearly gave me a heart attack.'

'Wrong. Password.'

Miranda sidled past her. Good thing her earlier black mood had passed, and she was instead in the mood for dancing and laughing.

Stevie was at the computer. Cat was searching for the coffee beans, which Blinkey had hidden as usual.

'Guess what Karen sent my way?'

'Doughnuts?' asked Cat hopefully. She was always hungry around midday.

'Well, something in a bag, but more of a douchebag than delicious.'

'Douchebag?' asked Cat. 'Something for showering?'

'More human,' said Miranda, 'certainly someone you might want to drown.'

'Ah,' said Cat, 'is that what I would call a spiv?'

'Not exactly,' said Stevie, 'it comes from incel culture, which means the involuntarily celibate male. A bit less successful than a spiv.'

Cat laughed. 'So, what did the douchebag do?'

Miranda told them all about her trip up the hill with the dog. All three women laughed joyfully when the dog came to her defence, but Cat said, 'I hope your dog wasn't hurt. Sounds like this chap might be quite poisonous.'

'Certainly, I think his information might have been,' said Miranda.

'I'm glad you didn't pay the douchebag for his information,' said Cat, her repressive voice reminding Miranda of Mrs Pogle. 'You should never pay for things that relate to morality. It opens you up to blackmail.'

'Besides,' said Stevie, 'most things he could give you, I can find on the Internet for free.'

'So, what have we found out about this DB?'

Miranda grinned. 'DB, very à la mode, Cat. His name is Clinton Steman and he works in Soho as a barman. Obviously, he's not working now because bars are closed. But it seems he's been working as a barman since the 1960s, so he must have quite a lot of information.'

'Why would a barman have lots of information?' asked Cat.

Miranda turned to her in amazement. 'That you even ask that shows how little time you spend in bars. They get info in two main ways. Firstly, customers talk to them. The more unhappy the client, the more information they give away. Secondly, barmen listen. It doesn't matter how busy they are, their ears are always open. And the more a barman needs money, the more he refines his hearing. I would say Putrid Clinton was a pretty ideal sponge.'

'But is it stuff we would want?' asked Stevie.

'True. He used to work in Soho, but in the late seventies he moved ... wait for it ... to a bridge club.'

'He became a bridge expert?' Cat's voice exuded disbelief.

'No, he worked behind the bar. More information there and you don't have to concentrate on the game.'

'How do you know this?' said Stevie.

'Ah, there are other methods of getting information than the Internet,' said Miranda, waggling her shoulders joyfully. 'I used what Cat would call the dog and bone.'

'Indeed,' said Cat, 'and are you going to tell us who was the woofa?'

'As you know, I left school early to help my mother in the shop, so my sisters could get a proper education.'

'Yes.'

'So, do you remember my youngest sister, the one who did really well at school and got to university?'

'Yes,' said Cat and Stevie simultaneously, 'the one who was always correcting our mistakes.'

Miranda laughed. 'Well, she was young, pert, they do that.'

'Hmm!'

'Anyway,' continued Miranda, 'she joined the police a couple of years ago on their graduate scheme. And, luckily, she feels indebted to me, so once I discovered from the shop that Clinton Steman was the douchebag's name, she did some ferreting around for me. She discovered that Steman is one of their "knowns". He has a list of small infringements and crimes, some blackmail and scams, but nothing large. But, because he sometimes helps them out, they tend to know where he's working.'

'Wow! Really? He was a sort of grass? And is he now a detective?'

'She thought it unlikely, given he's pushing eighty, and, she pointed out, if you want to do anything with security you need a licence; a man with a record simply wouldn't get one. But anyway, there's more and this is particularly interesting. Guess who joined the bridge club in 1998?'

'Not Silas?' said Cat.

Miranda pouted. 'No, not Silas, but Karl Deliverer.'

'Wow! He joined a bridge club in London. Why?'

'I can only guess he was looking for Silas. We're assuming Silas played bridge – he may not have been very good but perhaps he took lessons. If Silas is Simian, then he is now very good at bridge. So, he learnt very well.'

'Interesting. But why go to London? And why wait until 1998?' asked Cat.

'Both good questions,' said Miranda. 'But if you were running away from Sussex in the sixties, where would you go? Which town seemed like the Golden Mecca? London, wasn't it? London, the most cosmopolitan and free town of the country.'

'Could be,' said Cat. 'How did your sister know Karl joined the bridge club in London?'

'It was in Steman's notes. Obviously there was a connection between them since Karl employed him as a detective.'

Cat made a face. 'Increases your admiration of police sleuthing, doesn't it?'

'Stevie,' said Miranda, 'can you find out if Silas was a member of the same club?'

'I'll try,' she said. 'I wonder what name he would use. Silas Deliverer. Or Silas something else?'

'Or,' said Miranda, 'something completely different. Karl must have thought he would run into Silas while there. And, of course, he no doubt enjoyed the bridge.'

'So, this is where Clinton met Karl. I wonder who got

information from whom?' said Cat. 'Was he trying to sell you something about Karl or Silas?'

'I'm not sure, but my sister said she'd keep an eye on when he was next in custody – quite a frequent happening, apparently. She'll let me know.'

'Well,' said Cat, 'one for pre-Internet sleuthing. Have you got anything else for Stevie to look up, so she doesn't fall into depression?'

'We still haven't found Terry Plump for me to eliminate from my investigation,' said Miranda pinching her chin.

'I'll look for him,' said Stevie absentmindedly mirroring her friend, 'but it would be helpful if you could remember something about him. His job? Interests? Anything.'

'I'll try. But any memory of him is eluding me. He seems to be slipping through life like a tea leaf in the night.'

'Funny girl!'

'Also,' said Miranda waggling her eyebrows - something Felix had recently learnt at school- 'see what you can find out about Le Duce in Soho and the Gigolo in King's Road, also Jack's Club, opposite Le Duce on good old Terry Termi-nal. Our DB worked in all of those places from the sixties to the eighties.'

Stevie nodded. 'That seems within the range of my magic.'

'Brilliant' said Miranda, 'and, also, can you research train lines from Midhurst and where they went in July 1963, including freight-only lines.'

'No problem.'

'Cool. Particularly out of North Shore and see where you could go from there.'

'Where was the jacket found?' asked Stevie.

'Camden. I'd bet my dog's life on the fact there *is* a

connection between Karl's boat being in the bay on Friday 26 July 1963 and George's boat being stolen.'

'The mysterious Silas,' said Cat, making some more coffee. 'The by-blow who slipped through life like a ghost.'

'Cat!' said Stevie sharply. 'We don't talk about by-blows nowadays.'

Cat looked embarrassed. 'Sorry – what should I say? Love child? Lucky mistake?'

'Why mention it at all, unless you want to bring up the problem of being a single mother?'

'You know,' said Cat, changing the subject with some haste, 'there was something else in George's story.'

'Yes?' said Stevie.

'He said something about not wanting to get his own back on Karl because his boat was scuttled a year later. Who do you think did that? Brian? The mysterious Silas or Karl himself? Perhaps hoping for an insurance payout.'

'Good point,' said Miranda. 'Are there records about that sort of thing on the Internet, Stevie?'

'From 1964? I doubt it. But I'll have a look at a few history sites and see if I can find any old boys who might remember the time. As we can see from George, they're very good sources of unusual information.'

'Museums are still closed,' said Cat.

'Yes,' said Miranda, 'unfortunately, or we could go over to the sailing museum near Tangmere and browse around or talk to the volunteers.'

'It's a flying museum,' said Stevie.

'I know, but when I last went there ...'

'You went to a flying museum?'

'OK, OK, you're not the only one with interests. I may not like flying but I am interested in things ...'

'Oh yeah? What did you go there for?'

'My Polish grandfather was a pilot in the war and he flew Spitfires. I was told Tangmere had information about them, and it was true. While I was there, I noticed that there was a lot sailing as well as flying information. But it's all irrelevant since the museum is closed.'

'Never mind, I'll have a look. Could be that they have contacts or experts with interest in scuttled boat in the 1960s.'

CHAPTER 26

BICYCLING IN THE MUD AND
COMING OUT CLEAN

Since the start of lockdown, everyone in the village had tried to use the shop as much as possible. So, the next day, after dropping Felix off at school, Miranda crossed the square to the shop.

In some ways the village was much as for time immemorial: old men with newspapers chatting about the state of the government, women walking dogs and couples lounging by the well. But now the men and women wore masks and gloves, and the pub had 'Remember to hand sanitize before entry' over the door jamb, left over from the days between lockdowns when you could still visit.

In the middle of the square, two of the mud-splattering bikers from yesterday stood drinking coffee from polystyrene mugs, talking about their bikes.

Miranda stared down at her mud-splattered coat, then sprinted over towards them. 'Hey, you guys. Look at this!' She swept her hand down her side. 'That was the result of meeting you three lovely gentlemen yesterday. What happened to bikers' etiquette?'

The two men looked up, startled. 'Sorry,' mumbled

yellow jersey, refusing to meet Miranda's angry eyes. 'We didn't see you until it was too late. That mud was awful though, wasn't it! No fun walking or cycling in that.'

'To be fair,' said blue jersey, looking straight at Miranda, 'it wasn't exactly our fault. A guy with a dog said he'd race us up the hill, so what could we do? We had to take the challenge.'

'A guy with a dog?'

'Yes, the one in the middle ... sadly I got knocked back at the beginning and never made it up. Charlie here beat us all.'

'Really? You didn't know the other guy? And what dog?'

'Oh,' said yellow jersey, 'didn't you see the dog in his basket? I thought it was too big for a bicycle basket, but he said it was used to boats, so it would be fine, and certainly it wasn't any trouble.'

'Wasn't he part of your group, then?'

'No, we met him while we were having a coffee. Take-away, of course.' He smirked. 'But he stopped to chat when I asked about the dog, and then he made his challenge. After the top of the hill, he zipped off and we lost him.'

'I see. Thanks,' said Miranda, continuing to the shop.

She didn't know what to make of that. Seemed like the guy with the dog wanted to push her into the wood so she would find the dog tied to a tree. Why? Was it just that he wasn't a bad guy and didn't want the dog to suffer, in which case why tie it under a tree, or was there some other reason?

As Miranda drove over to the school to pick up Felix, thoughts about the mysterious biker colluded with thoughts about the putrid Clinton Steman. Was there a connection there? They were both strangers who had turned up in the village at roughly the same time. Steman was clearly linked to the Deliverers, but was the biker too? Was that why he wanted her to find the dog and hear George's story?

Felix was waiting for her at the gate, playing with a stick he was jamming into a hole in the wooden fence. So much for the school keeping an eye on the youngsters, thought Miranda bitterly; still, she'd rather not see the ghastly Pogle if she could avoid it. 'How was the day?'

'Good,' said Felix, 'I'm going to be an astronaut. But I might still help you find murderers. I'd be good at that. I could pretend to be a dead body and then ...'

'Thanks, Felix. Why an astronaut?'

'So I can see the world as it really is. Mrs Pogle says if you look from above you see things clearer. She said you get angry because you have a close-range view. Small size, she said. Or was it small eyes?'

Miranda twinkled tightly. 'Did she?' She might well have words with Mrs Pogle tomorrow. 'Does Mrs Pogle have a dog?'

'No. She likes hedgehogs – she's got an albino one. He lives in the school.'

Miranda sneered. 'No wonder she's a bit prickly. Know what's wrong with Mrs Pogle?' said Miranda, hurrying on in case Felix tried to answer. 'She's got her humour-mode button turned off.'

Felix yawned. 'What's for tea, Mum?'

After Miranda had fed and bathed the children and they were all in bed, she checked her emails.

There was one from Stevie sent around lunchtime entitled 'COVID good and bad.'

Inside it said:

Good news: my mother's been offered her second jab. I'm about to

drive her over to Portsmouth, back 5 p.m. if you want to talk
about point two.
Bad news: Frank, Cat's boyfriend, has tested positive for COVID.
He had achy muscles and a headache this morning, so Cat drove
him over to Chichester and they both got tested. She hasn't got the
results yet but she's pretty sure he positive, so she's going to self-
isolate and says we'd better not see her, except on Zoom, for the
next ten days. She says she feels fine, a bit tired but just in case.
She is a bit of a PPPP person. Incidentally, that means Prior
Planning Prevents Piss-ups and
is very important for pilots. LOL.

Since it was now past seven, Miranda gave Stevie a call. 'How are Cat and Frank, any news?'

'I sent her a WhatsApp. She said she's OK, just achy and headaches, she's going to self-isolate, drink lots of water and hope to clear anything there out of her system.'

'And Frank?'

'Sounds like he might have the "exhausted" version. Apparently he found it hard to get up this morning and he's gone to his bed for a few days.'

'Lucky their dogs are so old,' said Miranda. 'I couldn't leave mine without a walk for a few days.'

Stevie wasn't interested in anything you couldn't take flying. She murmured, 'Yeah, right.'

'You found anything on Silas yet? Or Terry Plump?' asked Miranda.

'Not Silas. Even the Internet, magic though you and Cat think it, couldn't find a man who might be called Silas, who might have been born in India or Nepal in the 1950s and might be an illegitimate son of Karl Deliverer. Might have the surname Deliverer or might have another, totally different surname. But I'm working on it.'

'Ah. OK. So, you did find something on Terry Plump.'

'Yes. If I found the right one, he's about forty-five to fifty in age and has a father in his late eighties who is in a home in Norfolk.'

'Why Norfolk?'

Stevie grimaced. 'End to my magic! Guessing ...maybe he lived up there. Finding that he was in the home at all was a piece of luck.'

'Such as?'

'Well, I was fiddling away on the Internet looking for Silases who might have belonged to bridge clubs in London in the 1990s and I came across Terry Plump, who belonged to the same bridge club as Karl in London. It couldn't be our boy because he was probably born in the late 1980s and they don't cater for kids at this club. But I thought it was quite possible father and son had the same name. Then in 2010, he was no longer a member of the club. However, it seems the London club is often relocated for weekends, and it did one of these trips to Norfolk in 2018. There was Terry Plump back on the players list again. He won the tournament as well. That was lucky because the local paper took it up and wrote an article about him entitled "Man with Dementia wins Bridge Tournament".'

'You're pulling my leg,' said Miranda. 'He's got dementia and he won a bridge tournament. Doesn't say much for the other players.'

'Um,' said Stevie. 'Thinking of my mother's dementia I thought that too. But then I read the article. The journalist had done his work. He interviewed a neurologist, who explained that even someone who can't look after themself on a day-to-day level could still be an ace bridge player, if he already was before the illness. Who knew, eh?'

Miranda nodded even though Stevie couldn't see her. 'And did this lead to Terry Plump junior?'

'Sort of, in that there is a Terry Plump selling a house near the home in Norfolk. I wondered if that might be our boy. Perhaps his father has died or doesn't look likely to come out of the home.'

'Um, OK,' said Miranda. 'I suppose he could still have been playing bridge with us through BBO. No need to be in the same village after all.'

'Except ...'

'Except what?'

'Simian played bridge with us using Brian's IP address. He could have set the game up, that was done on a VPN, but he couldn't have played the game.'

'Bother!' said Miranda, walking to the fridge to get a bottle of wine. 'So, unless he zipped back to the village it's unlikely to be him playing bridge.'

''Fraid so. Suppose he could have come back to the village. But doesn't seem very likely with all those COVID policemen jumping out to get you. Why would he want to use Brian's modem to play bridge when he could use his own?'

'Yeah. I guess we can almost cross him off the list. But I still want to talk to him. No chance a mobile number was on his house advert.'

'Nope.'

Miranda sounded so down that Stevie hurried to cheer her up with her other news.

'However, I did find something about what Karl did during the war.'

'You did? What?'

'Well, he was in the Essex Yeomanry. They were in Dunkirk in 1940. Then he seems to have been separated from his unit – they even marked him as a deserter. He found his way back and continued with his unit, but not until 1944, when they were in Arnhem. It was impossible to find out where he was between 1940 and 44.'

'He went missing for four years?'

'Yes. But don't start saying he might have got out to India or Nepal to father children ... how would he get there?'

'He could. If his unit sent him. I was talking to someone the other day whose father was sent to work in Burma in the middle of the war.'

'Yes. But Karl had been reported missing.'

'Could be undercover,' said Miranda determinedly.

'True.'

'However, let's suppose for a moment he did actually go missing for four years, that's quite a heap of time. Especially during a war. How did he live?'

'That's what I thought. I looked on Google Maps and the distance between Dunkirk and Arnhem is 307 miles and would take sixty-three hours to walk. Mind you, that's information now when there are roads. If you were trying to avoid capture, plus trying to find food ... it would take much longer.'

Miranda tried to imagine wartime roads, pretty much lanes in the films Phillip liked so much. Where would you sleep? Was there was the same endless mud as they had round here? That would slow up the pace a fair bit.

Stevie was talking again. 'I looked up what World War Two deserters did do. There seem to have been quite a few of them, enough anyway to have a website or two about them. It seems that some hooked up with French or Italian women, lived in their houses and pretended to be locals.'

'Really. But if Karl Deliverer did that, he must have later let his new girl go and taken on Hannah instead.'

'Yes, good point. It seems that at some point he must have been wounded because at the end of 1944 he was in a field hospital, which is where he met Hannah and where they married.'

'How romantic,' said Miranda.

'Um, maybe. My mother said wartime made you romantic,' said Stevie. 'Not that she was old enough to be there, but she got that from my father.'

Miranda chewed her cheeks, trying to imagine Blinkey as a romantic young woman. 'Sounds like an excuse for flirting.'

'There must have been an attraction,' said Stevie. 'Besides the fact they both spoke fluent German and French.'

'Who did?'

'Karl and Hannah, pay attention! Anyway, he was demobbed after the war. Not a regular soldier.'

'Hang on,' said Miranda. 'He went missing for four years and he spoke fluent German and French. Odd, wasn't it, that if he went missing for four years, he wasn't punished? Didn't they kill them for deserting? Maybe he really was under-cover. Or alternatively, could he have defected? Joined the Germans? People did, for money, fear all sorts of reasons ... That might explain the crystal meth and stuff Pete found in the attic, if he was working for the other side.'

'Wow,' said Stevie, 'that's quite something. We need far more evidence before we can suggest that to Karen. I'll keep looking.'

'By the way,' said Miranda, 'you said Essex Yeomanry. Did he live in Essex then?'

'Yes, he appears to have lived in Jaywick in Essex before

the war. He learnt to sail there. He was part of a local club, learnt on something called Eights, if that means anything to you.'

'Nothing. But just going back to his wartime.'

'Yes?'

'Could you find out if he defected to the other side? On the Internet?'

'Hmm, maybe. I'm not sure where you'd get information like that. War Office? Would that even be released yet? We probably need someone alive at the time.'

'Yes, no,' said Miranda, 'we're running out of people alive at the period. People who could give us clues. Charlotte talked about a Friar Jacques over at the monastery, I wonder if he's still alive.'

CHAPTER 27
FATHERS OF PERPETUAL INDULGENCE

Miranda rang Mrs Hearthop's house. She, if anyone, would know if Friar Jacques was still breathing. Stevie had discovered there was a Friar Jacques living in the monastery, but it could be someone else with the same name. Neither of the women knew much about religion and they didn't want to disturb the sick Cat, but they had a vague feeling that friars didn't keep their own names when they left 'civilian' life but were 'reborn' with new ones.

Overall, it seemed more fruitful to call Mrs Hearthop who, Miranda expected, would be in perfect health until the day she dropped down dead, rather than rely on the vagaries of the Internet.

Jean answered the phone at the Hearthop house. 'Oh, yes,' she said in reply to Miranda's question, 'he's not only alive, he visits here every Friday. Usually stays to lunch. He doesn't seem any more worried about the virus than Mrs H, right.'

'How old is he, do you think?'

'Must be top eighties,' said Jean. 'Younger than her, but not by much, 'eh.'

'Thanks. I don't suppose he has a mobile number?'

'You suppose right. You can either ring the monastery, or just turn up, 'eh. They receive visitors. There aren't many of them still living there now.'

Miranda parked her car outside the monastery, fitting her Polo between rows of weeds and fallen bricks. Didn't look like many visitors came searching for the friars either.

The door to the monastery was probably the only part left from its original building. An impressive piece of carved oak, it looked out of place in the centre of the modern brick building with its double-glazed plastic-framed windows. Miranda put on her mask and lifted the knocker. The monastery had a speakeasy hatch in the door. It was lifted immediately and a mouth said, 'Hello?'

'I'm looking for Friar Jacques,' said Miranda, trying not to giggle.

'That's me,' said the voice, 'come in.'

Brought up with Robin Hood and *Blackadder*, Miranda expected to see a rotund tonsured man with a huge personality, but Friar Jacques was slim, wrinkled, and had the small amount of thinning grey hair you would expect on any man in his late eighties. Apart from the habit he could have been anyone. He wasn't smiling either. He took a pace back, staring at her masked face.

'I'd prefer,' he said, shocking Miranda with the gentleness of his voice, 'that you removed the boundaries between us.'

'Oh,' said Miranda, 'but I wore it for you. For your protection.'

'Then please remove it,' said the friar. 'I'm slightly deaf and it helps if I can see your lips moving.'

To her surprise he appeared to be sneering, but then he lowered his head, and she could only hear his voice, not see his confusing facial expression.

'I hope you don't mind,' he continued. 'I have had both vaccinations.'

Miranda was on the point of telling him that he could still infect her, but she ripped off the mask instead. If she hadn't got the virus from Cat, she was unlikely to get it from this man, with whom she would not share hugs and kisses.

He led her into a huge empty room that must once have been a refectory bustling with monks and friars but now felt like a football stadium under COVID. He offered her some tea from a machine, which she refused. They sat down on basic wooden chairs at a plain wooden table.

'Why did you wish to see Friar Jacques?

'Oh, I'm a ... I'm a detective, Miranda.' Jacques referring to himself in the third person disorientated her. 'I'm, er ... from the SeeMs Detective Agency and we've been employed to find out why Brian Deliverer might have committed suicide. I mean, that is what the police concluded from the evidence.'

Jacques nodded. He had sad eyes. 'I see. The current rule is that there is no impediment to receiving a Catholic funeral or being buried in a Catholic cemetery after dying by suicide. That has now been removed from Canon Law, although it was in the Code of 1983.'

'Ah, right,' said Miranda, wishing she'd thought to ask Jean what Friar Jacques was like before she visited. She took a deep breath and tried to regain control of the conversation. 'Tell me about Karl Deliverer.'

The friar nodded, then looked away towards the hills.

For a moment Miranda wondered if she'd lost him completely, then he said, 'Friar Jacques was his confessor. There will be certain questions he cannot answer.'

Miranda was silent. She hadn't expected that. Had Karl confessed to killing his son, and now Jacques was unable to tell anyone? Had he lived with such a burden until he died?

'OK,' she said, 'then perhaps I could ask you questions, and you can tell me if they are allowed or not.'

He inclined his head.

'Was Karl Deliverer a religious man? Did he attend services here?'

'Yes, indeed. He was both pious and generous. He had not been brought up in the Christian faith himself but was originally Jewish. However, when he married Hannah, which he did during the war, he converted and became very devout. We never had any doubts about his sincerity here in the monastery.'

'I see,' said Miranda, feeling extremely full of doubt herself. Everything she'd heard about Karl Deliverer so far seemed to suggest he was a pretty angry man. 'And his children?'

'They came to services regularly.'

'I see. Can I ask you about Silas?'

The friar nodded and Miranda saw his face change, becoming slightly grey.

'Do you know where Silas went to school?'

'Yes, here.'

'Here?'

'Yes, we had a junior school, although there were only four children in it: Brian and Francis Deliverer, Silas and Charlotte Hearthop. The Deliverer boys and Miss Hearthop left at ten to go to schools elsewhere, but Silas stayed here. He was brilliant at languages, particularly Latin and Greek, and I think Karl hoped he might enter the church. Sadly, that was not to be.'

'No,' said Miranda. 'When did you last see him?'

Jacques's face dropped and for a moment Miranda thought he might cry.

'July 1963. When school started again, in September, he did not return.'

'Any idea where he went?' asked Miranda. 'Some suggested he returned to India.'

Jacques's lips smiled gently but the emotion didn't rise to his eyes, which registered pain instead. 'Can you return to a place you have never been?'

'He wasn't Indian?' Why had she thought that? Was it India that Pete said? Or Charlotte?

'He was from Nepal,' said Jacques. 'Karl and Francis went out to Nepal for a holiday in 1957. We, at the monastery, gave them an introduction to the Christian community. The Nepalese are mostly Buddhist. However, Silas's father was from the small Christian fraternity still practising in the country. Unfortunately, his father had been killed and his mother remarried. Her new husband was a Buddhist and did not wish to give the young Christian boy a home. The consequence of this was that he was then living with a Sherpa who was of the Christian faith.

'When this Sherpa met Karl, he was clearly impressed by him as a devout and kindly man. The Sherpa asked Karl to take Silas home with him. He hoped Karl would give Silas a better life, a life away from the poverty of his homeland. The Sherpa's family were very poor, and they could not afford another mouth to feed. They did it for the best. You do understand that? People now misread the past. Mores have changed. We older people perhaps do not understand the present, but that does not mean that our way was wrong.'

Miranda nodded. 'So, he wasn't Karl's child?'

The priest shook his head. 'We have heard that is what people thought, but no, it was an act of charity and devout faith by Karl.' He looked into Miranda's eyes. 'You may have heard that Karl was an angry man, even a savage man, but he also had kindness and charity in his heart. He was a devout believer. Human beings are complex creatures.'

Miranda dropped her eyes; for some reason she could not hold the intensity of the holy man's gaze. 'Did he adopt Silas?'

For a moment the friar paused. Then he continued in a firm voice as though trying to convince himself as well as her. 'Karl did not feel it was necessary. Having brought the boy out on his passport as though one of his children and given him a comfortable home, he thought that was suffi-cient. He told us he saw no reason to weigh the boy down with paperwork.'

'Paperwork?' Miranda could hardly believe anyone alive today would say such a thing. Even living in a monastery, Jacques must have heard of the Windrush scandal, people sent back to the Caribbean. People who had lived here their whole lives, often more than fifty years, owing to lack of paperwork. 'But that would make it so difficult for him later. Would he be allowed to stay in Britain?'

The friar looked at her, his eyes slightly closed. 'You are familiar,' he said, 'with the case of *Willcock versus Muckle* in 1950, which showed up the futility of keeping wartime legis-lation on in peacetime.'

Miranda shook her head. 'I was born in 1982,' she said.

Jacques sneered openly this time. 'It is the privilege of the young to behave as though life started with the death of Elvis Presley, or perhaps even that is too long ago for someone born in 1982.' Miranda thought he made it sound like a sin. 'It is important to learn from history. If you can leave your twenty-first-century perspective for a while, then perhaps Friar Jacques can attempt to explain the way Karl saw life.'

He gave her a jackal-like smile. 'Karl was in Holland just before the war. There he discovered how easy it was to find the Jews, because they had their religion on their identity papers. Obviously, since he was himself Jewish, this was very worrying for him. He vowed never to burden the boy with that kind of bureaucracy. He did not think about the possibility of work because he intended Silas to enter the church.'

'I see,' said Miranda, although she felt there was a deep arrogance in anyone who would make a future for a child, and one to whom he had not even given the benefit of his name. 'What surname did Silas take, then?'

'We called him Deliverer Minimus. If he had another surname we were not informed and did not ask.'

Miranda rested her chin on her hand thoughtfully. The friar sat up straight in his chair and didn't lounge like her. Did their different poses mean anything, she wondered? 'What were the Deliverer boys like at school?'

Again, the friar looked away, as though he hoped to find inspiration from the surroundings. 'Brian worked hard. He was a nice, polite boy, kind to his mother, obedient to his father. He would always do well in life, and indeed he went on to become an accountant and we are told that he was always in demand.'

'And Francis?'

'Francis,' said the priest, and again he looked to the

heavens for help. 'He sang like an angel, but he was not an angel in his behaviour.'

'Oh?'

'Francis was very good at singing and acting, and perhaps he could have been good at many things, but he chose to skip off school. Even when he was only five or six years old, he would disappear and not return. He told us all sorts of lies to cover where he really was ...'

'And where was he?' asked Miranda.

'Playing cards,' said the priest. 'He was playing bridge.'

'Bridge? At five?'

'Yes.'

'I don't understand. Karl played bridge too. It's not a forbidden game. Why would Francis need to disappear to play bridge?'

'Because he wanted to do only three things: sing, act or play bridge. He would disappear off to clubs with adult men, and when we found him, he was acting, singing and playing cards. He was a great disappointment, not only to his father, but to us in the school.'

'At five years old?' said Miranda, trying, and failing, to see Felix in such a senario. 'He absconded to clubs? At five years old – how did he get there?'

The friar looked at the far-off hills again. 'He was the son of a devil. He flirted with the novitiates and other church members until they were under his power. They were the ones he led astray.'

Miranda shook her head. The cold feeling in her stomach was making her slightly queasy. 'Five years old? *He* led *them* astray?'

The friar looked back at her. He opened his mouth to say something, and then closed it. When he spoke again, she wondered what he had planned to say.

'Mozart,' he said, 'composed his first piece of music at five years old.'

She almost laughed at the ridiculous comparison, but he looked deeply into her eyes, forcing her to hold his gaze. 'Francis was a wholly unusual boy. Never in my eighty-seven years have I come across another boy so determined to live life by his own rules.'

'But, but,' said Miranda, she felt herself floundering, this was all so surreal, she grasped at the only normality in the Friar's words, 'wasn't bridge a good thing? He must have been counting, so improving his maths, and ...and he played bridge at home.'

The friar coughed. 'The boy needed to be obedient, to do what he was bid, to honour his father's words. Again, as times change so does perspective. Now, perhaps, Francis would be lauded as an individual, as someone expressing himself and teaching himself in his own way. But we were there to teach him the ways of the Lord, obedience and chastity. As you will know from Deuteronomy 10: *"What does the Lord your God require from you, but to fear the Lord your God ... to serve the Lord your God with all your heart and with all your soul, and to keep the Lord's commandments and His statutes"*. Francis failed all these things and more.'

Cat, thought Miranda, with her religious upbringing, might have done better here than her. She doubted if anyone in her family had ever visited a church except as a tourist.

'Is that why Francis was buried outside the walls of the cemetery?'

Yet again the friar lifted his eyes to the hills. This time he was frowning. He said, 'Have you seen his grave?' Without waiting for an answer, he continued, jumping up with an agile movement. 'Come.'

Miranda got up stiffly and followed the friar out of the monastery into the graveyard. He moved so fast she could hardly keep up with him. As before, the burial ground was empty apart from the same old man cleaning the stones. The friar marched up to the wall at the far end of the cemetery.

'Look at that stone,' said the priest, his arm drawing a spectacular flourish. 'Marble.' He turned round and shouted at her. 'Marble! Marble! Who gives their son a marble stone? Only a man who loves his son despite his inequities – despite his evil ways. Francis may have disappointed his father, but his father still wanted the best for him, even in death.'

'But it was outside the cemetery walls, until the boundary moved?'

'Young sinners may spend time in purgatory learning the errors of their ways,' said Jacques. 'Karl and the friars both hoped that the Lord, who understands and forgives our foolish ways, would allow the boy into Heaven after a sufficient period. Certainly, after some years we allowed him back into the fold. And now I must return to my duties.'

'But wait,' she said. There were still so many questions about Karl Deliverer and his relationship with his son. Oddly, just one popped into her mind. 'Did Karl Deliverer kill Francis?'

The friar stopped. He stood completely silent for a moment and then he said, 'No, Karl Deliverer did not kill his son.'

He bowed his head and marched off, leaving her standing there by the grave of the mysterious young man who had aroused so many differing emotions.

When Miranda got to the car, she rang Stevie. 'Are we absolutely certain Francis Deliverer was Karl's son?'

'What?'

'I'm coming over. There is something dead creepy about Friar Jacques. I actually wonder if he's religious at all – the way he talks is weird.'

'OK,' said Stevie.

Even after putting the phone down, Miranda didn't start the car but sat staring at the poorly adapted old building in front of her. Perhaps Cat, with her great religious knowledge, would have had more insight into the Friar's mind, but her instinct told her Jacques hadn't told her everything. What did he know that he wouldn't say? And why?

CHAPTER 28

SIGNS AND SIGNALS OF
BURNING IN HELL

Miranda was yet again walking up the hill with her dog. Walking seemed so endless at this time of year. There should be a hobby, she thought, of mud-walking, where you gained points for miles endured, for depth of mud and the amount of muscle power generated. These could be converted into air miles and she and Phillip could fly off somewhere hot and sultry, without kids or dogs. Recapture their original love. Bliss.

She shivered as the cold breeze swept through the missing teeth on her zip. OK, the wind had dried the mud somewhat, and it did make walking easier, but it would be lovely if the sun came out and she felt warm.

Her mobile rang, displaying 'Jeff, fire investigator'.

'Hi, Jeff, how are you feeling?'

'Oh, Miranda, you know it's me?'

'I do indeed. You feeling better?'

'Much better, pet. Thanks so much for cutting the wife's hair. She's like a new woman after that. Now, what was it you wanted? I worked on the Karl Deliverer case – it was an odd

one and one of the few we had to admit baffled us. How can
I help?'

Miranda moved her phone to the other ear, checking the
dog was still with her and hadn't scampered off. 'Pete said
there was a rumour it might have been arson, not an accident. Was that so?'

'Good old Pete, you can't tell a builder anything – leaky!'
He laughed. 'We were a bit puzzled over that one, surely.
Two problems: first the two ignition sites, one upstairs - a
magnifying glass caught the sun and ignited some tissues -
the other downstairs, in the living room. Theory was, he fell
over in the living room and his cigar ignited the old carpet –
it was pretty threadbare and some traces of whisky were
found. It's possible both things happened at the same time.
Sometimes one site can spill over onto another, but not
when one is upstairs and the other is downstairs. But you
never want to jump to conclusions. Reality is a strange crea-
ture and so is fire.'

'Is it possible that one site was happening anyway, and
then Karl's fall caused the other?' Miranda asked, she was a
bit out of her comfort zone here, but it sounded logical.

'Possible, but unusual. Other things too. When Karl's
body was found he was lying on the floor surrounded by
glass, and the docs thought he'd cut his head running into a
mirror. The way the smoke covered the mirror glass and its
cracking showed that it was already broken before the fire.
There were bits all around Karl's body, as though he had run
into the mirror at speed, which seems odd indoors.'

'Perhaps he was drunk.'

'He was drinking, but that was not unusual. The docs
said post-mortem showed a lot of whisky in the stomach,
but the liver damage showed he was a heavy drinker,
wouldn't have as much effect as on someone who didn't

drink a lot. His head was badly cut, but, although he might have knocked himself out, he would not have died from that injury.'

'So, what were the other problems?'

'Well, love, there was the position of the body. The head was turned towards a cloth, which we identified as a smoke source and stuck on the rag were burnt pieces of glove. No other bits of glove anywhere. The window was open too, which had fanned the flames, and there was dirt the other side of the window, soot that had been probably knocked off a shoe. Scuffed too. Like someone was trying to hide the evidence.'

'Oh.'

'And another thing – right up your street as it happens.'

'What's that?'

'Looked like he was playing cards. Reconstruction reckoned, from the way the cards fell on the floor, it was set for a game with four players.'

'What? How on earth? How did they know there were four players? Were there any other bodies?'

Miranda wanted to jump to the idea they were playing bridge, with Karl it was possible, although solitaire sounded more sensible, but even if so, why?

'Nope. It was the position of the chairs and the way the cards were bunched. No other glasses though so, unless he was with three fellas on the waggon, looks like he was playing against himself. I've seen weirder in my time. Scoot round from one seat to another.' He laughed. 'And then there was an open packet of drugs beside him, but no trace in the bloodstream.'

'What sort of drugs? Painkillers? Did you think ...?'

'No. Nothing like that, these had a brand name –

Pervitin. Real old stuff. Wouldn't have any effect now. Long
past the sell-by date.' He chuckled.

Miranda frowned. Here was that Pervitin again. What
had Pete said about it? It was in Karl's loft, but it made no
sense for Karl to get it from the loft, not if he was playing
cards alone. Miranda could imagine herself with a group of
friends going upstairs in a larky mood to fetch the old stuff
and show it off, but Karl wasn't that sort of person, was he?
Or, had she totally misjudged him and he was a comedian at
heart and all this was a great bit joke. Nice but unlikely.

'What about the upstairs fire?' Miranda asked.

'That looked like the sun's rays being magnified. It was
an old house, with dry dusty contents. It's rare, but it
happens, even from reflections from chips in window glass.
We've had several in our time.'

Miranda nodded, thinking.

'It took the roof off,' Jeff said. 'Those old beams, they
went up like straw. Whatever was in that attic was well gone,
I can tell you.'

'So, you and the police thought Karl might have been
murdered?'

'Not to put too fine a point on it, yes. When there are so
many signs of human interaction in a fire space you have to
ask the question. No one wants to jump to conclusions, and
we didn't find anything to lead to a suspect, but the case is
still open.'

'Did the police take fingerprints? Or can't you take
fingerprints in a fire?'

'Oh no, you definitely can. Sometimes a fire is good for
fingerprints, if you get my meaning. You get the soot on
walls or floors in which there are footprints, handprints,
and fingerprints. Also, you might see soot outside a door
that's much lighter than inside the fire room, which shows

that someone closed the door during the fire. In this case the window was open, which both magnified the fire and would have allowed egress. Marks outside too.' He sighed. 'We were pretty certain that there was at least one other person in the room at the time of the fire, but we couldn't find him.'

Miranda frowned. 'At least one other person?'

'Yes, may sound odd, love, but there were a couple of things we thought showed the presence of more than one person.'

'What sort of things?' *Bridge players, perhaps?*

'Well, for one thing, it looked like a door between the two fire sites had been opened and closed while the upstairs fire was raging but not the downstairs. Then, the window was opened after the second fire had ignited.'

'Couldn't one person have done both those things?'

'He could, but there was more. Footmarks going away from the house and onto the footpath, but then also tyre tracks over the gravel and onto the road. We were pretty sure that indicated two people, one walking, one driving.'

Silas and a friend, perhaps, thought Miranda. One who could drive him back to London, if that was where he was now. Could Silas have come back after all these years and taken his revenge on the man who might, or might not, have been his biological father, and certainly was his guardian, although that term now had a more sinister overtone.

'Oh,' said Jeff, just before Miranda ended the call, 'there was one other thing in the post-mortem.'

'What was that?'

'He'd been in a fire before. They found old burns on his right arm, as though he'd been defending himself against a burning object. It was quite deep, would certainly have needed treatment, the doctors said. And there was some writing under the burn. They couldn't read it, but it looked like numbers.'

'Thanks, Jeff,' said Miranda.

Writing? Numbers? Could Karl have belonged to some cabal, and they wanted something – money, perhaps – and they came back and killed him? Could this be nothing at all to do with Silas?

CHAPTER 29
GLORIA CALLING

C at was sitting in bed reading a book on wildflowers when the phone rang. Her test had been negative, but Frank had tested positive for COVID so she'd been right to self-isolate. He was now living, sleeping really, since he did little else, in the spare room. She masked up to take him food that he never ate, and mugs of soup.

She wasn't sure if it was the proximity to disease or the fact that they had passed the hospital where Charlie died only five years ago, but she felt miserable. She was glad of an excuse to lie in bed and read; she really didn't feel like doing anything else. Charlie had done everything for her, or redone it, since she so often got it wrong. Frank was so different; when she did things wrong, he just laughed and said it didn't matter.

She stared out of the window, wishing she could get rid of the ball of pain that had lodged itself in her solar plexus and refused to move. She couldn't even be bothered to put on lipstick; she just didn't care. She felt tears forming and dug her nails into her arm. When the phone rang, she stared at it, unsure if she could be bothered to answer. Reluctantly she looked at the face.

It was Gloria. How did that girl always know when she needed someone? She was unique.

Cat answered it. Put on her happy voice. 'Hello, darling. How are you? And how are all the Little Family?'

Gloria and her complicated throuple with Cat's children were known to Cat as the 'Little Family' even though, Gloria having given birth to another boy under COVID, they now numbered five. Cat couldn't bear to use the word 'throuple'.

'We are all fine. Worried about you. Stevie told me Frank had COVID. How are you feeling?'

'Fine, I have a headache, but I tested negative, so I'm fine. Frank does nothing but sleep, which I assume is good news.'

'Yes, yes,' said Gloria, 'and in yourself? Are you eating, Cat? Drinking enough water.'

Cat felt her defences rising like hackles. 'Yeah. I'm fine. Frank's the one who's ill.'

'So,' said Gloria after a short pause, 'in your email you said you had some questions for me. The kids are both asleep, and I wondered if this was a good time?'

'Thanks,' said Cat, realising she had been harsh and that Gloria had noticed. 'Yes, indeed. You have perfect timing as usual.'

She lay down and rested the phone beside her on the pillow. 'One question was why an apparently happy grand-father would commit suicide, and the other was about the type of pills he used and how long it would take for them to be effective.'

'Oh good, nothing large then! Honestly, Cat, why do people take their own lives? We could discuss that for hours. It's such a complicated subject. I'll give you my own personal view, but don't take this as anything other than that. OK?' She stopped and perhaps arranged herself more comfortably before continuing. 'One thing is when people's expectations don't meet with their realities that can lead them to feel desperate. I don't mean they will necessarily kill themselves, but they feel like doing it.'

Cat wondered if Gloria remembered that she had tried to end it all and was saved by Miranda, or if it was all too long ago and too unimportant. Probably she had forgotten, Cat thought feeling unloved.

Gloria was continuing. 'My belief is that the underlying problem is their fear that they have lost the power to control the world around them. Worse still, they cannot envision it ever changing for the better, only for the worse. Whatever happens draws them lower.'

Yup, thought Cat, *that was how it was for me. Charlie was dead after that long fight from MND, and my children were better off without me. If I died, they could get money from the house, and they would benefit from that more than me alive.*

'Usually there's a catalyst, an activator – sometimes as little as the coffee machine breaking down, or a broken glass can push them over the edge. However, when I say it like that it sounds so insufficient for something that causes so much havoc, not only to themselves but everyone around them. The people who love them so much.'

She paused, and Cat felt guilty. Of course Gloria remembered. Listen to the timbre of her voice: love. She was her sensitive, caring daughter-in-law. Gloria didn't forget things like that. What *is* wrong with me today?

'Why do you ask?' said Gloria. 'Is this relevant to your hobby?'

Cat's family referred to the detective agency as 'Mum's hobby'. It was pointless telling them that the detective agency had found lots of stolen dogs, unearthed gangs behind fly-tipping, solved murder cases and made an income for its agents; they just found it funny.

Cat could hear the amusement growing in Gloria's voice. Yup, she really did remember. Cat's mood flipped, she swelled with happiness. Talking to Gloria always made her feel better. Perhaps that also worked for her patients; she had some chemistry that made other people happy.

'So,' she said. 'How long would it take for the amitriptyline pills to work? Could someone who had taken them still be able, for example, read a story to his granddaughter?'

'As to the second, yes, if he was conscious. How long? I can find out. Off the top of my head, I'd say an hour or two, but I'll let you know.'

'How would someone force another person to kill themselves in a way that would leave no trace?'

'Oh, Cat! That's not a medical question. Willpower perhaps? The threat of something worse. Honestly. What *is* going on in that village of yours?'

Cat gave Gloria a rundown of everything that had happened in the case so far.

'Hm,' said Gloria when she'd finished. 'So, the question is what triggered it there and then? You said the amitriptyline had been sitting in the cupboard for a couple of years. Why suddenly take them now? Especially since his note said that this related to something that happened in his childhood. Any chance he was being blackmailed?'

'That is quite possible.'

They talked about the case for a while, then Gloria said, 'Oh, I meant to say we'd decided to hold off the baptism until COVID things ease up at bit. We're thinking of asking Stevie to be a godmother – do you think that's a good idea?'

'Brilliant,' said Cat, trying to keep the relief out of her

voice. 'She's probably already thinking of flying lessons for the baby!'

Gloria laughed.

Cat stared at the ceiling. Although young people seemed to have no problem with the fact that both her son and her lesbian daughter loved and lived with the same woman, Cat knew that her generation found it vaguely shocking that her grandchildren had two 'fathers' and one mother. She preferred that as few people as possible knew about it. She knew it was silly, that it was like refusing to come out for gay people, but even so, she liked to keep her secrets. Stevie and Miranda had been in on the ups and downs of the Little Family since the beginning. She didn't mind them knowing things. They were her best friends. They felt like family – more, sometimes, than her real family.

'Who're the other godparents?'

'University friend of Victor, a lawyer friend of Vanessa's and a doctor I work with.'

'Cool, let me know when you name the day. I'm longing to see you all.'

She lay back on the pillows, exhausted but much happier, her mind dwelling on why Brian would kill himself. Unlike her, Brian had had no Miranda and Gloria to come to the rescue. What had made him so desperate that he went up and took all his wife's pills? What was the trigger that knocked him over the edge? A broken glass? Or perhaps a game of bridge?

Was that why there was a four-place card game on his table? Was it bridge? Did someone use it to push him to kill himself? Was it somehow related to the bridge game they were playing online?

* * *

'I've found out who owned the computer,' said Stevie on a Zoom call with Miranda at home and Cat sitting up in her bed. 'The one Simian was playing on, on Brian's modem. Or rather I've found out who it was registered to.'

'Who?' asked Cat, she didn't bother asking how Stevie knew, that was clearly modern magic!

'Silas Lama. That's the registered name and it traces back to a bank account.'

'Really?' said Miranda. 'Is that our Silas? If so, it means Silas got legal identity. I mean ... You can't open a bank account without passports, utility bills and all those things.'

'Sure,' said Stevie, 'but if you started with false papers, say from the 1960s, then you can start giving yourself legal papers and anything you need until you are fully legally formed. Particularly if you started in a time when people didn't expect money laundering and all the problems we have to deal with today.'

'Good point,' said Cat. 'So, are we now sure that Silas and Simian are one and the same person?'

'Looks like it,' said Stevie.

'Wow,' said Miranda. 'But then why would he come back? He ran away after Francis's death. Why did he run away? Was he responsible for Francis's death? If so, then presumably Brian knew about it. Why would he return?'

'All important points,' said Cat. 'But assume he was not responsible for Francis's death but was fearful he might be blamed. Was it now safe to return? What had changed matters? Why didn't he return after Karl's death?'

'And, of course,' said Miranda, 'having had information from creepy Clinton, did Silas now arrive in Brian's house and terrorise him into killing himself or actually murder him?'

'Perhaps. Or perhaps he knew something about Brian, that dreadful deed he wrote about in his suicide note.'

'It certainly doesn't square with what the friar said about Silas's kindly nature,' said Miranda. 'Not that I think anything he said was straight up,' she added, her mind replaying his last words.

'Fifty-seven years is a long time, people change,' said Stevie. 'Especially if they've been trying to survive in a difficult environment.'

'He was good at Latin and Greek, thought about taking the cloth,' said Miranda. 'Does that sound like a murderer? Didn't someone say, "show me the boy at seven and I'll show you the man"?'

'Aristotle,' said Cat. 'Give me a child until he is seven and I will show you the man. Bet the friar knows that.'

'But,' said Stevie, 'we don't know what happened to Silas once he got to London. Remember, he was thirteen years old, in a strange city, and having led a sheltered life. He might have been killed and become one of those corpses that are never identified.'

'Not if he had a bank account.'

'Unless someone found it useful to steal his identity and then kill him.'

'Oh. How awful if so,' said Cat, feeling tears regrouping in her eyes. 'Poor Silas. Not much of a life. Short and painful.'

'Well,' said Stevie rationally, 'let's hope that wasn't the case.'

'I wonder if we should look again at the bridge club,' said Miranda. 'There must be a reason Karl chose that one to enrol in, or did he enrol in all the bridge clubs in London?'

'Interesting point. I'll find out,' said Stevie, getting down to it on the computer.

Then she stopped. 'Incidentally, I meant to say. I found out what happened to all those computers.'

'Which computers?'

'You remember I found forty computers, all registered at Brian's address.'

'Yes.'

'Over the years they were all reregistered to the Salvation Army. Registered as donations from Brian Deliver on their charity list.'

'Why?'

'I rang the Sally Army,' said Stevie, 'talked to their donations manager. He was very helpful, although he wanted to explain that the kind of bargain Brian had with the SA would not happen now.'

'What?'

'It seems that Brian gave them regular donations, and in return they would let him know if a Silas Lama, or a Silas Deliverer or anyone looking Nepalese turned up in one of their homeless shelters. The manager said Brian did visit a few times but all the potential Silases were red herrings.'

'Wow, Brian! That's unexpected,' said Miranda, 'something so proactive. Searching for the missing boy. He must definitely have believed that Silas was alive then.'

'Ah,' said Cat, 'so he did have a hidden side. We all do!'

Miranda rolled her eyes.

CHAPTER 30
SEARCHING FOR SILAS

A week later, Cat felt safe enough to come into the office and there (having passed Blinkey's password test) she found Stevie beavering away on the Internet. Miranda was now looking for the coffee beans.

'News,' Stevie said.

'Great. What is it?'

'Well, interestingly, Karl not only signed up for all the bridge clubs in London, in places as far apart as Richmond and Dulwich, but also all the local clubs. He signed up with Chichester and Petersfield.'

'Looks like he and Brian were both looking for Silas. And Karl was becoming obsessed, but why wait so long? Why not look for him immediately after Francis's death?'

'Maybe something happened that changed his attitude.'

'Maybe. What, for example?'

'When did Hannah die?' asked Miranda.

'In 1989,' said Stevie. 'She died on Francis's grave, had a heart attack.'

'Really? Was that coincidence? Was there a post-mortem?' Cat asked.

'I don't know. I didn't think to look or ask anyone. Do you think her death is relevant?'

'Probably not,' said Cat. 'And when did he start joining the bridge clubs?'

'In the nineties.'

'Wait,' said Miranda, 'back up to Hannah for a moment. Did something shock her into dying on his grave? Did she see someone? Silas, perhaps?'

'Possible.'

'When was the tombstone erected?'

'I don't know. I think you'd have to ask Friar Jacques.'

'He said it was erected by Karl, but let's suppose for a moment he either lied or simply didn't know the truth. If Silas put it there, then Hannah would have no idea it was arriving. Then there it was. Suddenly, a mark of respect for her dead son.'

'Interesting point,' said Miranda, twisting her lips, 'and that would certainly be a catalyst for Karl to go charging up to London and try to find Silas. A Silas who was now back interfering in his life again. And presumably he would think this was revenge-orientated.'

'Hm,' said Miranda. 'We need to talk to Francis Deliverer. He was the one who put us on to the grave.'

Stevie sent another message to Francis Deliverer and cc'd his sister, asking if he could now talk to them about the family. He sent a message back saying two or three days.

'At least the time has shortened,' said Miranda.

'Or lengthened,' said Cat, 'depending on how you look at it. It's now been a month since he said next week.'

CHAPTER 31

LOOPING THROUGH
HISTORY

The weather had improved so much that Stevie was able to go flying in the Tiger Moth, a gift many years ago in the will of an old friend. Although Stevie had been on furlough since the beginning of the lockdown, COVID regulations in the UK had lightened. She was now allowed to fly privately, as long as either she was solo, or there was sufficient distance between her and a passenger. Regulations abroad were different and many of Stevie's USA pilot friends were able to fly more or less without restrictions, although it depended which state you lived in, and one or two had to wear masks in exams.

When Stevie got back, she was feeling relaxed and happy. Miranda and Cat were waiting for her, sitting in deck chairs outside the hangar.

'Flying suits you,' said Miranda, laughing at her beaming face.

'Too right. But I've got something for you two, too.'

'What's that?'

'Well, you remember that Friar Jacques said that Karl

had been Jewish and converted during the war after meeting Hannah.'

'Yes,' said Miranda.

'Well, I kept thinking about that. How many families living in Essex were Jewish before the Second World War? After the war, you could understand, but before? Why? So I looked it up.'

She got her laptop out of her flying bag and pulled up a page on an Essex site to show them.

'Apparently, in 1879, there was a huge resettlement of Jews to Essex from the East End of London. Five hundred people in all moved to Essex. It's not important to us, but it was all due to a very interesting land fraud. However, you can read that yourselves if you're interested. The important thing is that the Deliverers were Jewish. They were one of these families.'

'So that supports what Friar Jacques said.'

'Yup,' said Stevie, 'so then, having got myself all immersed in Karl's relations, I got on to Ancestry to find out if Mrs Hearthop was right about them being descended from one of Charles II's mistresses – I mean, how may Jewish mistresses did Charles II have? In that era, governments were pretty good at finding scapegoats and rich Jewish bankers have always made good enemies.'

'But hang on,' said Miranda, 'we don't know if there's any connection between the royal side and Judaism. Could have been two different sides of the family. Whether or not Charles II had Jewish mistresses, it doesn't prove a thing. Anyway, he might have just said that to Mrs Hearthop because he could see she was a snob.'

'No, you're right, and I couldn't find anything either way. But what I did find out explained why Karen didn't have any Deliverer cousins. Both Karl's brothers were killed early in the war. His parents had already died before the war.'

'No sisters?'

'Was one, but it's impossible to see when she died. It wasn't mentioned. She might still be alive. But her children wouldn't be Deliverers, anyway, they'd have taken the husband's name.'

'Poor Karl,' said Miranda. 'So sad to lose everyone in your family in the war.'

'Yes, but I don't think he was unusual. Quite a lot of people lost whole families in the first and second wars.'

'Still, sounds like Karen had plenty of cousins on her mother's side,' said Cat.

'Yes.

'Talking about family matters,' said Stevie, 'one of Miranda's relations may be going to help us with the boat-scuttling incident. I was mucking about on the Tangmere Aviation Museum site, good site incidentally, you might want to look at it. Anyway, I filled in the contact form and got hold of a Polish guy called Filip Novak. He was an engineer, and he knew all about boats, so I rang him and we had a great conversation. He's ninety-something and he loves aviation. We also compared living in Poland under the Nazis with living here under COVID regulations. It was very interesting.'

Cat looked for her lipstick.

'Guess the first thing shops ran out of?'

'Loo paper?'

'Spot on! Anyway, he invited me to come and have a coffee on his veranda.'

'Is that allowed?' asked Cat lowering her eyebrows. 'Was that wise?'

'It was OK, we've both had jabs.'

'You've had a jab?' Cat's voice jumped up a couple of octaves. 'How come?'

'Sorry, I didn't tell you because I thought you'd be pissed off – me getting a jab before you, and then Frank getting ill. But I'm my mother's carer, sort of. Normally, when I'm working, a shared carer, but now that flying is so restricted, I'm with her twenty-four-seven. Anyway, when they gave her the jab, they did me too. I've actually had both jabs.'

Cat wrinkled her nose but blew Stevie a kiss. 'It's OK, I'm not at all jealous, really. It's probably going to hurt me more when I have it. I guess it didn't hurt you at all.'

'No, I was fine and so was my mother.'

Cat gave up on the lipstick and nibbled the top lip instead. 'They say anyone who's had COVID itself suffers a lot from the jabs. Poor old Frank, 'eh. Still, I'm sure he'll find a joke about it. Go on with the story.'

'Well, we started chatting about flying and COVID, and I must have mentioned the Tiger Moth.'

'Oh,' said Miranda, 'how unlike you!'

'Ha ha. Anyway, when he heard that I had a Tiger Moth he said, "Oh, it was on my bucket list to fly a Tiger Moth." So, what could I do ...?'

'You've taken him flying?'

'Not yet, he's going to come next week. But he's the greatest fun – if you want you can come and meet him. He's got lots of stories about living in Poland in World War Two. Sounds horrendous. They had nothing. Absolutely nothing.'

Miranda rolled her eyes. 'No thanks. While I'd love to chat about Poland, I've spent time with aviation enthusiasts before and I know very well it will be five per cent on Poland and ninety-five per cent flying. I can think of better things to do than chat non-stop about the intricacies of rivets and bolts. That bit of investigation you can do alone. I might as well go and chat to another weird elder instead: Friar Jacques.'

'And the boat-scuttling incident?' said Cat.

'Oh, yes, sorry. It was before he got here but they all knew about it. Apparently, the boat was sitting in its usual position one night. Then the next morning it had gone. They found it, eventually, at the bottom of the sea in Portsmouth Harbour. Because it was a danger to shipping, they had to raise it, and it was all at Karl's expense because he had forgotten to insure it. The boat was ruined, and it cost him a pretty penny. The odd thing was the dinghy was missing. Divers couldn't find it in the harbour and, in the end, they guess it had been taken by whoever scuttled the boat. They never found out who did it.'

* * *

Karen called Stevie on WhatsApp. 'Hi, Karen.'

'Stevie, can I send you something odd? I know you do all the research and I'd like to find the reason behind this.'

'Sure. What is it?'

'My father's bank statements. From 2000 until 2019 he was paying money to an unknown recipient named only CCCH. I can't imagine why.'

'No problem, pitch them over.'

'Thanks, Stevie.'

Stevie looked up CCCH and discovered the initials fitted many places including a Catholic cemetery, a church and a care home. Only the care home was in the UK, and it was in Essex. Called the Cosy Curlew Care Home, it did seem the most likely recipient of a regular payment from Brian. Although, why? Karen wasn't always forthcoming with information, so there might be something else she hadn't mentioned.

Stevie rang Karen. 'Any elderly Deliverer relations in Essex?' she asked. 'Who might be in a care home? Need support?'

'No. Dad did once say Grandfather had two brothers, but they were both killed in the war. I've never heard of any other relations.'

'OK, thanks. I'll keep digging.'

CHAPTER 32
TERRY LOST

Now that COVID regulations had eased a bit, Miranda decided to drop round on Terry Plump, just to see if he'd returned. Her knock on the door was answered by a complete stranger.

'Hello?'

'Oh, hello, I was looking for Terry, Terry Plump. Does he still live here?'

'Yup, sure does. He's in Norfolk at the moment. His father's just died and he's trying to sell the house. As you can imagine, it's not the easiest time to sell a house.'

'No, guess not.'

The man balanced on one foot holding the door jamb. He seemed to be doing exercises. 'Can I help at all? I'm Terry's husband.'

'Husband?'

He grinned. 'Yup. I'm guessing you quite fancied Terry yourself. Am I right?'

'No, I just didn't know ...'

He winked at her. 'You didn't know he was gay, 'eh. Not that I'm surprised. There were so many beautiful girls at our wedding it was a farce. All broken-hearted. I think my lovely husband was a bit of a tease before he married. So, what did you want him for?'

'I'm from the SeeMs Detective Agency. We're working for Karen Middlebrow, looking into her father's death. I know this is a bit of a strange question, but do you know if Terry was playing bridge on 8 January?'

The man laughed. 'And I was worried you might think I was odd! Hang on, I'll find out.'

He pulled the phone out of his pocket and for a moment Miranda thought he was going to ring Terry, but instead he opened the calendar.

'Eighth of January?' He scrolled back a bit. 'Well, we spent Christmas up in Norfolk. His dad died on the following Monday, 30 December. It was nice, that last Christmas together. We weren't allowed in the home, but we had a picnic in the grounds and as the dayroom was on the ground floor and had large French windows, his dad and a couple of the others sat in the window. They could see us, and we them. OK, I'm not sure if his dad knew who we were, but it was still fun. We toasted each other. The matron let him have a glass of champagne and ... well, it was lovely.'

He wiped away a tear and Miranda nodded. She liked stories where the father died happy. It was such a contrast to her own family story.

Terry's husband strolled down a bit further and Miranda noticed what elegant hands he had. She shoved her own in her pockets.

'OK,' he said reading, 'so, then, the following week we were with him. And, as I say, he died on the Wednesday. We had another week sorting through the care home's needs, the funeral and the house. Then, ah yes, the house went on the market on 7 January. Not much interest while we were there. We drove back down here on the eighth. So yes, basically. We were both here on 8 January. Terry stayed a couple of days and then drove back on the Monday. He wanted to be in the house when it was being sold. Hopeful, I call that. What was it you asked me about 8 January?'

'Whether he was playing bridge online.'

The man twisted his face. 'Hm, could have been. He plays bridge online most days. He probably did. Do you want me to ask him and give you a call?'

'Yes, please,' said Miranda; she gave him her card.

He looked down at it. 'Well, hello! I've never seen a three-name card before. Is that a throuple?'

Miranda burst into laughter. 'No, we work together. I'm the one in the middle, Miranda.'

He grinned at her enigmatically. 'Right oh, Miranda. I'll call you when Terry calls me. Hope you don't mind, but he prefers it that way. He doesn't want to be disturbed when someone's going round the house. Actually, reception is pretty pants up there anyway. He usually calls me from his dad's landline.'

'Thanks.'

Miranda walked back to her house thinking it was possible then, that Terry was the one playing bridge. If his father was such an ace player that he won competitions, even when demented, Terry might be a better player than she realised.

CHAPTER 33
COSY CURLEW CARE HOME

The Cosy Curlew Care Home was owned by Mrs Caroline Curlew. Stevie found, to her surprise, that Mrs Curlew was a helicopter pilot and owned a small self-built helicopter called a Rotorway. If only it wasn't for lockdown, Stevie could have gone over to the home and enjoyed a useful discussion about the helicopter with the owner. She would easily strike up a rapport with another aviator, particularly one who had built her own machine. It was still possible, but not being there in person made it all more formal. However, there were always ways, even in lockdown, even on the phone, which Stevie hated using.

It wasn't long before Caroline Curlew and Stevie were deep in conversation about the Rotorway. Stevie had never flown a helicopter, mostly because of the cost, but the Rotorway sounded perfect. You could build it yourself (something Stevie loved doing) and learn to fly on it and all at a tiny percentage of the cost of a production helicopter. What was not to like? The girls could have chatted on their favourite subject all day, but Caroline remembered she had to work.

'Did you call me about flying? Or was there something else, Stevie dear?'

'You're right. I'm a detective, employed by a Karen Middlebrow. Her father was Brian Deliverer ...'

'Oh, my goodness, that lovely man. I read about his death. So, so awful. I had no idea he was unhappy. I must say he was the kindest, easiest man I have ever met, and so generous to Elsie. I'm so glad she died first. She would have been heartbroken if he had left her. But perhaps he wouldn't have done it if she was still alive. I certainly like to think so. Dear, dear man.'

Wow, thought Stevie, could we be talking about the same person? The stern angry Brian Deliverer. 'Elsie?' she asked. 'Who is Elsie?'

'His aunt. Elsie Deliverer. He used to visit her every week without fail ever since his father died. Oh, we miss him terribly.'

'Brian or his father?'

'Brian. Certainly not his father! He was not a nice man.'

'When did Elsie die?'

'Last year – 2019.'

'Can you tell me a bit about her?'

'Of course, happy to. I have all the patient's notes. Wait a tick while I find hers.' Caroline Curlew returned in a few moments. 'Right, here we have it. OK.' She read: 'Elsie Deliverer was born in 1930, with a form of non-verbal autism. She suffered from AOS, or apraxia of speech, and it was impossible for her to speak. She was, however, able communicate through other means.'

Caroline gave a small sigh. 'We're taking about a time long

ago when not being able to speak was equated with stupidity,'
she said. 'We have never thought Elsie even slightly stupid. In
fact, given the way she was able to communicate with us, she
was rather able. She was, of course, very small, but I think
that was due to her condition. Anyway, her family clearly
thought she would be better off in a home. The parents were
elderly and I suppose the boys, she had three older brothers,
too young. Since the Deliverer family were not wealthy, the
collegiate community banded together and formed a trust to
support Elsie throughout her life. After her parents died, she
was moved to CCCH, which was her home ever since.'

A rustling noise indicated that Caroline was putting
down the papers. 'I'm not an expert in these matters but I'm
told that the trust was cleverly set up and did well. Certainly,
it easily paid for Elsie's care. However, in the late sixties,
CCCH was contacted out of the blue by a Karl Deliverer. It
was before my time, but my mother ran the home then, and
she talked to him. At first, she thought he was kindly
offering to take Elsie into his home, but it turned out this
was incorrect.'

'Did he want to visit her?' Stevie asked. 'Must have been
nice to find your sister was alive after all this time.'

Stevie could hear Caroline grinding her teeth at the
other end of the phone.

'No, he rang to inform my mother that he had been
looking into the trust. It seems it was a discretionary trust
and, at the discretion of the trustees, any of Elsie's
surviving siblings could also benefit from the trust. I'm
pretty sure that the original intention had been that if one
of the siblings wanted to adopt Elsie into their family, then
they should receive the money that would pay for her
care. However, apparently Mr Karl Deliverer had
convinced the trustees, who were all Jewish like the family,

that owing to his injuries during the war he needed the money. Of course, they were very sympathetic to him because he had been in Auschwitz and still had the tattoo to prove it.'

'He had been in Auschwitz? Auschwitz the concentration camp? Really? And survived?' Odd, thought Stevie. Odd that Karl Deliverer had survived incarceration in Auschwitz but that no one had mentioned it was weirder than weird.

'How come he was in Auschwitz?' she asked Caroline Curlew. 'We knew he was Jewish but he was in the British Army. Didn't they protect him? How could he get over to Poland to get captured? This is all extraordinary.'

'I know,' said Caroline, 'my mother thought it odd too, but he had the tattoo. She couldn't gainsay it, could she? He said he was picked up when he lost his unit at Dunkirk and they discovered he was Jewish. He talked about long indescribable train journeys across to Poland.'

'Oh,' said Stevie.

It did explain Karl Deliverer's missing four years, if he'd been in Auschwitz. Even that brought up more questions, though. Why Auschwitz? And once in Auschwitz, how did he live so long? And how did he escape? They needed a team discussion over this one.

'Anyway,' Caroline continued, 'although this still left enough for Elsie's support, it did mean that she would not get all the extras she normally did, and inroads might have had to be made into the capital that supported the trust.'

Stevie gasped. 'But surely he couldn't make inroads into the capital, that had the potential to ruin the trust.'

'Exactly!'

'Oh, how awful, poor Elsie.'

'Indeed. Luckily, she knew very little about it. But my mother, and then me when I was old enough, had a lot of extra work, and the lawyer and stockbrokers had problems, especially when the market was doing badly.'

'So, what happened?'

'Karl Deliverer drained the trust of money. It was getting very touch and go, when – and I hate to say this – but God be praised, he died. It may be awful of me, Stevie, but I was so glad that with his death went the last possible external beneficiary. Now we weren't going to get any more surprises. Before, you know, we weren't prepared to help the trust function properly in case he got the money. But now he was dead, we all worked hard to try and regain enough money for Elsie's care. But sadly, it was impossible.

'Karl had taken so much money from the trust it was faltering. We were uncertain what to do – we couldn't just throw her on the streets. Then I had a brainwave. I looked on Ancestry to see if Karl Deliverer had any children. He did. I contacted Brian and the dear, dear man agreed to make up the deficit. Even more wonderful, he came and visited Elsie every week. It gave her a new lease of life, having a relation. It made her last nineteen years the happiest of her life.

'And that wonderful Brian gave us all such fun too. He brought us presents. You know, nothing huge but flowers, chocolates, doughnuts. He remembered our birthdays. Always helped with the tree at Christmas. What a lovely, lovely man he was.'

Stevie shook her head, glad that Caroline could not see her through the phone. This was a side of Brian Deliverer that no one else had seen. No longer the staid, angular man who could not communicate with his son or grandson. No longer the silent villager who snapped at his neighbours and complained about their hedges, but a kindly nephew who gave love and money to his aunt and her carers. How amazing was that?

Perhaps Cat's psychobabble was correct: Brian had another side and if he had another side, perhaps he could be the effervescent Simian. Could they be wrong about Silas? Could Silas be dead, and could Brian Deliverer have been Simian all along? But, if so, why did Brian keep looking for Silas?

CHAPTER 34
TERRY FOUND

Terry phoned Miranda that evening. 'Hi, Miranda, ages since I saw you in the pub. Perforce OK, with this frigging lockdown, but I can't wait to get back to having a beer of an evening. Norfolk's nice but it's not Owly Vale. I hear they've done up the pub. Got a long bar now! Like Singapore. Very posh. We'll be able to throw peanuts or whatever it was they did in Raffles.'

Miranda hadn't a clue what he was talking about. She'd only been out of England twice, once for her honeymoon in Jersey, and the other time for a family holiday to Poland, trying to find out more about her father's heritage.

Cat was the one who travelled, working as a translator after her first husband died. Cat's French mother had insisted she become at least bilingual, whereas Miranda's Polish father had insisted they did not learn Polish. When you immigrate, he used to say, you absorb the identity of the country, and the English are unilingual. Much good it did him. Or them.

'Thanks for calling me, Terry. Very sorry to hear about your father.'

'Yes, it's always sad. But it was a blessing in some ways, you know. He was quite away with the clouds. Hardly even knew me. Anyway, Kit said you dropped in about a bridge game. What did you want to know? Is this related to a missing dog?'

She laughed. 'No.' She was about to say 'missing parent' but thought it might be tactless in the circumstances. 'No, we're working for Karen Middlebrow – you know her?'

'Sure, Brian D's daughter. I expect his death was a bit of a blessing too if you know what I mean.'

Miranda frowned. She didn't. 'What do you mean? He was only seventy-odd.'

'Hm. How well do you know the Deliverer family?'

'Not at all. My husband and I moved here less than ten years ago. We're getting to know most people, but we hadn't got to know Brian and family apart from to say hello, and the occasional bridge game or village party.'

'No surprise there,' said Terry. 'He wasn't exactly Mr Life and Soul of the Party. You can take it from me that's it's frigging amazing Karen and Francis are so normal, given what they've come from. My dad used to talk about Karl as the Owly Vale monster! And as for strait-laced Brian ...' He gave a deep sigh. 'Believe me, his death's a blessing for the village and the family.' He stopped suddenly. 'So sorry, Miranda, got a bit carried away – I have history with that homophobic bastard! What did you want to know?'

Although she was curious, Miranda restrained herself from inquiring further into Brian and Terry's history; she could ask Cat and Stevie. They had both lived in the village far longer than her.

'Seems odd to ask, but were you playing bridge on 8 January at eight in the evening for a couple of hours?'

'Bound to have been. I play bridge pretty much every

night. I've got much better, you know. I'll never be like my
dad, a Four-Ace, but I do love the game. Did that help?'

Not really, thought Miranda, but she kept going. Could
he be this cool if he was deceiving her?

'Sorry to ask, but do you use BBO or some other site?'

He was silent for a moment. 'Hang on, let me think. On
Mondays I play with some cousins and we use BBO, then
Tuesdays and Wednesdays I play with robots, so that's Fun
Bridge. Thursdays, I play with some friends, but we use
Trickster. What day of the week was it?'

'Friday.'

'Oh, right. Nothing in the diary, but that doesn't mean
anything. I often forget to put things in. Kit's always telling
me off about it. Oh, hang on. Friday 8 January. That was the
day we drove down from Norfolk, wasn't it?'

'Yes, Kit said so.'

'He says *hi* by the way. He's a great guy. You wait until
pubs open and you can meet him. He'll make you laugh and
laugh. One of nature's comedians, is Kit. Anyway, that Friday
... You know, I don't think I did play bridge that evening. We
were pretty tired after that long drive. I think we just had
dinner, watched something on Netflix and went to bed. We
were pooped.'

'Thanks, Terry, look forward to seeing you in the pub
soon.'

Miranda stared at the wall. Another dead end. Unlikely
he was lying. So it seemed pretty certain that Silas was
Simian. There wasn't really anyone else in the listing. All
they had to do was find Silas.

Or perhaps, thought Miranda with a flash of inspiration,
they could lure him into finding them. He set up a bridge
game to entice them in, so they could set up another one to

lure him back. Question was, what bridge game would be so appealing he couldn't avoid it? She dealt out the pack. Perhaps she could find it in the cards.

CHAPTER 35
YOUR ACTUAL MR BENNETT

Again?' said Stevie, her usual piloty-mumble sharpened by frustration. 'Yes, I can set it out for you in BBO, that's quite easy to do, but haven't we done that Mr Bennett murder game to death?'

'Ha, ha,' said Cat, looking for her lipstick in her bag.

'No, I didn't mean ... Oh, OK. I'll become a BBO teacher and set it up for you.'

She shook her head and tapped hopefully on her computer, which was in the middle of a reboot.

'But seriously, Miranda,' said Cat, 'why do we have to do that game again? You say it will entice Silas to come and play again, but how will he even know we're playing?'

'Simple,' said Miranda, 'we tell Karen and Francis. One of them is in touch with him, must be. Simian/Silas knows too much about us – he appears to be leading us – but he couldn't do it if someone on the inside wasn't tipping him off.'

Cat frowned. 'You're making it sound like a spy movie. I thought we were Karen's employees. She's paying us to discover the truth.'

Miranda nodded. 'I didn't say that anyone knows the truth of what happened. I simply think that our client and her family are pushing us in the direction they believe we should look. You said yourself there seem to be too many coincidences. Anyway, we need to be on top of this, not let Simian lead us, hence the bridge game.'

'OK,' said Cat, 'I'm on. When?'

Two days later, all three women in their various houses tapped into a virtual game of bridge. Opposite Miranda was the red outline of an empty place, with 'Simian (Reserved)' in yellow letters. As they watched the place became grey and the first hands shuffled out.

'He's on,' said Miranda, opening WhatsApp.

Stevie's face appeared immediately, and a moment later so did Cat, and then, in the fourth box, there appeared the face of a monkey.

'Good evening,' said Simian, 'so we begin.'

All three girls put up a monkey filter.

Simian laughed. 'I say! This is a jape. Can't wait to play.'

Miranda pursed her lips. Her instinct was already shaking its head.

The first game began. The hands were well balanced, and Miranda was left to play one no trump. She made it. Simian made no comments on her play.

The next few games were similar. Simian spoke very little; when he did it was pertinent and unflamboyant. Miranda noticed he was not playing very well, often making silly mistakes. As she watched, a slow depression crept into her chest and, as soon as she was dummy, she went over to the fridge to get a bottle of wine. She could hardly be bothered to go through all the games before Mr Bennett's murder came up.

Stevie, who hadn't wanted to waste all evening playing

bridge, had put Mr Bennett's murder on as the fifth game of the series, and Miranda saw with delight her cards were the ace, ten, six and three of spades, ten, eight and three of hearts, four of diamonds, ace, nine, eight, four, two of clubs. Stevie had done it right. Simian would be Mr Bennett. Perhaps now he would show himself in his true colours.

The bidding went as expected. So did the play. Mr Bennett aka Simian went one down. Miranda took a deep gulp of wine. 'OK,' she said, 'let's all unveil.'

Everybody removed their Simian filters. Opposite Miranda sat Terry Plump.

'Hello, Terry,' said Miranda. 'Did you enjoy the game?'

'You betja,' he said, 'that was a laugh. Did I recognise the last game from somewhere? I think I've seen it before.'

Miranda fumed internally. Yet again Simian/Silas was one ahead of her.

'How did you come to be playing with us?' she asked.

Terry raised his eyebrows, his eyes dancing behind his glasses. 'You invited me. I got an email from you. Here, I'll read it to you.'

Clearly, he thought she, like his father, was suffering from dementia. He scrolled through his emails and pulled up the one.

'Dear Terry, now I know how keen you are on bridge, why don't you join us on Wednesday evening, 8 p.m. on BBO. Sign in as Simian, password is xxx. Can you wear the monkey filter on WhatsApp? See you there. No need to reply unless you are busy. Best, Miranda.'

'See. It even sounds like the way you speak. I can tell you I was chuffed. Not many people let me play in their games. That's why I have to play with robots twice a week. Thanks a lot, see you around. Bye.'

'Bye, Terry.'

Cat laughed quietly. 'Meet you tomorrow morning to discuss?'

'Might as well,' said Miranda.

As she lifted her glass, she heard Cat say, 'Without a hangover, preferably.'

The cow, thought Miranda, and took a doubly big gulp. It wasn't like she could have done any better. That Simian was a slippery git. She filled her glass again, to the brim.

CHAPTER 36
THE MONKEY'S PUZZLE

When Miranda and her hangover arrived at the office Blinkey jumped out. 'Password!'

'Oh ... Blinkey!'

'Correct. You may pass.'

Despite everything Miranda laughed. She went into the kitchen. Cat was already there drinking coffee, leaving kiss marks on the cup.

Stevie was on the computer. 'Something arrived for you,' she said, 'it was delivered by a courier. I asked where it came from, but he said he picked it up from the Amazon hanger with all his other deliveries.'

Miranda stared at the box sitting on the kitchen table.

'Do you think it's a bomb?' said Cat smiling like her Cheshire namesake. 'Should we call in the bomb disposal unit?'

Miranda grimaced. 'Very funny, Cat, not. That is the sort of humour I'd expect from Phillip, or your beloved Frank, not you.'

Cat laughed happily, accepting the tribute. 'Meow.'

Somewhat reluctantly Miranda opened the box. A little

green spur popped out of the opening. She pulled it out. 'A tree? A tiny tree.'

'Recognise it?' asked Cat.

Miranda could hear amusement in her voice. 'No, you're the plant expert. What is it?'

'A monkey puzzle tree.'

Miranda waggled her head, and then wished she hadn't. She looked for the coffee.

'There's an attachment,' said Stevie.

Miranda got her coffee and went back to the tree. A small white gift card was attached to its neck. She opened it. The card read 'Try harder, darling! It's difficult being a detective.'

'Did you send this, Cat?' For a moment Miranda felt even further down, then she suddenly stopped, her heart soared. 'Hang on – I won!'

'What do you mean?' asked the others.

'Simian knew about the game.'

'He could have done that through BBO,' said Stevie.

'How?'

'You can find out if your friends are playing, you only have to look.'

'But you're missing the point. Simian set up Terry as a patsy. That email was not from me but him. He told Terry not to reply, because he knew if he did, I would cancel the game. He came to our lead like a dog to a bone.' She grinned. The paracetamol seemed to have kicked in. 'Don't you see? This proves that Francis or Karen *are* in touch with Simian. Only they knew about the game. I'll bet it's Francis. I think we need to know more about Karen's older brother.'

'OK, good point,' said Cat nodding, 'but it also means something else.'

'What?'

'Well, if Terry isn't Simian then we need to find out who is. Remember that Simian has played bridge with you. Simian knows your style. Since we've got rid of all our possibles list, then it must be one of the women on your bridge circle.'

Miranda laughed. 'What? Dot Hargraves. Ninety if she's a day. Or Caroline who does all the good works in the village? Or Naomi, who works in the shop and walks dogs when their owners are busy? Which one looks most guilty?'

'No,' said Cat, 'OK, not them. But what if someone can't do a day? Don't you get in occasional players? Aren't some of them very good?'

Miranda thought for a while. 'We have had one or two, mostly not so good. There was one middle-aged girl who only came once. Dyed red hair, quite a joker. She knew lots of music from the past and talked a lot of cant we didn't recognise. I can't remember her name, but she was a very good player.'

'She,' said Cat. 'Better start a new possibles list.'

'OK, Cat, fair enough,' said Miranda. 'I'll ring up Dot and see if I can find out where she came from. And her name.'

CHAPTER 37
HEROES OF
COMMUNICATION ZERO

The speed at which Karen agreed to another Zoom call made the SeeMs detectives suspect she was wondering if they would ever find out anything about her father's death.

'First thing is,' said Miranda, 'did you know your grandfather was in Auschwitz?'

'Auschwitz?' said Karen, her voice rising in confusion. 'You mean the concentration camp?'

'Yes, the concentration camp in Poland.'

Karen sat silently for a while, staring at the screen as though hoping for revelation from there. Then she said slowly, 'That might explain why he was so grumpy. He didn't spend any time with us kids. Didn't like us.' She looked down at her hands. 'Francis might have known. But I doubt it. As I said before, neither my father, nor my grandfather really did chat. Orders. Necessities. But not casual time-of-day stuff.'

Miranda said nothing; a grandfather in a concentration camp was hardly casual, time-of-day stuff in her book.

'No. OK,' said Cat.

'You already know,' said Karen, her voice getting back its normal timbre, 'that Dad didn't tell us about the aunt Stevie found in Essex. The one he visited and paid for. No one even mentioned her existence. See what I mean? Our family wasn't like other families. The Heroes of Communication Zero, Francis and I used to call ourselves.'

She smiled and shrugged at the same time, reminding Miranda of a confused puppy.

'Can you tell us something about your brother, Karen?' Miranda asked.

'Sure,' Karen said, leaning back against the cushions, 'glad to. What do you need? You know a bit already. He's tall, thin, plays bridge well, has a great sense of humour and is generally good fun to be around. What else?'

'Why did he move to Australia?' Cat asked.

'Oh, he's sporty.'

Miranda chewed the inside of the cheek thoughtfully. 'We have sport here, too.'

Karen laughed. 'I don't think you understand. In Australia sport is a religion. It's everything, all you need. Here it's just, well, sport.'

Cat laughed too, but Miranda looked curiously at Karen's face. It was lit up with a kind of longing. 'Are you sporty too? Do you love sport?'

'Do I? I was captain of the girl's hockey team up to county level. I played tennis for my county. I studied sports physio at college but ... well, every physio in the UK, if they're sporty, wants to be a team physiotherapist. I don't have any connections.

So, I just work with geriatrics. It's very fulfilling but, well, you know.' She shrugged.

'Did you want to move to Australia, with your brother?'

Karen moued and Miranda almost expected her to say

whatever, but she actually said. 'How could I? First my mother was ill. Then my father was lonely. And he loved being with my daughter. Now, maybe, but the kids would have to agree. It can be hard uprooting a family, moving them away. Anyway, what else did you want to know about Francis?'

'What does he do for a living?' Cat asked.

'He's a pilot.'

Stevie made a funny noise – the sort of noise someone would make if they thought some incredibly important piece of information hadn't been imparted. Something she would've liked to have known. 'Who does he work for?' she asked. 'Which airline?'

'He doesn't. He's a helicopter pilot. He used to do all sorts of things, spraying, teaching at the local flying school, taking people around in smart choppers, but now he's become an Air Ambulance pilot. Training is much cheaper in Oz. Francis says it's the best thing he's ever done. Makes him feel so free. Is it relevant?'

'Not really,' said Miranda, ignoring Stevie's bolshie face. 'Do you know if he's ever been in touch with your grandfather's sometime adoptee Silas?'

'Not that I know of. You mentioned Silas before and I asked him in one of our family WhatsApp calls, but he said he'd never heard of a Silas.'

Miranda said nothing. It appeared that Francis was quite happy to chat away to his sister, but not to the detectives.

'Can you get him to talk to us soon, Karen? We really need his input.'

Karen's phone bleeped and she looked at it. 'Funny you should say that. I've just got a message from him.' She checked her watch. 'Odd time to send it. It's the middle of the night there.'

'What does it say?' asked Miranda.

Karen looked. She made a strange noise. 'It says *Palone-omee savvy*. Sounds like code,' she said. 'Does it mean anything to you?'

'Nothing,' said Miranda.

'Yes,' said Cat, 'just a minute. Let me think. Do you remember the children's book in Brian's cellar? That had some kind of code. Did you and Francis make that book?'

Karen shook her head. 'Not me, certainly. If it was in Dad's cellar it's more likely to be my father's generation. But it will be here. I've cleared out everything from his house except furniture, so the viewers can see it properly. I haven't had time to go through all his stuff yet, but if I didn't put it in the tip, or give it to the kids, it will be here.'

She left the room but returned almost immediately. 'My son had it. He's fascinated by it ... he thought it was some secret language and he's translated a lot of it, but some things were beyond him. I've given him my phone to look at.'

Her son came in holding the phone. 'Palone,' he said, 'is a woman. Omee is a man. So, I'm thinking Palone-omee is a priest. A man who dresses like a woman.'

Miranda looked at Cat and raised her eyebrows. Cat lowered hers in return, refusing to meet Miranda's look.

Hmm, Miranda thought, *only a Catholic boy would associate a man in a dress with a priest.*

'Savvy means knows or in the know,' Karen's son continued. 'So, it must mean the priest knows.'

'I see,' said Miranda, 'sounds like another trip to see Friar Jacques.'

CHAPTER 38

HANNAH'S HEART ATTACK

s Miranda drove towards the monastery her phone rang. It was Dot, the organiser of her women's bridge group.

'Hello, Dot, did you get my message?'

'Miranda darling, so nice to hear from you. To be brutally honest, I'd actually forgotten about that funny woman who played with us. Remember she was very keen on the song 'Gypsys, Tramps and Thieves'? Said she fell in love with her husband when she was playing it on the piano.'

'I'd forgotten,' said Miranda, 'can you remember her name?'

'I have to say I'd forgotten,' said Dot, 'but I rang the other girls and they remembered. They got her through the Chichester bridge club. Apparently, she used to live here years ago. It was a sort of trip down memory lane. Her name was Fran.'

'Thank you, Dot,' said Miranda, ending the call.

. . .

When Miranda arrived at the monastery Friar Jacques was outside in the graveyard. As usual it was empty, apart from the old man cleaning the graves. The friar looked up as she approached, and she saw a look of inevitability on his face.

'You were expecting me?' Miranda asked.

He sighed. 'You're a detective. It was only a matter of time. What do you want to know this time?'

'Where's Silas?'

The friar looked away at the hills. For a long time, he just stood there, staring. Eventually, he looked back at Miranda. 'The friar does not know. The only thing he can tell you is someone has a great interest in that family. That someone unknown keeps doing things with the Deliverer grave.'

'Doing things? What sort of things?'

'Cleaning it.'

'Cleaning it!' Miranda thought she was going to laugh. 'How awful.'

He turned around, looking for someone, but the old man who cleaned the graves had disappeared.

'That grave cleaner. We, the monastery, did not employ him. He comes all the time to clean the graves. I asked him why. He said he was paid to do it. Cash, he said. He gets most money for cleaning the Deliverer grave, so he does that one particularly well. But he also cleans the other graves. Presumably he's paid for them too. Or perhaps he just likes to see things clean.'

'Who employed him?' Miranda asked. She shook her head. Why would someone pay you to clean graves? Mostly they were tended by their relatives, or not tended at all after the close relatives died.

'He doesn't know. He picks up the money every week from a PO box.'

Miranda laughed. Wait until she told Cat about that. They *were* living in a spy film.

She turned back to the friar. 'Did Karl kill his son?'

'I've already answered that question,' said the friar, flexing his chest out like a sportsman.

'Who killed the person in the grave?' Miranda asked the question warily, used to Jacques's obfuscations.

'Brian Deliverer.'

Miranda gasped. 'Not an accident? Not Karl? How do you know?'

'Karl told me. As I said, he was a deeply devout man. He felt so bad for his children. Really, he blamed himself. I told him it was not his fault, but he was eaten up by guilt. In confession he told me everything. Normally anything said in confession remains there, but this time I feel I should speak out.

'It was on the boat. As I said, Francis was an evil boy and he started a fight with Silas. He knocked Silas overboard. Brian ran to Silas's defence. Although Brian was the bigger boy, Francis was a slippery customer and had often defeated Brian in a fight. Brian was scared. He grabbed a winch handle to protect himself against his brother. Francis came at him. Brian lashed out with the handle in a panic. The handle hit Francis on the temple and it was all over. Francis sank to the deck but not before, in one last thrash, he knocked Brian out. Brian could not remember any of it. Karl was left in the terrible position of telling him that he had accidentally killed his brother.'

'And what happened to Silas?'

'Karl searched the waters high and low for him. But he could not find him and had to conclude he drowned. Only now we realise he escaped somewhere and has come back to bother us. Perhaps he waited for Karl's death. Or perhaps he caused it.'

Miranda thought about this. She walked up to Frances's grave and looked at it. If Silas had really run away, wouldn't he want to be shot of the whole Deliverer family? Why would he pay someone to tend the grave? Once or twice, maybe, but still, fifty years later? Could it really be Silas? She turned her back on the grave and looked at the old man. Was it, instead, someone who could never distance himself from the family? Someone haunted by his own bloodline.

'Whose body do you think is in the grave?' she asked the friar.

'Francis Deliverer.'

'Then why is the name spelt wrong? It says Frances with an e not an i.'

The friar stared at her. He looked at the gravestone. He looked back at her and his face turned slowly grey. He shook his head in denial 'You don't understand,' he said. 'It was a mistake. Karl laughed about it, he said stupid Polish carver couldn't spell English names. It isn't a Polish name. He forgave him. Karl was a very forgiving man.'

'Then,' Miranda persisted, 'then why did Hannah have a heart attack when she saw that misspelling?'

Jacques's shoulders drooped and it seemed to Miranda that he shrank and aged before her. 'It is Francis Deliverer,' he repeated. 'It is. Karl told me himself. He said it was Francis. He did not deceive. Francis was the one who ...'

'Thank you,' said Miranda. She left the friar standing by the grave of Frances Deliverer.

CHAPTER 39
PALONE-OMEE

Miranda was about to call Cat and Stevie to update them when she got a call from Charlotte Hearthop. 'Hi, Miranda,' she said, once again sounding like someone half her age, 'I wondered if you'd like to come for a walk?'

Miranda sighed. The dreadful COVID was forcing her to take all this unrequired exercise. 'That would be cool. Shall I meet you at the wishing well in twenty minutes?'

'Lovely.'

As she walked towards the wishing well, Miranda tried to put together what she had heard. Something was wrong here. OK, it made sense now that Brian was haunted by his past, that he had killed his brother, and that in the end, he decided he had to kill himself. But, if he did, who was playing bridge? And why? What was the relevance of Mr Bennett's murder, the bridge game?

And what about the misspelling on the grave? Was Jacques right, it was a mistake? If so, why did Hannah collapse and die? And what had really happened on that fateful night in July 1963?

As she arrived, she mused to herself about the 'savvy' person. The words 'palone-omee'. A man in a dress? Or a combination of man and girl? A man in drag? A boyish girl? A lesbian?

Charlotte was waiting for her. They greeted each other by pointing elbows and started walking up the hill again. Charlotte shot ahead, leaving Miranda puffing behind. As they got to the top of the hill, Charlotte slowed down and waited for the detective.

'Shall we sit on a log and talk for a while?'

'Yes,' panted Miranda, 'that would be great.'

All around them trees had been felled, the victims of ash dieback, which had decimated much of the UK. The dog lifted his leg at the clean cut end of a thirty-foot tree and Charlotte watched him, clearly saddened by the degradation of such a natural treasure.

They sat down at the required two-metre distance, which Charlotte called six feet.

'I have something to tell you,' she said.

Miranda raised her eyebrows invitingly. 'I was about to call you. Only I visited Friar Jacques first. My mistake.'

Charlotte appeared to shrink a few inches. 'I wasn't completely honest with you,' she said, 'or rather I didn't tell you everything about the Deliverers. I thought now, after all this time it could hardly matter, but something happened yesterday that changed my mind.'

'What happened?'

Charlotte looked at her hands. She seemed to be deciding how to say something. Lifting her left hand, she massaged her chin thoughtfully.

Miranda waited, longing to jump in and talk but forcing herself to feel the power of silence on the interviewee.

'I saw a ghost,' said Charlotte and shoved her hands deep into her pockets.

Miranda did not completely understand what Charlotte meant. Was this another old-person oddity? Or was she being serious?

'The ghost told me you had been to see Friar Jacques.'

OK, thought Miranda, so the ghost is not Charlotte's imagination. She tensed, waiting to see what would come next.

Charlotte looked at Miranda. 'Miranda,' she said, 'was your family ever religious?'

'No.' Miranda shook her head. 'Not even the Polish part.'

'Well, I have to tell you religion is a wonderful thing. It can be a great support in times of suffering. It can lead to charity and kindness for the underprivileged. It does many important things. I have always believed in God, and I always will.' She moved slightly and sat on her hands like a child. 'But sometimes the people who preach, and those who are devout and believers ... are not what they seem. I'm sorry, I'm finding it difficult to explain this.'

'Take your time,' said Miranda, 'I'm listening. Is this about Francis?'

'Partly,' she said, 'but mostly about Karl Deliverer and Father Jacques.'

Miranda felt a surge of queasiness. 'Go on.'

'Karl Deliverer had a few problems. I think nowadays we would call them mental-health problems. Something happened to him in the war, I don't know what, but I do know it altered his life. War is a terrible thing. It shows the sides of men and women they don't need to know. It brings out the worst in some and the best in others.' She stopped, now clasping and unclasping her hands. 'In the case of Karl Deliverer, he changed his religion, converted from Judaism, became a Catholic and grew a rabid and avid hatred for gay men.' She bit her lip. 'It wasn't uncommon then. Because being gay was illegal nobody talked about it, and as nobody discussed it, people who were not gay assumed that it was all bad, bad, bad! And then, of course, there were the gay spies, Philby and Maclean.' She stopped. 'I'm not expressing this well.'

'I understand,' said Miranda, 'go on.'

'Karl had such a phobia about homosexuality that he would give lectures to his wife and children, and any visitor, including me, about the horrors of being homosexual. He would explain to us each wonderful new "cure" the medics created, how they worked and what were the effects. This wasn't as odd then as it would be now. People thought like that then. It seemed natural to cure what they considered an illness.' She paused. 'In fact, there are some countries that still try and "cure" homosexuality.'

'But you were very young to hear that sort of thing,' said Miranda gently. 'What age were you?'

'I was probably about thirteen or fourteen, so the boys were ten or eleven.'

'Too young,' said Miranda, again thinking about Felix. 'But what did Hannah say about this? Your mother said she had the money, so surely, she had the control? And your mother said Hannah used to dress Francis as a girl ... surely she would object to this homophobic behaviour.'

Charlotte stopped and looked at Miranda speculatively. 'How to explain the period when, fifty years later, things have changed so much,' she mused aloud. 'If only you young people read history you would know about people like the Chevalier d'Eon and Abbé de Choisy.'

Miranda stifled a giggle. Eon was an electricity company, she thought.

'OK,' Charlotte continued. 'Hannah was six years older than Karl, a blue-stocking as we then called it. Unusually for her generation she had been to university, but, when the war came, she wanted to do her duty, so she retrained as a nurse. She married Karl when she was almost thirty – in those days "on the shelf". She had the twins when she was nearly forty, almost a miracle in those days. I've heard the rumours that she dressed Francis as a girl, although I don't remember it, but I think it's more likely that he started wearing her clothes and she thought it was funny and bought some his size. He used to wear my clothes too and I loved it.'

'Oh! But what did Karl say? It doesn't seem to sit with his homophobia.'

'I don't think he knew about it.'

'But the tapes? There were pictures of the little girl sailing.'

Charlotte shrugged. 'I don't know. Maybe when Francis was young it seemed like a game. I suppose he didn't associate dressing up with homosexuality. Why would he? We didn't. Still don't.'

'No, go on. I interrupted you.'

'OK. Sometimes when we went sailing Francis would pretend to be a girl. We would take the dinghy somewhere, West Wittering maybe or one of the other sailing clubs. I think I mentioned he was a brilliant mimic, a great actor. Anyway, he used to call himself Fran. We would go into the club, Francis wearing one of my dresses, and he would pretend we were two schoolgirls who had just come over from Bosham. He would shilly-shally over all shy. Sometimes he approached people he already knew under the name of Francis, and, looking through his big eyes, start talking to them. Once Fran challenged two boys to a race. She would say things like, "Oh, I'm a bit of an amateur but I love speed. I'd really like to see how people race. I'm sure I could learn something if we tried to race you. Afterwards you could explain where we went wrong." Then, of course, once we were in the boat, she became he, if you'll forgive me, and he was such an ace sailor. We zipped way ahead, leaving the poor boys standing. Then Fran couldn't stop bragging about how two little girls had beaten the boys. It was hilarious.'

'Dangerous,' said Miranda, but she laughed. 'I see what you mean about Francis, but what about Hannah?'

'Yes, poor Hannah. Karl was so dominant. Hannah had a sense of humour and, at first, she would laugh at things, but slowly that wore away over the years of his ... today we would call it bullying or even mental abuse.' She shook her arms as though to dispel something. 'Karl had an ally in Friar Jacques. I don't know what Jacques said to you. He can be charming. He lunches with my mother every Friday and she considers him the best of the best, but I saw him at his worst.'

She stopped again, looking at Miranda thoughtfully. 'My mother must not know about this.'

'No,' said Miranda. Pretty safe, she was hardly on chatting terms with Mrs Hearthop. Did her non-detective side want to hear what was coming next? Probably not.

'May I ask you first,' said Charlotte, 'what Jacques told you about Francis?'

Was there was some detective code that should stop her telling Charlotte? Was she leading a witness? You heard it all the time in police stories, that the detective led the witness so his evidence could not be considered.

'He said Francis was the embodiment of evil,' said Miranda, 'that at five years old he was escaping to clubs and playing bridge ...'

'Bridge?'

'That's what he said.'

Charlotte gave a sudden spurt of sniggering that threat-ened to knock her off the log. 'Bridge? Bridge!' she repeated. 'Makes you think of the clubs of old ladies playing bridge as witches covens, doesn't it! Did you believe him?'

'I have an eight-year-old son,' said Miranda. 'He is naughty, but he would not be capable of escaping to clubs and leading on older men.'

Charlotte sighed. 'It could only be because Friar Jacques is so far from the world, so ... so protected ... that he thinks you would believe him. But ...'

Miranda nodded. She had a feeling she knew what was to come. 'Go on.'

'Francis was not a saint, that's for sure, and he did skip school and go and hang out with guys. He did play bridge but that's when he was ten or more. Besides, that wasn't from the monastery school but from the school in Peters-field, and they found ways of harnessing his talents and keeping him at school. That was their cleverness. In the early years the problems were more of naughtiness until ...'

She stopped again and Miranda felt forced to ask, 'Did Friar Jacques abuse Francis?'

'No,' said Charlotte, 'me.'

Miranda's hand flew to her mouth.

'Jacques like girls, not boys. I know it's more docu-mented that monks abused boys, but Jacques was unusual.'

'Of course! You were in the school too.'

'Yes, they wouldn't normally teach girls, but Jacques swayed it with the authorities as long as I left at ten. Well, that suited him fine – by ten he had no further interest in me.'

'You must hate him,' said Miranda, her emotions

bubbling in her chest so she could hardly breathe. 'Did you ever try and get him prosecuted?'

Charlotte half smiled. 'No. But you have to understand things are more complicated.'

'You mean protecting your mother.'

'No, not that, although it hasn't helped our relationship. But no, the relationship between Jacques and me was more complex.'

Miranda felt cold; her lungs hurt as she spat out the words: 'How so?' She had heard of victims falling for their abusers. She really hoped that was not true here.

'On one hand he abused me, but on the other he taught me. Not sex. I mean Latin and Greek.'

'Latin and Greek,' said Miranda raising her eyebrows. 'Sex in exchange for the Classics?'

Charlotte grimaced. 'When were you born?'

'1983.'

'Well, I was born in 1947, so my schooling started in 1952. Women didn't always get much schooling then. It very much depended on the parents. Culture has changed now, and for the better. Jacques persuaded my parents to let him teach me Latin and Greek, and he did. I was a good student. When I was ten, Jacques informed my parents I was extremely clever. He persuaded my parents to put me in for a scholarship to Wycombe Abbey. I came top. Perhaps you know the school?'

She stopped and Miranda shook her head. Her world did not encompass fee-paying schools.

'Well, it's a very competitive environment. Some girls shrivelled up and died. But I loved it. I thrived in that environment, and I went on to Oxford and studied law. I became a lawyer, something unusual, although not unheard of, in my generation. I was able to support myself without any input from my parents. Thanks to Jacques I have had both a good and a bad history. Look, I'm not saying I'm grateful to him, or indeed that I understand. I'm just telling it as it happened. Do you understand?'

She looked at Miranda, who did not understand. To her abuse was abuse. She did not speak, and Charlotte continued.

'Nothing is ever as straightforward as it seems. With every dark cloud there is a shaft of light.'

'Oh,' said Miranda. 'But what about the others?'

'Others?'

'The other girls Jacques will have abused since then. If you had exposed Jacques then, none of that would have happened.' Miranda felt herself getting angry. She forced her nails into her palm.

Charlotte's shoulders drooped slightly, but she continued. 'Imagine if I had told my parents about the abuse in 1957, when I was ten and leaving the school, or indeed when I was eighteen and starting at Somerville, do you think they would have believed me? Would anyone? What would have happened to me? I would have been labelled a liar, and I certainly wouldn't have been allowed to go to boarding school. Perhaps I too would have been given the "cure". Things were very different then.'

Miranda breathed deeply, forcing herself to calm down. 'No, I suppose you're right. I'm looking from a modern perspective. What about your parents? Do you think they knew?'

Charlotte shook herself. 'While it is possible to both know and not know, I doubt it. My parents thought Jacques was, as they called it then, not the marrying kind. That he was actually a paedophile would not have crossed their minds. I doubt if they even knew such a thing existed.'

'Oh, but the war. I mean, didn't that enlighten people?'

'Did it?' Charlotte looked at the dog. 'This isn't about me,' she said, 'but about Francis. One day, when I was ten, Francis came across the friar doing his worst with me in the graveyard. He attacked him. He was no match for him, but, after that time, Jacques did everything he could to make Francis seem like the devil. He was the one who encouraged him to skip school, to go out to clubs. But he was not five, but eight, and he didn't do it of his own volition. He left the school two years later. He didn't learn much in those last two years – nothing academic, I mean.'

'And so,' said Miranda, 'Jacques was never punished for his ... his crimes.'

Charlotte half laughed. 'Do you read the papers? How often are they? No, Jacques remained unpunished and until last week I thought Francis had been killed.'

'Until last week?'

'Yes. I met a ghost, as I said. I recognised him immediately.' She gave another snort.

'The ghost was Francis?' Miranda asked astounded. 'So, he's not dead? Who is then?'

'Silas. It's his body in the grave.'

CHAPTER 40

THE QUEEN OF CHICAGO BRIDGE

Charlotte's words came as a shock. Miranda didn't know what to say. She wished her colleagues were there so they could discuss it. Discussion always helped her process information. Since they were not there she continued doggedly on her own.

'But ... but ... Karl and Brian were both looking for Silas. Why would they do that if they knew he was dead?'

Charlotte looked into Miranda's eyes. 'I don't think Brian knew Silas was dead. I think he thought Francis was. I could be wrong, and I certainly don't know what happened on that boat. Karl, on the other hand, must have known what happened on the boat. Since Francis is still alive, he must have been looking for him. Perhaps he thought Francis would take Silas's name. That he would deny his Deliverer heritage.'

She ran her hands over the bark of the tree and as she did so exposed the FD/SL tree tattoo Miranda had seen earlier. She pointed at it, then continued with her story.

'Having seen Francis, I finally know something of how much he must have suffered, of the life he led after he escaped. But what he wanted was for me to tell you he did not kill Silas. He loved Silas. The real story was much more complicated.'

'So? Who killed Silas?'

'I think Francis wants to tell you that himself.'

'How did he survive? He was thirteen years old.'

'Yes, he was, but Jacques was right about one thing: Francis was very unusual. His story is ... well, I was going to say it's amazing. But it's not amazing – it's an example of the triumph of the human spirit. I wonder if any of you young people, for all your wokeness and the rest, would be able to live in the way he did.'

Miranda rolled her eyes. There they went again, oldies on a dream cloud, thinking they were the only ones who had ever suffered. She brought Charlotte back to the present day. 'So, who bought the gravestone? The marble one?'

'Look. I think Francis is going to tell you all this himself.'

'When?' asked Miranda, thinking bitterly of the younger ever-elusive nephew also called Francis. Would this older Francis evade them in the same way with promises of truth-telling?

'I don't know,' said Charlotte.

'OK, tell me just one thing then.'

'What?'

'Why did Hannah drop dead at the grave? Did she see her son and the joy killed her?'

'I'm not sure. But I'll tell you what I think happened. She was such a nice woman. So clever. So ... well, now we would say she had emotional intelligence.' Charlotte stirred on the log and then continued. 'In that family they talked in para-bles. They left each other messages. You probably saw the book the children wrote.'

She looked questioningly at Miranda who slowly realised she was talking about the secret language book.

'The one about the Queen of Rubber Bridge?'

'Yes. Francis and Silas made it. They showed it to me in great delight since it was an allegory about my mother and their father. We used to laugh about their bridge fights, and this was the culmination.' Her face softened and she put her hand to her cheek. 'Well, the secret language was Polari. And it was Hannah who taught them the new cant lingo that she'd learnt when she was nursing. She loved anything like that. She had such a great sense of humour. Something she passed on to her son.'

Charlotte hugged herself. 'When she saw the grave, she understood. She saw that Francis was sending her a message not from Heaven, but from Earth, in this case Essex where the stone was made. She also realised that Karl had been lying to her for twenty-six years. As I see it, she could not bear the pain and she dropped dead right there on the grave.'

'Oh. But couldn't Francis have told his mother himself? She visited the grave every fortnight.'

'Perhaps he could. You need to ask him.'

'And the bridge game? Mr Bennett's murder. How was that relevant?'

'Sorry, I don't play. I saw all the trouble it caused.'

Miranda ground her teeth. All these Deliverers and friends seemed to be putting her off again and again. 'Will Francis really tell me the real story?'

'Yes, he wants to. He says he's been trying to tell you for ages, but you were very slow at getting the clues.'

'He what? Bloody cheek!'

Charlotte laughed. 'That's Francis for you.'

'Well, hell,' said Miranda.

Charlotte smiled at her. 'Francis is on a journey now, but he said he will meet you on Zoom in two or three days. I'm sorry I can't be more specific.'

'A journey,' said Miranda; was this yet another put-off? Clues indeed. Pah! 'Where?'

Charlotte looked at her. 'You know, don't you? You're a good detective, you have good intuition, but you don't always let it win, you try and over-rationalise it. Trust yourself.'

As if that wasn't the outside of enough. Hecky decky, as Felix would say. Clearly Charlotte was another clever dick like Cat.

'OK. I suppose I should thank you. Will Francis send me a link? For Zoom?'

Charlotte laughed. 'How pragmatic. Yes, he will. Thank you, Miranda. Your faith in us has helped us finally get the truth out, and retribution made. Keep going, Miranda. If you don't give up you will become a good detective.'

Retribution? thought Miranda. Not really, not after all these years. Who suffered? Who got revenge? Was Charlotte as well balanced as she seemed?

'Good luck, Miranda,' said Charlotte and she got up and walked away, aiming for the next hill.

Miranda turned to walk down into the village.

When she got home, she checked the pod emails. There was one from the professor, once again no cheerful *Top of the morning*; it started: 'Oh, dear me, this is a bad time for our locality. I must tell you the sad news that Friar Jacques died yesterday afternoon. He was found slumped over the grave of Frances Deliverer having had a heart attack.'

So definitely no chance of retribution, thought Miranda. What would Jacques have said? 'Vengeance is mine, sayeth the Lord'.

CHAPTER 41
TOBER SHOWMAN AND PILOTS

K nowing that Stevie had been flying with Filip Novak, the other two girls dilly-dallied around on their way to the airfield in case they found themselves caught into a five-hour chat about flying, but when they arrived, he had just left.

'He helped me clean off the Tiger,' said Stevie giving Cat a stern look. 'No one ever does that after a flight. You didn't, did you, Cat?'

'No,' said Cat, miming cleaning her whiskers. 'Too busy eating cream.'

'We had the greatest flight,' Stevie said, wrinkling her nose at Cat. 'He loved it. He really is the greatest fun. I may well take him flying again.'

'You took him flying in your old biplane?' said Miranda disgustedly. 'At his age. You might have given him a heart attack. Did you do loops?'

'Yes, he wanted to.'

Pharr!

'Anyway, flying the Tiger Moth is very socially distanced.

He was in the front seat, I was in the back seat, and we were four metres apart and outside. Perfect.'

Cat restrained herself from asking how a man in his nineties climbed into the elderly biplane without help from the pilot, and just shook her head. 'Did he tell you his story through the Gosport speaking tube?'

'Ha, ha,' said Stevie. She and Cat had had many happy hours of miscommunication through the WW2 trainer's only method of transmission: a rubber blowhole. 'No, we had a coffee afterwards, he'd brought a thermos. He was so excited that his words flew. His story was interesting.'

'Go on.'

'Well, the first funny thing was that he was an avid bridge player. Apparently, it was a big thing in Polish families before World War Two. Who knew 'eh? Anyway, he joined the bridge club in Chichester and guess who walked in one day ...'

As Stevie told Filip's story both girls grew quiet; even Miranda found no reason to interrupt. When she had finished, they were silent.

'Wow,' said Cat eventually, 'I think that's something we need to tell both Karen and Francis about. I wonder what their reaction will be.'

CHAPTER 42
SHUSH BAG

The email from Frank@Anglinout.com said 'We look forward to another instructive bridge game' and contained a link for a Zoom meeting in two days' time.

Would they really play bridge, wondered Miranda sceptically? Was there another game that could form a parable for what really happened to the four men on the night of 26 July 1963?

Two days later, all three girls were in Cat's kitchen. They would normally have met in Stevie's kitchen, but her mother's new carer said it was not safe. Or rather, she'd said, 'I may be on Grade Two payments, but no one ever informed me that that meant putting up with squirrels in the loft, a dog that smells like a dead fox and a dotty old woman shouting *Password?* every time I enter the room. So, I'm not having two extra germ-carrying unvaccinated dog detectives in my kitchen. Right?'

Stevie said pacifically that was fine and the girls went

over to the other side of the village to Cat's house. Once in Cat's beautifully airy kitchen, the girls wondered why they didn't usually meet there. The Internet worked, they could find the coffee without searching the house in unlikely places, and no one asked for the password every time they left the room.

They got up the Zoom link and were let into the meeting. And there in front of them were Karen, on one side of the world, and two clones on the other. The only difference between the two men called Francis seemed to be that one was in his forties and the other in his seventies. Nice for the younger Francis to see how he was going to age, thought Cat: rather well apparently.

'Welcome, SeeMs Team,' said Francis the older. 'I wanted to wear a monkey mask, but Frank said it was better this way.'

The girls all laughed, but rather in the mode of children in the headmistress's office than four people sharing an in-joke.

'Are you in Australia?' asked Miranda.

'Guilty as charged,' said Francis the older doing a little bow. 'Been back here for a couple of days now.'

'How? Australia has strong quarantine rules.'

'You met me,' said Francis smirking. 'I am capable of having many lives, many faces. Rules, my dears, are there to improve a person's life, not to limit it.' He snorted. 'I must have inherited that belief from my father. Possibly the only thing we had in common.'

Frank, formerly Francis the Younger, frowned. 'I'm sorry, Miranda. Even at seventy he's impossible to rein in. But he has had two jabs and I promise to keep him isolated here for the requisite time. I know a lot of older people don't believe in this self-isolation, but my wife and I do. Our children are young, vulnerable.'

Hm, thought Cat, *someone else who sneaked in and got a jab before me.*

'OK,' said Miranda. 'Tell us what happened.'

'OK,' said Francis. 'Before I start, please remember two things. This happened fifty-seven years ago, and memory does adapt and change with time. The main issues will not deviate, but perhaps I was unfair to Karl. He had many issues to deal with in his life, and we all find it hard to overcome our personal biases. The other thing I want you to bear in mind is that I am a pacifist, but that does not mean I do not facilitate. Keep those things in mind as I tell you my view of the truth. I apologise if you hear more than one voice in this tale, but I cannot tell a story without employing my actors.' Once again he swept a bow before them.

Francis started in Karl's voice. Although none of the girls knew Karl, they saw an overbearing giant growing in front of them. They were surprised to discover he had side whiskers.

Karl loved his children with a fierce passion. He never wanted them to suffer the way he had, but they were so naughty, so rebellious, especially Francis. Brian he could cope with, a good, serious little boy who studied hard and wanted to please his father. But Francis, he was different. Francis was half animal, half child. From the moment he was born, he had stolen Brian's air. Funny and clever. Refusing to conform or be put down. He was the baby who cried all night. The one his mother spent her waking hours consoling. But, as he grew older, he was also the one who entertained her most, who won every fight, not with his puny muscles, but with his charm and cheeky banter.

He would never sleep. Even now when he was thirteen, the little rogue was making so much noise he was keeping them awake.

Karl was going to stop this noise now, or the boy would lose his privileges.

He walked into Francis's room and stopped dead.

Francis was there, in bed, and so was Silas, and there was no doubt from their position that they were not just keeping each other warm.

Karl could not speak.

For several moments he just stared at the boys as he stood at the door, shaking his head in horrified disbelief. Had all his warnings of the powers of the Devil gone unheeded? Had they?

The boys must have sensed his presence and they rolled apart. Silas looked terrified. His eyes opened wide and his head flew about like a trapped animal looking for escape. Francis tried to pull the boy behind the shelter of his slim body.

The movement awoke Karl from his reverie. He gave a wolfish howl.

He charged into the room, no longer responsible for his actions, and grabbed Silas, pulling him out of the bed by his shoulders. He dragged Silas to his own room, lifted him up and threw him onto the floor so hard the boy bounced

Silas remained completely still, a petrified sparrow curled up in a ball.

Whatever Karl might have done next was forestalled by his son. Francis had followed them into the room. He crept up behind his father and grabbed his father's arm. 'Father …' he began, 'I can—'

Karl whipped around, punching wildly and knocking his son to the floor. He slammed Silas's door shut and locked it.

He picked up Francis and carried him back to his room, where he chucked him on the bed like an unwanted pillow.

'I will deal with you later,' he said.

He left and Francis heard the door being locked. He stared at the wooden mullions unable to process what had just happened.

CHAPTER 43
YOUR ACTUAL TRUTH 1963

Francis's story

Very early in the morning, I heard my bedroom door being opened, quietly, surreptitiously. That sort of movement was not Karl, but someone who feared him.

A hand slipped through the door pushing a plate of food, a mug, and a bucket. A bucket! My mother thought of everything. I laughed. 'Mother ...'

Even as I started to speak, she whipped back and relocked the door. Another terrified cuckoo in Karl's nest.

I gobbled down my food, hoping that Silas had some. Would my mother care as much about her adoptee as her own flesh and blood?

Nothing happened for the rest of the day, and I was truly grateful for my mother's foresight with the bucket.

Then, in the late afternoon, the door was unlocked. My father stood there, large, cold, and magnificent. 'Get your sailing gear,' he said, 'and Silas's.'

I ran down the stairs, out the door and into the outhouse

where the sailing equipment was kept, my physical actions automatic, my mind replaying everything I had gone over in my room. How should I save Silas? Could I push father off the boat? How? What would happen then? Were we going to be given the 'cure'? Were we going to hospital by boat?

Brian was already in the sailing hut when I got down there. He looked at me, I thought with distain, but he didn't speak.

'Are we going sailing now?' I asked.

'The tide is high,' was all Brian replied, leaning over to get his gear.

We got all our sailing kit and walked out to the car, I stumbled with so much tackle in my arms but Brian never once attempted to help me with the larger load.

Silas was already in the car, huddled in the front seat next to Karl. Apart from a purplish bruise on his temple he looked OK, but his eyes were large and wide like some terrified mouse.

Brian and I got into the back. No one spoke. Tension encircled the car and held us in an ice bubble, so even breathing gave me stabs of sharp pain.

Karl drove straight to the boat park at Bosham. It was dusk so it was virtually empty; a few people waved as we passed but they were more absorbed in their own boats than worried by a late-sailing family.

All three of us boys knew what to do, we had done it so often. We pushed the dinghy on its trailer out to the slip, put the kit on it, rowed everything out to the Swan and stored it without a word passing between us. For one moment, I was able to share a glance with Silas. Then my father loomed over us, and Silas shut down, returning to the jerky movements of the scared sparrow.

I undid the ropes, while Karl started the Swan's engine.

Silas usually did the ropes while I piloted the boat out of the port, but that evening I took the ropes. I was so frightened that father might leave the boy behind. As the boat slid away from its mooring I jumped quickly on board. I thought that I too was in danger of being left; so little did I understand my father.

The wind was light, and Karl motored all the way out of the channel. He didn't speak at all; even as we took up the buoys and stored them in the lockers his eyes never left the channel ahead.

He continued motoring up the Portsmouth coast. The sun was setting and the sky starting to darken to a deep engulfing purple that normally we would have joked about. Normally, we would have brought out the camera and fooled about in its beams, Silas and I both thinking of our future lives as film directors.

But today nothing was normal. No one spoke, except to give or receive orders.

When we arrived at Steephill Cove, Karl shouted at Brian to drop the anchor. However, Brian, sitting on deck in the dying sun, had fallen asleep, so I jumped up and did the job and Silas leapt up to help me. We were still so skinny and unmuscled, very different from the already powerful Brian that it took both of us to let down the rusty anchor chain and prevent it from falling too fast.

Karl's glance jarred on us like a boat on the rocks, checking us, dissecting us, before returning to the wheel with who knows what dark thoughts in his head.

Having secured the anchor, I went down to the galley and started cooking on the elderly stove, while the others finished the boat. I had decided I was going to treat this as an ordinary sailing evening. In my mind, I think I hoped that if I pretended nothing had happened, then perhaps it would be true.

Once supper was over, Karl got out a pack of cards. This was not unusual, but still I felt my heart thump painfully in my chest. I'm an optimist by nature and it was easy to convince myself that father was returning to normal. My rationale rejected the hope, but I pushed it down.

We sat down to play bridge.

We boys drank lemon juice from little bottles. Karl drank whisky. Every time he put his tumbler down, it did a little metallic dance against the coaster. The words *the dance of time* repeated in my head. How much time did we have?

We played hand after hand as the night became darker, and then hand after hand as it became lighter again with the rising moon. Twice we swapped partners, but only between Brian and Silas. Silas and I were not allowed to play together. Karl had played in most hands, but finally he got the chance to be dummy. Sometimes I ask myself, had he never had the chance to be dummy, would what happened next have been avoided? Would we have sailed home, a happy family once again?

In the following hand, he picked up the cards he had previously shuffled and began dealing. I knew exactly what game would be played next, and on a normal night I would have sniggered and sung out, but tonight we were all wrapped in a steel blanket of silence.

'I hardly needed to turn over my cards,' said Francis. 'The only question was would I or would Silas be Mrs Bennett, the murderer? And who would be the murder victim? Brian or Karl?

'The game was thus: my hand was ace, ten, six, three

spades, ten, eight, five hearts, four diamonds, ace, nine, eight, four, two clubs.

'Silas had four spades, queen, nine, four hearts, king, jack, seven, six, three diamonds, queen, seven, five, three clubs.

'Do I need to describe the other hands, Miranda?'

'No.'

'Good, then I'll go on.

'As a family, we had discussed Mr Bennett's murder over a card game very often. I'd always said Mr Bennett could have won and avoided being killed, but my father disagreed. Now, I thought, he was going to show me he could win as Mr Bennett. We were that kind of family, we talked in parables and acted out our feelings. Feelings and open speech were frowned upon in our house, except in games and proxies.'

Francis paused and turned away from the screen. When he turned back his face looked younger, more innocent, almost like a child.

'You must understand,' he said, 'how important Mr Bennett's murder was to us as a family. Dad used that murder over a bridge game as a parable for his family. In his eyes the devastation of the murder showed the consequence of not obeying the father figure. Silas and I used to laugh at that. It was clear to us that he was wrong. What it showed us was the consequence of mistreating and bullying your family.

'You girls found the book we wrote in Polari, Silas and I? You realise now that we used it as our secret language. But Brian didn't get it. He was often left behind and, in the end, I think, it killed him.'

'Go on,' said Miranda, but she understood he was trying to emphasise the power of Polari: once used as a language of survival, now, the language of excitement and intrigue.

Francis shook his head and continued the story. 'Karl played Mr Bennett, and just like Mr Bennett, he went down. For the first time since Karl found us in bed, I spoke unguardedly, but my speech was as inflammatory as that of the original Mrs Bennett. "You could have made that, Dad," I said. "If you'd listened to my idea."

'Karl lunged at me with his left hand, every fibre of fury suddenly given an opportunity to vent. I ducked. The blow missed me, but his fist continued to Silas. It caught him full on the chin and he fell backwards hitting his head on the galley. I jumped up to help Silas, but my father, who had paused for a moment, held by the enormity of his deed, rounded on me. It was as though my sympathy for Silas had reminded him what a sinner I was.

'"Sit down, you pervert," he screamed at me. "Haven't you caused enough trouble?"

'I sat down, unable to do anything else, immobilised by fear. Even at this distance in time I remember the feeling that I would not live until morning. I wished I had been able to say goodbye to my mother.

'Brian got up and put the kettle on the hob. In the evening Karl usually gave us boys cocoa. Clearly, for Brian, this night was no different from any other.

'Karl picked up Silas and took him to his berth, dumped him on the bed and returned to make the cocoa. He gave us both a mug and went to the medicine chest, found some antiseptic and went into Silas's cabin, shutting the door.

'I have always hated cocoa and, as I had been doing for years, I handed my mug to my brother, who gulped it down. Probably this was the only thing Brian had ever done in defiance of our father. I think, now, that Karl drugged the cocoa.

'Brian went to our shared cabin, and I waited to see if

Karl would come out of Silas's. As soon as Karl heard our cabin door click shut, he came out. Then stopped, seeing me sitting there.

'"Go to bed, boy," he said, his voice gentle and kind. He stood in the galley, waiting until I joined Brian in our cabin. Once there I heard his footsteps retreating to his cabin in the bow.

'Brian was already asleep. He gave a snorty slurp and started snoring.

'I sat on the bunk, my mind reliving the events of the evening. I wanted to check on Silas, but I was afraid to go out until my father fell asleep. The doors on a boat are such noisy flags of movement. I lay back, still fully clothed, waiting.'

CHAPTER 44

SWIMMING IN COLD WATERS

I must have drifted off. But suddenly I was awake. Something had woken me, but I wasn't sure what. I listened carefully. The boat was silent apart from the wind singing in the wires. I got up and crept quietly into Silas's room, half afraid that my father would have locked the door. But the door opened easily and silently, as though the hinges had been greased.

The room was empty.

I stared at it. I couldn't understand what was happening.

Then a cold hand clutched my heart. I ran into my father's room.

But it too was empty.

I stood in my father's room my heart beating like an orchestra. I knew I couldn't stay trapped in there, so I moved into the galley, listening. And then I heard a swishing noise on deck. It was not like anything I recognised.

As I crept up the steps, I saw Karl illuminated by the moonlight. At first, I couldn't understand what he was doing. He was standing at the pulpit, holding what appeared to be a pike over the water. Slowly I realised it was the boathook and he was pushing something down.

I moved closer and looked down into the water, following the line of the boathook. And saw a swollen bloated face.

I screamed. I ran at Karl and knocked him onto the deck. That he fell at all amazed me, he was at least twice my size, but he wasn't expecting me.

He jumped up like a much younger man. The face that looked at me was wild, crazy, his eyes lit with the lust of killing.

He was laughing. I hear it in my dreams sometimes. His laugh.

'Your boyfriend is beyond your help now,' he yelled at me. 'You won't be able to corrupt him any further.'

I looked down at Silas, saw him bobbing in the water, turned face down like a dead man.

Then, my father came up gently beside me. He put his arms around my shoulders. For just a moment I tried to believe it was an accident, and he was somehow apologising. And then he pushed me overboard.

I grabbed onto Silas as I fell under the water, but he felt blobby in my grasp. I thought I might be sick, right there under the water.

As I came up for air, I heard my father's voice.

'You can spend the night in the water! You filthy pervert! Wash your sins clean.'

He laughed and laughed. Maniacal, crazy! He sat down on the deck, the boathook in his hand, watching me, waiting for me to return.

I was terrified, but hearing his voice stabilised me. It was too late for Silas, but I could still save myself. In the distance there was a shoreline. I had always been a good, strong swimmer and the water was completely still that night, with plenty of moonlight. I swam over to the shore and climbed out.

When I looked back, the boat looked so far away. I stared at it. Even then, I hadn't quite accepted that my father had killed Silas and tried to kill me. I stared at the distance, wondering if my father could see me. He wasn't on deck anymore, but perhaps he had watched me swim. I wondered if he would follow me.

The dinghy was on the other side of the deck, and it occurred to me that at that moment Karl could be loosening the ties and about to launch it into the water to follow me.

I ran into the woods.

However, just a small amount of exploration showed me why Karl wouldn't bother to follow me. This was a very tiny island, with no connection to either the Isle of Wight or the Mainland. I was isolated and I couldn't go anywhere. It was too far to swim anywhere, and I was stuck. Karl would be able to come over in the morning with Brian, his faithful bloodhound, track me down and take me back.

My father must have chosen this place for exactly that reason. I shuddered as the enormity of the whole thing burst on me; the amount of pre-planning that it required. This was not murder in the heat of the moment, but a cold-blooded, brutally planned execution. And I was next. How could I not be? I was a witness to Silas's murder, and there was no way I would not speak out. I would enrol Charlotte too, to help me and to tell everyone about Jacques.

However, even as I thought these things, reality clanged into me like the door of the hospital where I no doubt would be sent. I would not be believed, even if I did speak out. My father would say Silas was washed overboard. Brian would support him, and I would be sent for 'the cure'.

Either part of my brain would be cut out or I would be given aversion therapy, or perhaps both.

No one in our household was ignorant of *the cure*. Once a month Karl would get his family into the drawing room up in the old house on Signals Hill. There we would be told the latest atrocities performed by homosexuals and the latest treatments. None of us had any doubt that homosexuals were responsible for most of the ills of the world. Undoubtedly, both Stalin and Hitler had been homosexual.

I didn't cry. Life was now too serious for tears.

I considered drowning myself then. Anything would be better than the cure.

I considered trying to swim to the far shore of the mainland, but I was already shivering, and I knew I would die of hypothermia before I got there.

But I was thirteen, at thirteen you don't give up so easily. And I was an optimist. I knew I had to look for an alternative.

I walked around the island, wondering what to do. Then, to my amazement, I nearly fell over a couple having sex.

They were so engrossed they heard nothing.

I backed off fast. But thinking.

If they'd got there, there must be a boat.

With such a small island, it didn't take long to find the boat. Even though it was tucked away in a small cove, where it should be invisible from the land or sea, I found it. Desperation makes you very clever.

I slipped into the boat and found two joyous things. Sitting in the bottom of the boat were a jacket and a pair of shoes. The shoes were much too big, but they were shoes and, once I got over to the mainland, it would be much less suspicious to be walking in overlarge shoes, than to be barefoot.

There was an outboard motor attached to the boat. I was about to start it, when my natural warning system engaged. The couple, deeply engrossed though they were, might well hear the throb of the engine and realise their boat was being stolen. So, I grabbed the oars and rowed away towards the mainland until the island was only a dot on my eyeballs. At least rowing warmed me, and I stopped shivering and started thinking. I knew if I could get to North Shore I could walk to the train station, it was only a couple of miles, and from there I could get to the brickworks and on to Midhurst. From Midhurst I could go anywhere, perhaps even London.

I started the motor and drove the boat over to North Shore. I motored right up the beach, pulling up the engine at the last minute so I didn't damage it. I didn't want the couple to lose their boat. I was very grateful to them and their love. All love, I repeated to myself, is precious.

No doubt someone would find the boat in the morning and go looking for the couple. I was sure they would be fine.

I slipped on the jacket and shoes. Looking in the pockets I found, to my delight, the man had left his wallet there, and lots of money. An unexpected bonus! If I hadn't abandoned Karl's God many years before I would have thought that this was His gift.

I apologised out loud to the unknown owner, but my need was far greater than his.

The dawn was breaking as I arrived at the station. It was five o'clock on Saturday morning 27th July 1963, and I was thirteen and a half years old.

The waiting room was already open. So, I went in and sat down on a bench. I didn't want to sleep in case I missed the train. However, I slipped off into a doze and was woken by an old woman shaking my shoulder.

'Are you getting on the train, child?' she asked.

I bowed my head in affirmation.

'It's here. Come on.'

Politely, I offered to help her with her bag. She nodded at me and gave me a sandwich as a reward.

'Thank you,' I said, wolfing it down so fast she offered me another.

'So,' she said, 'what takes you to London? You're very young to be travelling alone.'

'My mother,' I said hastily, cursing the woman's natural nosiness. 'I'm going to join her there.'

The old woman smiled. Her curiosity satisfied, she soon fell asleep. I wished that my lie was indeed the truth.

I arrived in London on Saturday morning 27th July 1963.

'Does that mean anything to you?' asked Francis, suddenly breaking off from his story.

'Well,' said Stevie diffidently, 'the first Gay Pride march was on 27th July, but not until 1970, so it can't be that.'

'Clever girl,' said Francis amused. 'However, as you said, I was seven years too early. No, actually for most people nothing special happened on that day but for my family it was the day the world changed.'

He laughed but Miranda didn't think he was happy.

I had never been to London before. I thought because I was streetwise in Petersfield, I'd be fine in London. I had no idea.

No one had told me that if you're the prey, rather than

the predator, you must let your personality meld into the background. I thought I would go to London and conquer.

I did know one thing about London. I knew that on Saturday night the silent queer community – we weren't called gay then – all met in Piccadilly under the Eros statue. So that was where I was planning to be on Saturday night, that night.

The biggest town I'd ever seen was Chichester. I wasn't prepared for the size of London. I thought that when I got off the train at Clapham Junction, I'd be able to walk to Piccadilly. Of course, I didn't know the way, but I asked. Sometimes people were suspicious, and they moved away from the ragged child in a too-big jacket and shoes. I avoided policemen. Suspicious people circumvent, suspicious policemen arrest. Eventually, a bus driver told me which bus to take for Piccadilly, and later a kind woman showed me where the Tube station was. I was lucky. I had some kindness, but I also met the opposite.

So, at midnight that Saturday I was under the Eros statue, looking like, I suppose, a sucker for the plucking.

What can I say? How can you defend innocence? Two good-looking boys in jeans came up.

'Hey boss, whatja doing?' said one, while the other complimented my clothes as 'outta sight'. That too-big jacket was now an emblem of my cool.

They were so groovy, so mellow. We ran up and down on the statue, kissed Eros, climbed and laughed. They teased me about my shoes. They flirted with me. Bumped hips. After a while they asked me if I'd anywhere to stay.

Of course, I said no, just arrived in London.

They were so surprised. 'What a bummer. No place to stay but you found yourself here, that's far out.'

'Right place, right time, you dig it right. Hey, Jason, this boy's a gas, perhaps we could give him some slack?'

'Hey, man, we don't have much room, but our place is yours, what you think, Jason?'

'Too right.'

And then they escorted me to a doorway in an alley, just round the corner. They said it was the entrance to their flats. One of them started looking for his key, while the other slipped his hand down my trousers ... Well, you probably know what happened.

I know now they called it 'rolling a queer'. It was a jolly night out for straight men.

Bit of a jape! Bit of a laugh!

Beat him up, knock him out and take his money.

CHAPTER 45

GYPSYS, TRAMPS AND THIEVES?

I woke up in a doorway with a dog licking my face.

'Monty,' said a child's voice. 'Come here.'

I opened my eyes. There was a girl, about seven or eight years old, sitting on the ground beside me and looking at me. 'Have you run away from school?' she asked.

'No,' I said, 'I'm too old for school. I'm eighteen.'

'Fibber,' she said, 'my brother's eighteen and he's twice your size.'

I said nothing.

'Do you want a sweet?'

'Yes, please,' I said, and tried to move my arm. I forced a scream back into my throat as razor pain shot through my body. Was my arm broken? As the myriad of aches competed for attention, so last night's evils returned to my memory. Gingerly, I lifted my hand. My arm still worked. I put my hand in the jacket pocket.

Empty.

All the money I'd stolen from the unknown man had now been stolen from me by another unknown hand. My father's God was having a good day. Retribution is mine, sayeth the Lord.

Jacques would have cheered.

Back on the street, a noise brought me back to reality; where there are children, there are mothers. This girl's mother appeared from the shadows, staring down at me.

I stared back. I'd never seen anything like this. Our West Sussex village or even Petersfield or Chichester had no one even remotely like her.

For a start, she was black. In fact, as I was to discover, she was light skinned, only half black, and 'could pass as white', but I had no parameters. And she was dressed in a way that would definitely have embarrassed my mother. I stared at her.

'Well, ducky,' she said. 'You had a downer. Someone didn't like you much last night.'

I must have looked like a frightened fawn, covered in blood and half dead.

She laughed at me. 'Got anywhere to live?'

I shook my head, although even that hurt like hell. I was starting to see the first question anyone asked in London is 'got anywhere to live?' Why was that?

She snarled at me. 'Got any money?'

I was about to say, no, everything was taken, and then I remembered. I'd bought some thick socks to fill out my shoes and got a ten-bob note as change. Not wanting to get out the wallet and expose my sudden wealth, I'd stuffed the note into my socks. It was still there.

I pulled it out and now she laughed. 'OK, ducks! You've found yourself a home.'

That was the start of my education.

Bev lived in Soho, in a small war-damaged terrace with

mould on the walls and ceiling. She rented the whole house and took in lodgers. We walked there with the girl and the dog. Bev took me into the bathroom, covered me with Dettol, patched me up with Elastoplast. She sat me down in a kitchen that smelt of old cabbage and said, 'OK, kid, now, what can you do?'

'Do?'

'Yeah. Do. I'm not a bleeding charity. You can't go to school or they'll drag you back home or wherever you've run from. So, you need to work. Got it?'

'Yes.'

'So, what can you do?'

'I can play bridge,' I said, and then, pulling out everything I could think of, 'I can sing and I can do imitations.'

'Can you?' said Bev. 'OK. You'll need to teach me to play bridge too, then, sonny, we'll be on solid ground.'

I taught bridge to Bev and her daughter Claire and whichever lodger was living there. Bev was quick, clever, and ingenious. In another world she would have been running a company, but in 1960s London she was a prostitute, a landlady, a thief, and a mother. She soon got the hang of bridge and we made up our own conventions, which would easily defeat any opponents. My mother had taught me the basics of Polari and Bev already knew the rest. She and I used it to communicate while we fleeced our clients at bridge.

For eleven years Bev and I played the pubs and clubs. One day I would be Fran. Another day I would be Carile, Scarlet, or one of the boys. I was such a good actor that no one ever knew the same person played with Bev but wearing a new disguise. We made money and if we upset anyone, we changed our appearance and our lodging. It wasn't hard and

it was fun. Only towards the end it was getting more dangerous. We played a lot in Jack's Club. He used to protect us,
but he kept warning us we were running too near the line.
He was the only person who saw through my disguises. And
the reason he did became clear when I was twenty-three,
and we fell in love. When you really love someone, you see
through their pretence to the person beneath.

He took me out of the criminal life. He'd been warning
Bev to get another partner, and by then I was ready to play
bridge without the cheating. Bev couldn't see it. So, when
Jack sold the club, she went on with different partners. But,
without my expertise and Jack's protection she was vulnerable. She was arrested shortly after I left the scene and died
in jail.

Francis stopped and took a drink of water.

The girls were silent, stunned. Even the nephew looked
awed. Perhaps he hadn't heard the full story before. There
was a gulping noise and Cat realised Karen was crying,
unmuted.

'How come you weren't arrested?' asked Cat.

'I no longer existed. Fran, Carile, the lovely Scarlet Rose,
Roger and the others had become Silas. A charming, quiet,
sensible boy from Nepal.

'The following year it was again getting too hot, so Jack
and I moved to Australia and travelled around Asia for ten
years as a married couple. We did make occasional trips
back to Britain, but mostly we stayed away.'

He stretched his arms out. 'I loved being a woman. I
hated giving it up. You know what they say? It's a drag not
dressing up.'

Miranda laughed. Even while she hated the father, she thought the idea of the wicked son dressing up and escaping from under his patrician father's nose great fun, amusing. 'Did you ever come back to see what was happening down here? Before, I mean, before we met you as Simian.'

'Yes,' said Francis smiling at her. 'You know I did. You bought me Tea, a local beer. You talked to me about your children, how much they missed having a grandfather. I liked that. Kind, I thought. And another time we played bridge with Dot and the others.'

Miranda made a noise. 'Yes. But that was only about a year ago. Your parents were dead then. Didn't you come before?'

'Yes,' said Francis, 'I did. I came quite often while my mother was alive. I actually wanted to see her, to talk to her, but before I did ...'

He stopped. For a moment Miranda thought he might cry, but he continued with just a lilt in his voice. 'I hadn't realised how all that time in bed would have weakened her heart.'

He shuffled in his seat. 'She visited my grave every week. I didn't realise that at first, but I got to know her timing. Exactly the same time every seven days – Karl's bridge day.

'At first, I was confused. Why would she weep so piteously over Silas's grave? It was several years before I asked one of the friars – not Jacques, obviously, but there were more friars there in those days – who she was and who she was crying for.

'What he told me shocked me profoundly. He told me it was the grave of her son, Francis Deliverer.

'Until the monk told me my mother was crying over Francis Deliverer's grave, I had no idea my father had passed off Silas's death as mine. I knew he would say it was an accident, and that Brian would support him. But I never thought Karl would lie to the Holy Church, that he would blacken his immortal soul in that way. That was a shock for me.

'Obviously, he lied to my mother too. She wasn't an actor who could pretend to weep for show. Her tears were real. She believed I was dead.

'That's when I thought I would donate a gravestone with Silas's name on it, so my mother would know I was still alive. That was in 1969, so the grave was still outside the walls.

'It took a while to make the gravestone, but the etcher had done his work, and next time I visited it came with me. I planted it over the little bunches of flowers my mother had brought there.

'However, Jacques must have told my father, because when I came down the following week, the stone had gone. There were bits of it still in the ground and flakes of granite around the site – clear signs Karl had destroyed it with huge angry bashes. But the important thing for him was that there was nothing to indicate who lay beneath.'

'Hang on,' said Miranda, 'wasn't Jacques curious about why someone would put a stone to Silas over your grave?'

'Probably, but my father could be very convincing, and Jacques would want to believe whatever he said. I sometimes wonder if Jacques was in love with my father. Platonically, naturally. We can all deceive ourselves easily when we're in love.'

'Why didn't you speak to your mother?' asked Cat. She hoped that her own son would feel capable of talking to her.

'Such a good question,' Francis said, 'and I have no answer. Perhaps I feared for her safety if Karl realised we had met, or my own. I can't answer you, Cat, I don't know.'

He continued with the story. 'The next time I visited, in the seventies, they had moved the boundary. The grave was now inside the walls. But, of course, without a tombstone.'

He stopped speaking and Miranda took advantage of the silence to ask, 'Why?'

Francis took off his glasses and cleaned them with his handkerchief. 'Why what? Move the boundary? A novitiate told me that a local farmer had been converted and he gave the church a strip of his land. I always wondered if my father paid for it. He couldn't risk someone digging up the body even then, so he got the walls moved. My father was nothing if not ingenious.'

'Perhaps,' said Stevie quietly, 'he used the money he had stolen from the Deliverer family trust.'

'What about your mother?' asked Miranda. 'Did she still keep visiting?'

'Yes. So, then I hit on another idea. Since Karl would destroy anything with the truth on it, I would invent a new fiction. I had to wait a bit, until I had money. But by the mid-1980s I could afford an expensive marble tablet. I had it made by AK Lander in Essex. The place seeming particularly appropriate since it was my father's stomping ground in his youth. In 1989, they took it over to the graveyard. Since I requested it in my father's name, I assume Jacques saw no reason to alert him. Anyway, there was no problem putting it in place. I know you girls saw it. It's attractive, isn't it? I wanted to give Silas the best stone, even if I couldn't yet give him a name.'

'We did see it,' said Miranda. 'Was that why you had *Frances* etched on it? The female version of your name.'

'Yes. I'm not sure if Karl noticed, but my mother did. Sadly, I think that's what killed her.'

'You didn't approach her, then?' asked Miranda.

'No. I still didn't feel safe enough. I still feared that Karl might come after me, even though I'd taken a new name, Silas Lama, and a legal, if you can call it that, identity.'

'So, your mother died. When? Was that 1989?'

'Yes. That was when I decided to kill my father.'

CHAPTER 46
THE KILLING OF FATHER KARL

The younger Francis looked at his uncle and the frown on his face reminded Miranda of Brian. 'You killed Karl?'

'Maybe, or maybe I just hastened his descent into Hell. Where, if there is one, he is surely abiding now.'

'But he didn't die until 2000,' said Miranda. 'Why did you wait eleven years?'

'Between the thought and the action falls the shadow,' said Francis.

'Elliot,' murmured Cat, but Miranda was still puzzled.

'OK,' said Francis, 'that was when I started thinking about it, but what really jolted me into action was when he started looking for me.'

'When he joined the bridge clubs?'

'Yes, but more importantly when he employed that little runt Clinton Steman as a detective. Clinton who worked for Jack all those years and had been a sharpy omee all the time. A grass. It sickens me. How could such a lowlife be an investigator? Probably my father's idea. His idea was probably "use a pervert to catch a pervert".'

'I met him,' said Miranda.

Francis nodded. 'Bad luck. Even though being gay was legal by then, it didn't mean my father, or his church either, thought it was acceptable. Clinton had known me since I was thirteen. He knew plenty.' Francis sighed. 'I trusted him. He had photos of me, of Jack, even of Bev. What a lowlife.'

Miranda nodded. No doubt the photographs he wanted her to buy.

'When my father started looking for me, I felt that same awful dread I had back on the boat all those years ago. I didn't want to kill my father, but if it was going to be him or me, then it would be him.

'After my mother died, Karl only went out to play bridge at one of his clubs or to buy food. So, one morning, when he went shopping, I entered the house.'

'How?' Stevie asked. 'Did you break in?'

'No need. He never locked the house. Never had. He considered it a challenge to see if anyone dared usurp his authority. I knew that.

'I went into the library, which was where he sat, day and night, as he had always done. Any time, other than when he was in bed, he sat in that room. I got the cards out and laid them on the table.'

'Mr Bennett's murder?' asked Miranda.

'Correct. I also fetched one of those large Victorian mirrors with legs from upstairs.' He rolled his shoulders as though they were stiff. Then he went on.

After a couple of hours, I heard Karl's car draw up. He went into the kitchen with his bags. He came in, poured himself a whisky, lit a cigar and walked over to the table. At first, I imagine, he thought he had simply left the cards out. Then he saw which game was on the table. He dropped his glass. Whisky spilt all over the cards and the floor.

He looked up. 'Francis,' he said, 'where are you?'

Mimicking my mother's voice, I said, 'Karl, you told me he was dead.'

As I watched, his face lost all its colour. He closed his eyes and his chin drooped. He appeared to shrink – I thought he was having a heart attack, that remorse for my mother's pain had finally shattered his overwhelming self-belief. But I had misjudged the man. A moment later my father swelled up like a cartoon cat. He regenerated into an enormous mass of energy and swung around, his eyes darting across his face, his hands grabbing, he reached out for me. 'Where are you, you little devil? You don't fool me. You never did. I didn't spawn you. Your mother slept with the devil.'

Still in my mother's voice, I said, 'Karl, you killed him, you killed Silas. You killed us all. Why? We were a happy family. But you killed us.'

He ran to the fireplace and picked up a poker. 'I should have killed you last time. Like your perverted friend. I revel in his death. I'm glad I cleared the world of another obscene influence. Where are you? That's it. This time you won't get away, you debauched vitiate, you ...'

He stopped because he saw me in front of the table. In the position where Mrs Bennett should be. There I was. Laughing at him.

He lunged across the table, leading with the poker. He launched his whole body weight towards me and smashed into the heavy Victorian mirror. He fell back. Blood poured from his head. There was glass everywhere.

'Francis,' he said, nothing else.

I went over to his body. He appeared to be unconscious.

The cigar had fallen on the floor and gone out. I leant over him. Checking his breathing, I didn't think to ask myself why he would be dead when he only hit the mirror ... but by then I too was in a highly anxious state.

He grabbed my arm.

I shot back and knocked into the table. Brought a mass of cards floating down like leaves onto my father. He lay still, although the cards could hardly have hurt him.

I smashed my hand into his face. He didn't move. However, the poker was still in his clenched hand and I wasn't sure whether he was bluffing. I knew what a madman he was when aroused and I had certainly aroused him.

I was so frightened that my mind has completely erased what happened next, and only came back into my body as I was running out the door. I stopped for a moment. Then I thought I heard something inside and I ran off down the footpath. I didn't stop until I was far enough away from the house to be out of sight. I collapsed down, shaking, wondering what I had hoped to achieve. Why did I go back? Was I hoping he would fall on me in tears and confess his faults? Was I hoping for a prodigal-son-like reunion?

I think I was.

I don't know how long I sat there, but it must have been some time because the clouds came over the sun and I grew cold. After a while I heard a noise. It sounded like a rushing stream. I couldn't identify it. My back started to feel slightly warm, as though the sun had come out of the clouds, but it hadn't.

I got up and looked back.

The whole house was on fire. I couldn't believe it. What had happened? I wanted to run back towards the house, but it was too late. The house was old and the wood must have been as dry as tinder. I couldn't even get close to the house, the flames were so hot.

I turned round and ran down the footpath into the village. I went straight into the pub, yelling that Signals House was on fire. They went out saw the red horizon and knew I was right. There was an auxiliary fire truck left over from the war, which they used for farm fires and others, and they got that fired up and raced up the hill. But it was all too late. By the time they got up there the house was in ruins and my father with it.

Francis blew a raspberry. 'He got a funeral he didn't deserve and was placed next to his wife in the churchyard. Not where Silas is, but right up by the monastery, in recognition of all his generosity over the years.'

'And you?' asked Miranda. 'Did you go to the funeral?'

'Yes, as a middle-aged woman. No one asks questions of strange middle-aged women. Perhaps they thought I was his mistress.' Francis laughed. 'I talked a lot to my friend Charlotte, but I left when I felt her start to recognise me.'

'But,' said Miranda, 'this time she did recognise you. She said she'd seen a ghost.'

'Yes. This time I needed her. Perhaps we could have justice after all these years. It was too late for my father, but Jacques was still available. Sadly, he died before that happened.'

'Did he see you?'

Francis shook his head 'No, I was on my way to the graveyard, but he died first. I like to think he finally accepted his sins, but I doubt it.'

'And now,' said Miranda, 'we come to the beginning of the story. To Brian and the bridge game. Why? And how?'

CHAPTER 47
BRIAN MAKES A VIDEO

R ight,' said Francis, 'time for a tea break, cookies and coffee for Stevie and Cat. A glass of wine for Miranda, and then we will show a short but telling video.'

'Did you make it?' asked Miranda.

'No, Brian made it on his phone before he died.'

'You did see him then?' said Miranda.

Cat echoed, 'So he did have a phone.'

'Yes, he was in the house when we four chums played bridge together. Sorry, girls, but there *was* a ghost at our feast.'

Miranda laughed.

'I'll show you the video first,' said Francis, 'then we can have our round table discussion.'

With that he posted the video.

Brian's video

Brian appeared staring at the screen as though he didn't know what to do with it. He sat for so long the girls started to wonder if the battery would run out or he would die first.

Then he spoke. 'Dear Karen and Francises,' he said, as though he was dictating a letter. 'I'm so sorry, I killed Granddad.

'No, I said that wrong. I'm not sorry I killed him, I should have done it years ago, but suddenly the opportunity presented itself, and I took it.

'I was only at the house because of the shopping. I was in Chichester with Emma and Karen, you remember, Karen, we were looking for a dress for you, for some occasion. The girls went in and out, on and on, from shop to shop. I got so bored I thought I'd pop back up to Dad and take over the picture he'd asked me to get him. It was in the boot already.

'But, as I drove up towards the house, I saw someone running away down the footpath. My heart gave a leap. I was pretty sure I recognised that run even after all this time. A detective chap, Clinton Steman, had been trying to black-mail me, and he said it was on behalf of someone from my past. Of course, I now know it was you, Francis, but when I saw the running man, I thought Silas.

'I went into the house. Dad was on the floor, uncon-scious. I checked his pulse. He was alive. I went upstairs to the attic and found the sachets of Pervitin. I ripped one open and poured the contents away, then I put the empty pack beside Dad. I thought if it was found they would think he'd gone off on a trip and accidentally killed himself.

'I got his cigar and took it to the fire, relit it and held it to the carpet until it ignited. My gloves did get slightly burnt, but that didn't matter. As you will discover, I have ten or twenty pairs of gloves. I dropped that pair in the river in Chichester. No one ever found them.

'I knew people generally die of smoke inhalation, rather

than the fire itself, so I got a damp cloth and put it near the fire. It lit. Then it started smoking. I put it next to Dad's body. I turned Dad's head towards the smoking cloth, and then I thumped him in the stomach. He gave an involuntary gulp, inhaling deeply. I had to hope that would do the trick. Clearly it did.'

Brian stopped and took another gulp from his whisky glass.

'I left the rag there. If it didn't burn, and was found, it would be just another clue that would either lead to Silas or me. In some ways I didn't care. If it did lead to me, I would have been relieved. I was fed up with my life. I was totally in Father's power. He could quell me with a raised eyebrow and a snarl, simply because I was so afraid of what he might say.

'Now I would either be free of him, or in jail.

'Having set up the fire, I opened the window to increase the breeze and climbed out. I scuffed my prints in the mud. In the best case, they should lead to Silas, not to me. Then I went back to Chichester.

'Luckily the place where I had parked was still vacant, and when I joined Emma and Karen, they didn't even know I'd been and gone. Later, when the police asked us what we were doing, they both said immediately we'd all been shop-ping all day. Shows how vital I was to them!'

He grunted and drank some more whisky, topping up his glass from the bottle beside him without stopping the video.

'Perhaps I should stop now. Let Francis tell you the truth, but I want to make you understand the way I saw what happened.

'OK, back to 1963. The day that ended my childhood.

'I woke up on the boat. Francis and I shared a berth, but

he had gone. I stretched in the sunlight that was pouring in through the porthole. I looked out and could see that it was still a little misty but that it was going to be a lovely day. To my surprise, as I rolled over, I saw the winch handle. How odd. I must have taken it to bed by mistake. I laughed, feeling a swelling sense of happiness, probably for the last time in my life.

'I got up and went into the galley. Father was sitting there, his head in his hands.

"Oh, my dear Brian," he said lifting his head to look at me, sympathy in his eyes. "How are you, dear boy?"

'I was flummoxed, as much by the kindness in his tone as the words.

"'Yes, yes, thank you, sir," I stammered. We always called him *sir* or *governor*. It sounds odd now, old fashioned, but Karl liked it.

'He gave me a surprised look. "You managed to sleep then?"

"'Yes, sir."

"'Oh, the optimism of youth," he said, with that same compassionate smile playing in his eyes.

'I didn't question him. We were not encouraged to question. The best we could do was create a parable, but I wasn't good at that. I didn't have the imagination. I used to ask Francis to do it for me if I needed to ask questions. But usually, I just accepted that Karl would tell me the truth.

"'Is Francis on deck?" I asked. "Does he need some help?"

'My father looked at me and his face drooped. I can still see it now, thinning and lengthening before my eyes. "Francis?" he said. "Francis?"

'For a moment I wondered if he had gone mad, forgotten he had two sons, his mind going back to the days when we were children. When mother dressed Francis as a girl. I stood, my hands hanging by my sides, waiting ineffectually, uncertain what to do or say.

'Then father continued. "My poor, poor boy."

'He jumped up and took me gently by the shoulder, led me to the bench. "Sit down, my boy, and I'll get you a coffee. What do you remember about last night?"

'He put the coffee pot on the stove and looked at me, waiting.

'I wanted to please him, so I said, "We played bridge, I think, and then we went to bed."

'I did remember he had hit Silas, but I thought it would be tactless to mention it.

'He looked at me in complete horror. "Is that all you remember?"

'"Yes." I did remember we had hot chocolate, but I didn't think he meant anything as trivial as that.

'"So," he said, "you don't remember that Francis hit Silas when he lost the game? Do you remember that he was Mr Bennett and Silas was Mrs Bennett?"

'I said, *no* because I thought Father had been Mr Bennett and Francis had been Mrs Bennett, but I knew Father could not be wrong. He after all had dealt the cards.

'"Oh dear," said father and gave me my coffee. "Shall I tell you what happened?" His voice was so sympathetic and his face so completely open that I fell into his truth, and having once fallen, I could never reclaim the truth as my own again.

'"Francis lost the game," said Father. "Silas laughed at him. He said, 'You could have done it if ...' He never got any further because Francis took a swipe at him, knocked him off the bench and onto the edge of the cupboard behind. He cut his head and fell down. I went over to care for him, but

Francis made to hit him again. You were furious. Your sense of honour surfaced, and you grabbed at Francis, trying to stop his arm. But you recall what a slimy boy he was. He slid out of your grasp and ran up onto the deck. You followed him. I called, 'Boys, please.'

"'But you were both so angry that you didn't hear me. I tended to Silas for a while, taking him off to his bed and laying him down with something over his wound. When I came out, I heard you boys fighting on the deck.

"'I went up to stop you, but it was too late. You, being the stronger boy, had just sent a final blow onto your brother and knocked him clean into the water. I grabbed you. Otherwise, you would have jumped in after him. I was frightened you might try and drown him.

"'I calmed you down and led you below deck. You went into your cabin. You're such a nice boy, you said, 'It's OK, sir, leave me, I'll be OK. You'd better go and see if Francis is all right.' So I gave you the emergency medical kit and went on deck.

"'To my surprise, Francis was still in the water. I could see his body bobbing around face down in the water. I got the boathook and managed to get him near the side, then I dragged him up on deck, but he was dead.'"

"'Dead?" I said, immediately correcting myself. "Dead, sir?"

'I couldn't believe it. Francis, dead. It didn't make sense.

"'Drowned, dear boy, and what a mess he looked. I couldn't even recognise him. He was such a mess of pulp and putrefaction." He stopped and looked at me more gently than I'd ever known.

"'But I don't blame you at all, my son, it was not your fault. It was either him or you. I understand that. He was a wicked, wicked boy. My only hope is that he will go to purgatory and be cleansed and, in the fullness of time, receive benefaction from God and be allowed into Heaven. His poor, poor soul."

'I could hardly breathe. I was staring at him, gasping for air. I killed Francis. I killed Francis. It was all I could think.

'"Come," he said, and he took me on deck. Francis's body lay under a tarpaulin. Father pulled back the canvas cover and there he lay. A mess of human parts more ghoulish than anything I've ever seen. I turned away and threw up on the deck. Again. And again.

'Father was very kind. He covered Francis back up. He wiped up the mess on the deck and he got me below, forcing me to sit down and drink my coffee. All the while he talked to me, telling me it was an accident, and he totally understood that. But that probably other people wouldn't understand that, that I might be prosecuted for murder or, at best, manslaughter. He was saying something about the minimum age having been raised this year, but I couldn't take anything in. I was simply sitting there shocked and unable to move or think.

'"So," he said, "we'll have to avoid that. I can't lose both my sons."

'And he smiled.

'I remember that smile. It shone out at me like a beacon of hope. Father was going to help me. It would be OK.

'"I am going to tell everyone that the boom hit Francis while we were sailing, knocked him out and by the time we were able to turn the boat and get back to him, he was dead," he said. "You will support me totally and we will get through. We will tell your mother the same story. Do you understand?"

'I stared at him.

"'Do you understand?" he said again, and this time his voice was fiercer.

"'Yes, yes, sir," I said. "Francis was hit by the boom and drowned. So awful. Poor Francis. He must have been knocked out. Yes, yes. Sir."

'Father nodded. "Good."

'But I suddenly had a thought. "But what will Silas say?"

'Something flashed through Father's eyes. At least that's how I remember it when I relive that morning, which I do, again and again, but perhaps it's a false memory. And then he said, "Silas has gone."

"'Gone?" I repeated. I didn't understand anything. "Gone where?"

'My father gave a deep sigh. "Where indeed? Ungrateful boy. He upped and left. After all we have done for him, this is the way he repays us. It breaks my heart."

"'Perhaps," I said, "we could say Silas killed Francis and ran away."

'I can't imagine what got into me. To try and make anything even close to a contradiction of my father's idea must have meant I was deeply in shock.

'He turned white. For the first time ever, I saw him as an old man. "I'll forget you ever said that," he said, in a voice so cold I felt like I had murdered him too.

"'Sorry, sir."

'He nodded, his face transforming as he saw I was following his lead.

"'Don't worry, son, that's the shock talking. OK, now we must sail back and tell everyone the awful news."

'Somehow, I got up and helped with the boat. I was never as good as Francis anyway, but with his body lying there on deck it was impossible for me to turn the winch handles or lift the buoys. Annoyed by my fumbling around the deck, Father decided to motor all the way, even though there was a fair onshore wind blowing.'

Brian stopped. He looked down at the video as though wondering if it was still working.

'Until the day Francis turned up at my door, I thought I'd killed him, and Silas had run away. I had no idea I was the patsy for Father. Even now I find it hard to believe, and yet Francis is next door playing bridge with three detectives. I'm the one who died along with Silas.'

He lay back against the sofa cushions.

The video stopped. Either he stopped it, or the battery ran out.

CHAPTER 48

GASLIGHTS FOR MR BENNETT

W oof,' said Francis. 'Poor Brian. The original gaslighter, that was our dad. I always wonder – had I taken the drug in the hot chocolate, would Karl have thrown me overboard? Would he have drowned his own son? I should have guessed, but despite all I saw, everything he said on those homophobic evening talks, I never thought my father could be that bad.'

'How did you find out?' asked Miranda.

'Brian told me.'

'He was shocked to see you?'

'Totally. Totally! I slipped into his house and laid out the Mr Bennett's murder card game. I thought he would see it and be glad. The prodigal son, or in this case brother, returned. Then I went upstairs to make myself a bed. I thought I would stay the night. I thought we would sit up, exchanging stories. Laughing over the mistakes. How little I understood my brother.

'Brian came in while I was still upstairs. He saw the game laid out. He thought it was Silas. He told me he had been terrified about what might happen, what Silas would do to him. After all, he thought he had seen Silas at Karl's house and that was why Karl was unconscious.

He rushed to the bathroom and took an overdose of his wife's depression pills. He was still in the bathroom when I went downstairs. He must have heard me moving. He dropped the suicide note and left it there, which was why I never found it. He followed me down, expecting to see Silas.

'When he saw me, all the colour drained out of his face. He staggered and gagged. I thought he was going to be sick or collapse. I caught him and led him to the sofa. Gave him some whisky. Then he told me his story.

'I asked him to play bridge in my place, but he said he had to read to his granddaughter, and we would talk later. So, I went to play bridge with you, and he to read to Orla. He told me he was going to make a video while I played and that we could discuss it afterwards. He seemed pathetically pleased to see me.

'Poor Brian, I suppose that even now, even after all these years, he couldn't bring himself to talk about things. When I came back from playing bridge, he was dead. I was terrified. I thought I'd be blamed. I grabbed his phone and fled.

'Of course, Brian, a very conventional man, would not have understood, nor believed, that the roving dishonest life quite suited me. I suppose I have my father to thank for that, at least.'

'Poor Dad,' said Frank. 'No wonder he had such problems with life. And yet he called me Francis as though he wanted to revive the dead.'

'I think he did,' said his uncle, 'and yet when he did, it brought back the most awful memories, especially when you started looking like me. Poor Brian, how he must...'

'And,' Karen broke in, speaking quickly, 'that's why he first doted on my son Tom, and then, when he started to look like my brother, began to hate him. All because of you, Uncle Francis.'

'Exactly that,' said Francis, 'exactly that. Poor Brian, indeed, and what a devil my father really was. What could have happened to my father to turn him so evil that he would kill one boy and make another boy take the blame?'

The detectives looked at each. Then all tried to speak at once.

'You say, Miranda,' said Cat, 'you're the lead detective.'

Miranda laughed and her heart swelled. She put her hand on Cat's shoulder and squeezed it. 'Thank you, Cat. And Stevie, I'll need your input.' She smiled at her computer wizard.

Slowly she turned towards the family on the Zoom call. She knew even as she started to speak that what she was about to tell them would change not only their lives but also what they knew and felt about each other. For one moment she remained suspended in thought, wondering if it would be better to leave them in ignorance. Then Cat coughed and Miranda knew she had to tell them the truth.

'We can help you there,' she said slowly. 'We know what happened to your father in the war.'

CHAPTER 49

THE SINS OF THE FATHERS

S tevie was trying to find out,' Miranda said, 'who scuttled the boat. We know it wasn't George, although he was angry with Karl for leaving him and Sally on the island, because the boat was scuttled before he got a chance to "square up to him" as he called it. He said his job had been done "by another hand", but he didn't know who.'

'I can answer that one,' said Francis. 'I stole it. Took it out into Portsmouth Harbour and pulled out the bung. Rowed the dinghy back to shore, and left it to sink, just as my father left me to sink. End of.'

Stevie laughed, taking over the story. 'Such a simple solution. Not knowing that, I filled in the contact page on the Tangmere Museum site. Filip Novak, who also volunteers at the Chichester bridge club, answered. He loves bridge, almost as much as flying. Wants to challenge us to a game once lockdown is over.'

She grinned, apparently embarrassed at this total audience attention. Cat and Miranda usually spent most of their time interrupting her statements.

'Filip was born in Warsaw in Poland in 1922. Before the war he lived with his parents and older brother, Janusz. His parents were killed in the bombing in September 1940. Filip only escaped because he was staying with a friend, and he remained with them through the war. However, his older brother, Janusz, had already left home and, Filip thought, joined the resistance. He's a bit vague, both about the age and what Janusz did, but as he is ninety-eight you will have to forgive him.

'So, after the war, Filip decided to try and find his brother. The first news was very bad. Janusz had been caught by the Nazis on a raid and sent to Auschwitz.'

'Was he Jewish?' asked Cat.

'No, Catholic, but lots of Catholic Poles were interned in Auschwitz,' Stevie said. 'Filip was devastated. Not many people made it through Auschwitz. Looked like he had lost both his brother and his parents in the war. He went to the former concentration camp. The locals had kept it as a museum, determined to prevent those atrocities ever happening again. No one had heard of Janusz Novak, but Filip kept ferreting around.

'One day he was lucky. He was in a bar in Oswiecim in 1948, talking to the owner. Some guys came in and the owner called them over. He told Filip they were local guys who had been in the Polish Resistance.' Stevie stopped. 'His story was much longer than this. I'm just giving bullet points. These guys told him about an escaped prisoner in 1940 – a real hothead. Some of locals who helped him ended up in Auschwitz in his place. After all sorts of questions and answers he became certain this hothead was his brother Janusz. So now he felt certain Janusz was still alive, he redoubled his efforts to find him.'

'Interesting,' said Miranda. 'Must have been so wild in

post-war Europe. Stealing cars to get home, creeping through checkpoints, bandits everywhere—'

Cat coughed.

'Yes,' said Stevie. 'Anyway, Janusz seems to have got back to the resistance. He did several more jobs including on the Eastern Front, then they lost trace of him. He didn't appear to have been recaptured, but no one could find what happened to him. Not that that was unusual then. Lots of people just disappeared.

'Filip wouldn't give up. He kept looking. Then, about a year later Filip found a record of his brother in Lublin. Then nothing again, but all the time people were helping him and directing him to others. Someone told him Janusz left Lublin for Prague. Then he went across the Swiss border. He found news of him in Switzerland and then the trail went cold. Someone told him that lots of Poles went over to France to help the resistance there.

'He booked a room in a guesthouse in France, run by an old woman. As usual he was busy telling everyone of his search, when the owner said, "Back in 1944 I went out to feed the cattle and I heard a noise in one of the empty barns. I wasn't surprised. Lots of deserters hid in my barns over the years. I think they knew I was good to them, and they were useful to have around."

She told him that she had found two of them in the barn, speaking French, but one was clearly English and she thought the other one was Polish, although he claimed to be French. But she'd seen a lot of deserters through the war years and his accent was, heavy like a Pole.

She said the Englishman was very nice, he showed her his tag and eventually he admitted he had deserted his unit in 1940.

. . .

Apparently, she thought she might have a relationship with him, he was so kind and big, good for the farm.

So, Flip was getting hopeful. This might be his brother with the Englishman. But then, her story took a turn.

Apparently, two days later, the barn where the men were sleeping went up in fire.

She and the farm girls rushed out, but the flames were huge and by the time the fire trolley arrived everything had gone up in the flames.

Flip was devastated. He asked what had happened to the men's bodies. Did anyone identify them? Apparently, she shrugged and reminded him that this was wartime. They buried what remains there were in the field.

'Filip was despondent. After escaping Auschwitz, it seemed his brother had died anyway. And in a simple barn fire.

'By 1949, Filip was homeless and, he told me, enjoying his research. He decided to try and find out where the English guy came from. Since the French woman was not completely sure if there were one or two bodies it might be he had survived. Maybe he would know something about Filip's brother. He also liked the idea of settling in Britain. A lot of Poles moved there. He couldn't go home to Poland, which was now in Soviet hands, and he was penniless.

'The French woman had told him that the Englishman, whose name was Karl Deliverer, was in the Essex Yeomanry. So, Filip went over to Essex and there he discovered not only that Karl Deliverer was alive, but that he had rejoined his unit in 1944 at Arnhem.'

'Didn't they shoot deserters?' asked Frank.

'Apparently not,' said Stevie. 'Or perhaps not that late on in the war. When he rejoined them, they were just recovering from a terrible fight, with a large proportion of the unit killed or captured and perhaps they were grateful for anyone, even a deserter.

'When they discovered he spoke fluent German and French, they moved him to intelligence.' She stopped for a moment. 'This is Filip's story. He is ninety-eight, so if it sounds outlandish well, perhaps it's all lies, but wartime makes for oddities. Somewhere along the line, Karl Deliverer had been wounded in the arm. Burnt. And either because of that, or something else he was sent to the field hospital. In hospital he met and married Hannah. He converted to Catholicism because she was Catholic.'

'What religion was he before?' asked Frank.

'Jewish,' said Miranda.

'Not ideal for him then, being sent into Germany.'

Odd, thought Miranda, that the children didn't even know what religion their grandfather was, but clearly they were a very uncommunicative family.

'No,' said Stevie. 'But to return to Filip. He had been an engineer during the war and found it easy to get a job. Bombed-out Britain was being rebuilt, and they needed engineers, builders, architects and so forth. His first job was in Basildon, and later he moved to Ongar. All these places were growing, and he was meticulous in his work, so employers liked him. As Poland was now part of the Soviet Empire, he was able to apply for British citizenship and he got it.

'For a while he moved around and then he met a lovely girl who lived in Chichester. He married her, but they couldn't have any children, which was a great sorrow in both their lives. Eventually, he ended up volunteering at the Tangmere Museum and in the local bridge club. The Novaks were all demon bridge players in Poland.

'One day, he thinks it was around the late 1980s but

could be as late as early 1990, he was working in the bridge club when a man came in wanting to join. Filip looked up and there he was, his brother Janusz. He says he recognised him immediately, even though he was much older and had got rid of his beard.

'Filip could hardly believe it. He thought his brother was dead. He wondered if the French woman had made a mistake and both men survived.

'Anyway, Filip didn't say anything but asked the man to sign the register. His brother signed the name "Karl Deliverer".

'Filip said he nearly had a heart attack seeing that name. He had to think it through big time. He concluded that Karl Deliverer had not survived, but his brother had, and he had taken Deliverer's dog tag and impersonated him.'

'Hang on,' said Frank, whose whole family history was being relocated in one quick story. 'How? I mean, did they look alike? And what about Deliverer relations? There must have been some. This can't be true. You can't just take over someone's identity.'

'Can't you?' asked his uncle smoothly.

Miranda spoke. 'All the relations had died, either before or during the war. There was only a sister left, and she was autistic. She lived in a home, for which the money was supplied from a trust. We'll come back to that one. Karen knows about it already.

'Whether they looked alike ... no idea. Presumably not, since Filip recognised his brother as not being Deliverer. Go on with Filip's story, Stevie.'

'Well,' said Stevie, 'Filip says it was easy to find Karl's address. So, a few days later he went up to Signals Hill. He stood outside, waiting until he could see his brother was alone in the drawing room and he knocked on the window.

'His brother came to the window. Cool like, he said, "Hello, can I help you?" Then he added, "I believe I recognise you from the bridge club."

'Filip says he laughed then. He said his brother was always a lying, cheating git and if the rest of the family hadn't died, he wouldn't have looked for him.

'He spoke in Polish, and immediately he could see his brother understood him. His brother tried a few obfuscations, but Filip was up on him every time and eventually, Filip said, "OK, if you won't admit it, let's go to the Notary and see who is right."

'Then suddenly Janusz was all loving brother, offering him money. And then, Janusz Novak told his brother his story ...'

CHAPTER 50
POLAND 1943

Janusz Novak's story

I met Karl Deliverer in France in 1943. He was a deserter. He'd shacked up with a French woman who had fallen in love with him. She protected him for several years and taught him French and German. Unfortunately, she died of pneumonia in 1944.

'When her house was bombed, Karl managed to escape but he was hiding in a ditch when I met him. We quickly saw we were blood brothers, who would be happier travelling together. In the time we travelled together we got to know each other very well.'

Filip laughed here and said, 'Of course, my dear, that is rubbish. Janusz got to know all about Karl Deliverer, but no doubt my brother gave him some sob story about being a French Jewish refugee escaping from the Nazis. He was always a good linguist. That story would make Deliverer trust him implicitly, thinking, if the worst came to the worst, he could give up the French Jew and save himself, even though he was Jewish too. These were brutal times.'

Back to Janusz's story.

'The Englishman said he was worried about carrying his dog tag, in case he was caught. So, he suggested to me that we play bridge to see who wore it. We played bridge. I lost, and so I kindly agreed to take the other man's identity and shortly afterwards the barn burnt down. I burnt my arm trying to get the British man out, but he died anyway.'

'Sounds like fiction to me,' said the older Francis. 'For a start, Dad would never admit to losing a bridge game unless he'd actually won it. Then, why on earth would the Englishman play for his identity? I expect my father stole his tag and papers, killed him, and burnt down the barn to cover his handiwork. He could easily burn his own arm. He was probably thinking to pass himself off as a Frenchman, then thought he might be better off joining the English-man's unit, since by then the British were winning the war and there were groups of mercenaries everywhere.'

Stevie moued. 'It is true his arm was burnt, but under the burn was his Auschwitz tattoo – they told me it was still visible if you pulled at the flesh a bit – and he used it to claim money from Elsie Deliverer's trust. But I'll email you the details of that. Anyway, Filip admits that he found himself a source of income that didn't dry up until 2000.'

'He blackmailed his brother?' said Cat.

'Yup.'

'Nice family!'

'I wonder,' said Miranda, 'if Janusz/Karl paid his brother from the money he was getting from Elsie's trust. A nice circular honesty in that, don't you think?'

'I wonder if your mother knew that she was married to Janusz Novak, not Karl Deliverer,' said Frank.

'Doubt it,' said Francis. 'She would have let it slip. Besides, it was quite common in that generation to keep war histories silent. Look at all the revelations currently coming out about people who worked in Bletchley Park, or SOE. We still don't really know what he did, just that he probably killed the real Karl Deliverer and certainly that he took his identity. At least we know our mother was who she said she was – she had far too many relations to be lying.'

'But what about the tattoo from Auschwitz? How would he explain that to her?'

Francis laughed. 'If Dad could convince Brian that he had killed me, and everyone that Silas's body was mine, why would he baulk at a small thing like a tattoo?'

'Maybe,' said Karen, her voice sounding gentle against the boys' cynicism, 'she wanted to believe him because she loved him, so whatever he told her worked.'

'Yes,' said Francis laughing, 'like all my patsies, they wanted to believe I was stupid, a bad bridge player, and so they got fleeced.'

'Shall we change our name?' asked Frank.

'No,' said Karen, 'I don't think we should tell anybody anything. This is our story.'

Her brother nodded. 'OK,' he said. 'Also, Karen, I've been thinking. Later, when COVID is over and we can travel again, you can come over here and meet your new uncle. Perhaps you might want to live here too. A physiotherapist and a tradesman will score high on the points system.'

Karen's laugh held a lot of repressed desire. 'Oh, I'd love to. But it does depend on the kids and my darling hubby too. Although ... Orla did say she wants to see a kangaroo. There has been a lot of interest in Dad's house. If we sell it, well. Well ... One can dream, right?'

CHAPTER 51
YOUR ACTUAL AUSTRALIA

A few days later Karen sent the detectives a WhatsApp asking for a Zoom as soon as possible. When the detectives zoomed in, they found the Francises already online.

Karen was the first to speak. 'I've been going through all Dad's things and I found something.' She paused. 'Dad had done a DNA test. He also did one for someone else – Elsie Deliverer.'

The detectives gasped. 'So he knew. He knew about his father, and yet ...'

Karen shook her head. 'I told you he didn't share things.'

She looked at her brother. He put his palms up; *whatever* seemed to emanate from him.

'But,' said Cat, 'what was the date of the DNA testing?'

'The report says September 2000.'

'Interesting,' said Stevie, 'as soon as he met her. He must have been suspicious that they were not related.'

'And yet,' said Cat, 'he still kept paying for her. Trying to right the damage his father had done to her family. What a good-hearted man he really was.'

'Any idea why?' asked Miranda. 'What made him suspect?'

'Her size, maybe,' said Stevie. 'Apparently she was a tiny little bird, and we know he was large, as was his dad.'

'Poor Brian,' said Francis. 'My father has a lot to answer for. However, I wanted to tell you one more thing. I've been musing over it for the last couple of days. You remember Pete the builder said that his father was at school with Karl Deliverer, that's right 'eh?'

'Yes,' said Miranda, 'and Karl didn't recognise him afterwards. I thought it was trauma left over from the war, but it makes sense now we know he was a different person.'

'That's right. But also, you said Karl Deliverer was rabidly anti-gay and, of course, my father was too. I kept thinking about this. Was it coincidence you got two such reactionary views in both the people who were at one time Karl Deliverer? And then I was reading a book about Polari, and I came across a chapter about the war. The writer, who had interviewed many gay people from the war, discovered that some straight men liked a little "relaxation" with gays during that period. I had to wonder, in the time that Janusz and Karl travelled together – did they share a little relaxation? Were they filled with horror afterwards, and is that why my father killed the Englishman?'

'Could be,' said Miranda, her eye-rolling unseen by the Zoomers abroad.

Once again, an old person was offering up a weird idea. People who lived in the sixties had some pretty odd beliefs. Thank Heavens she was born in a far more rational time. More likely, she thought, Karl was simply a mad dictator who couldn't bear to be worsted.

'We've decided what to do with Silas's grave,' Karen

broke in. 'A headstone with his own name on it. But what about you, Uncle Francis, do we tell everyone you're alive?'

'Why not? It will be irrelevant to most people. How many are still alive from the 1960s?'

'Charlotte, her mother, the Draytons.'

Francis inclined his head. 'Charlotte already knows. She might like to visit us here. Her mother won't be the least surprised to hear anything bad about my father ... in fact she might well already know. Someone who insisted on playing Chicago bridge rather than rubber bridge clearly came from dubious stock.'

The three laughed together and Miranda's heart suffused with sympathy. Perhaps Australia would be their new Eden, somewhere they could start again and forget the horrors of the past.

'What happened to Jack?' Miranda asked. 'Your lover.'

And, as the detectives watched, Francis changed into yet another person.

'My darling Jack,' said Fran flirting with them through long eyelashes. 'Yes, he's still alive. He's ninety now, you know, but *so* good for his age. He puts us all in the shade, which is where he is now. Sitting on the terrace, in the shade, setting out a new card game. Don't you love him? He thinks he can beat me at bridge. What a sweetheart!'

GLOSSARY

Polari terms

There is some of the speech known as Polari in this book
and, although most of it should be understandable from the
context, I have also compiled a glossary of terms.

It is notable how many terms there were for police-
man/policewoman/police station etc. There are also many
different terms for body parts both male and female. A lot of
Polari was applied with irony, such as That's Your Actual
French as a put down for those trying to appear sophisticated.

Polari Words: English
Almond rocks socks
Aspro, aspra prostitute
Aunt nell 1. Listen. 2. Ear
Aunt nelly fakes earrings
Auntie older gay man
Barnet hair
Barney fight

Beak a judge

Betty bracelets the police

Bevvy 1. A drink 2. A public house

Bevvy omee a drunkard

Bins spectacles

Bona good

Bona rack a gay club with a good reputation

Bona vardering looking good

Butch masculine (sometimes referring to women)

Cabouche car

Camp funny, flamboyant

Camp name an opposite-sex name given to a Polari speaker usually given to reflect an aspect of their personality, appearance or identity

Cark it to die

Corybungus bottom

Cottage public lavatory or urinal

Cottaging sex in public lavatories or hanging around there for sex

Diddle gin

Diddle cove barman or dispenser of gin

Dilly Piccadilly

Dilly boy rent boy or male prostitute

Dizzy scatter-brained

Dog and bone telephone

Dowry a lot. The word can be used to upgrade any adjective

Drag principally to wear clothes from the opposite sex but also the clothes themselves and can refer to a state of being

Ecaf, eek face

Fabulosa wonderful

Fake riah a wig

Farting crackers trousers

Fashioned riah wig

Fathers of Perpetual Indulgence a reference to Sisters of Perpetual Indulgence, a charity of gay street performers set up in 1979 in San Francisco

Full eke wearing make-up

Gloria God

Got your number 1. Sussed you out 2. To identify someone as gay

Hearing cheat ear

Hilda handcuffs the police

Jennifer justice the police

Jubes breasts

Lady a gay man

Lallie leg

Lappers hands

Letties lodgings

Lily law the police

Lily pad police station

Mais oui of course, see also **your actual French**

Matlock mender a dentist

Matlocks teeth

Meese ugly

Metzers money

Meshingener crazy

Metties wealth

Minces eyes

Molly gay man

Nada none

Nada in the vada nothing to see

Nanti dinarly no money

Nanti polari don't speak

Nawks bosom

Nelly feminine gay man

Nochy night

Ogale/ogle eyes

Ogale fakes/ogle fakes spectacles

Ogle filters sunglasses

Ogle riah/ogle riders eyelashes/eyebrows

Ogle riah fakes false eyelashes

Omee-palone/homee-palone a gay man

Omee/omia man

Onk nose

Opals eyes

Orderly to leave or go

Orderly daughters the police

Palone-omee a lesbian

Palone a woman or girl

Parker to pay

Parkering ninty wages

Plates feet ie plates of meat in Cockney rhyming slang

Polari the gay language

Polari lobes ears

Polari pipe a telephone

Queer ken prison

Quongs testicles

Rattling cove a taxi

Real girl a biological female

Rent boy/renter male prostitute

Riah hair

Riah shusher hair dresser

Round and Round the Horne refers to the Kenneth Williams radio play from 1965 to 1968 Round the Horne, which used Polari although never letting on that it was a gay language.

Rough trade masculine, working-class partner

Savvy to know

Savvy? Do you understand/know

Scharda what a pity

Setter seven

Sharp/sharper 1. To steal. 2. A policeman

Sharping-omee a policeman

She he, she, they, it

Sheesh affected

Shush to steal

Shush bag swag bag

Tat rubbish

Tea leaf thief

That's your actual French phrase used to highlight that speak was trying to appear sophisticated by speaking French

The Killing of Father Karl this refers to the 1968 film The Killing of Sister George, an iconic LGBT film.

Thumping cheat heart

Tober omee 1.rent collector 2. Landlord

Tober showmen travelling musicians

Treash term of endearment

Tres sheeshwahz very chic

Trundling cheat car

Vada/varda/varder to look

Vada bona looking good

Vaf look at that wonderful thing

Vogue a cigarette or to light a cigarette

Vonka nose

Wallop to dance

Willets breasts

Winkle small penis

Wonga money from questionable sources

Yashmacks, Pontefract and a little bit of fish refers to things that appear different from reality, Pontefract, for example, while appearing to be a staid Yorkshire town is apparently the sexiest place in the UK!

Yews eyes

Your actual intensifying phrase. For example, your actual Australia

Zelda 1. A woman 2. A witch

Zhoosh 1. Clothing 2. Trim or ornament

Zhooshy showy

Zhooshy tart woman showing off

Bridge Terms used in the book

Seating positions reflect points of the compass, hence: **north, south, east, west.**

Bidding an auction after the hands are dealt, but before they are played. Each player decides how many tricks he and his partner are likely to win and makes a bid on this basis.

Dummy one of the players, but one who is sitting that game out while his partner, the winner of the auction, plays the hand. Dummy's hand is laid down on the bridge table for all players to see.

Overcall making a call after your opponent has made an opening bid. Only the first such bid counts as an overcall.

Points cards in a bridge game have points depending on how important they are, thus the ace has four points, the kind three points, the queen two and the jack one. When you count up these points it tells you the value of your hand.

Signals these can be legal and known to all the players and thus part of the auction, or illegal and surreptitious and hence cheating.

Tricks you win tricks. In a Polari context this is also a reference to doing tricks i.e. sex for payment.

Vulnerable If your contract goes down one trick and you are not vulnerable your opponents get 50 points per trick. If you are vulnerable and lose you give your opponents 100 points per trick.

Mr Bennett's murder. In 1929, Mrs Bennett killed her husband with his own gun after his poor bidding and worse play in a hand of bridge. Although there were witnesses to the shooting, Mrs Bennett was acquitted on the grounds that the gun went off accidentally. She also collected his life insurance of $30,000.

Though Myrtle Bennett was exonerated of the murder of her husband, she failed to set the precedent that would have made the shooting of a bridge partner justifiable in the eyes of the law -- provided it could be proved the victim's play had provoked a murderous response!

ACKNOWLEDGMENTS

I want to thank all the people who helped me in so many ways with this book. Firstly, the editorial staff at Reedsy: Kat Gordon for her amazing editorial insight, Lesley Jones for her thoughtful and thorough line editing, John Martin for his proof reading and Kari Brownlie for her covers. Secondly, the beta readers including Shaun Baines, Caitlin Macleod at Fiverr and thirdly the staff and the other authors at Jericho Writers, who gave so much advice and help about writing, editing and general ways of looking at your own work.

A lot of research was necessary to understand the gay world of the 1960s and I would like to thank Paul Baker for his book Fabulosa, The Story of Polari, Britain's Secret Gay Language, Alkarim Jivani for It's not Unusual, a History of Lesbian and Gay Britain in the Twentieth Century, Elon Green for Last Call, a True story of Love, Lust and Murder in Queer New York, and Helen Boyd for My Husband Betty, Love, Sex and Life with a Crossdresser.

My thanks for medical expertise to Janie Grant and Caroline Veitch. For all the intricacies of bridge to the Andrew Robson Bridge Club in Fulham, where I learnt to play bridge and did several courses, and to Edmund Sixsmith for some endearing insights into playing the game. For police procedure, my thanks to Graham Nunn, and all in the crime writers' section of Jericho Writers.

For support, to my husband Gerald Cheyne and Malvina Nicca and our dogs, who all kept me sane during the writing, re-writing and editing process.

ABOUT THE AUTHOR

This is Gina Cheyne's second crime novel and the second in the SeeMs Detective Agency series. The first one, The Mystery of the Lost Husbands, came out in 2021.

Gina, whose name came from her mother's admiration for Gina Lollobrigida, was born in London with a longing to see the world. However, after travelling for many years she realised it was impossible to visit every country even if you never stopped moving.

She now lives in West Sussex with her husband and dogs. She has written under various names and for many years edited a lifestyle magazine and taught flying on both planes and helicopters.

She has been awarded the HAI Lightspeed Salute to Excellence in Communications Award 2022.

ALSO BY GINA CHEYNE

The Mystery of the Lost Husbands

Biscuit and Oscar Learn to Fly

Max and Biscuit fly to India

Pugwash Runs Away to Sea